THE WORDSMITH

Alan Ayer

ISBN: 1540852407
ISBN 13: 9781540852403
Library of Congress Control Number: 2016920326
CreateSpace Independent Publishing Platform
North Charleston, South Carolina

For Alice

1

Walt hated signing books for his fans. Every time he released a new book, there were the obligatory book tours and signings. He didn't mind the talk shows or radio interviews, but he hated the book signings.

To be honest, he didn't mind the long lines of fans always telling him how great he was. That was not an issue. The problem was the questions. "Where do you get your ideas?" was the one that irritated him the most. He really couldn't tell them. He hadn't had an idea for a book ever in his life. If any of his fans knew where his ideas came from, they would flip out.

A thin, forty-year-old woman with straight hair and dull brown eyes stood in front of him. She was saying something about being his biggest fan. He smiled and nodded and grabbed the book she was holding out to him.

"Make it out to Liz," she said, smiling a stupid grin at him.

"To Liz, my favorite fan. Best wishes, Walt," Walt wrote. He closed the book and handed it back to her.

"Thank you so much," Liz said, still grinning at him with that stupid grin. She turned to the left and walked off.

The next person was a short, plump man with no hair on the top of his head. His face was red, and he was breathing hard. He wore black cargo shorts and a shirt that just covered his ample belly.

"Hi. Please make it out to Ryan. I loved the book. I stayed home from work to finish it," Ryan said in a voice that was much deeper than Walt thought it would be.

"Thank you," Walt said. He signed the book, "Ryan, thank you for the nice words.—Walt."

As Walt handed the book back to Ryan, Ryan asked Walt the question he hated most. "Where do you come up with such wonderful novels?"

Walt said, "I don't. All my novels are written by someone else. I have no original ideas." He smiled as he said it.

Ryan laughed and turned and walked away.

On it went. Walt had about five things he signed. He had been doing this for about twenty years, and at first he had agonized over what to write when he signed his books. After a while he realized it didn't matter at all. He sometimes would just sign his name if he was feeling particularly pissed off, but he was in a semigood mood tonight. This was the last signing of the book tour, and tonight he would get to fly home. No more adoring fans to deal with. So he could make it through this. No problem.

Sometimes even these signings were not so bad. Occasionally he would meet a single, attractive woman in the line. He would have his publicist pull her aside and ask if she would be interested in having dinner with Walt. She always said yes. Single young women were always enamored of the famous author. They falsely believed he was a genius. But he wasn't, and he didn't care. He still would take them to whatever hotel he was staying in after dinner, and most of the time, he would get lucky. He would make up some bullshit about how he came up with his ideas and how the world was his muse, and they would be so turned on. It was great.

But he was flying home tonight, so none of that would be happening. He tried never to look at the line while he signed. That seemed to make everything go slower. He just signed one after the other, and eventually he was through the line.

So it went tonight. He looked up, and everyone was gone. He had managed to get every book signed, and his hand didn't hurt too badly. His publicist called for an Uber, and they rode to the airport together.

Mitch Conner had been his publicist since he started. Mitch was a no-nonsense man and enjoyed the money Walt made for him. Mitch knew what Walt wanted, often before Walt did.

"Glad to be done with this?" Mitch asked with a grin. He knew the answer. Walt's mood had changed the second he was done.

"Hell, yes," Walt answered. "This seems to take longer every time."

Mitch knew what he meant. Since they had started doing this some twenty years ago, the book market had grown so much tougher. Walt had ten number one best sellers and over twenty top-five books, but he still had to go out and press the flesh to sell each book. But it worked. He always sold a ton of books. He had even sold two screenplays. The movies turned out OK—not great—but that was the director's and the studio's fault. The stories in the screenplays had been great.

When they arrived at the airport, they shook hands and went in separate directions. Walt was flying back to his home in Southern California, and Mitch was headed to New York. They would send occasional e-mails, but otherwise he would not see Walt until Walt was almost finished with his next book.

Mitch was always one of the first people to read each new Walt Erickson book. Walt valued Mitch's opinion. The books were always great, and it was nice that Walt let him be one of the first to read them.

Mitch watched Walt disappear into the crowd. Then he turned and walked toward his flight. He was also glad it was over. As these trips went on, Walt became more of an asshole, and because Mitch was with him most of the time, he got the most of it. Walt would start picking on little things—the location of the hotel room, Walt's seat on the flight. Mitch would always solve the problems, but he was glad this was over. He could finally destress and get some sleep. He'd earned it.

Walt was glad to finally be heading home. He liked Mitch a lot, but after three months on the road with him, he was sick of him.

Walt's flight did not leave for a few hours, so he checked in, got through security, and headed to his gate. At the gate he looked for a nearby bar and sat down for a few drinks. He ordered a cognac. He asked for whatever house cognac they had and pulled out his iPhone and began watching Netflix. Walt hated reading.

The cognac went down easily, and by the time the flight was boarding, he was on his third drink. This would make the flight so much faster, he thought. He never had any trouble sleeping on a plane, and the alcohol would make it much easier.

Once he got on the plane, he sat in his first-class seat and ordered another cognac. The plane took off, and once they reached cruising altitude, he finished his cognac and fell asleep.

Two hours later the plane began its decent. He was told to bring his seat to the upright position, and a few minutes later, they landed.

Once they taxied to the gate, he stood, got his bag, and was one of the first people off the plane. He'd called for an Uber as soon as they let him turn his phone back on, so it would be waiting when he got outside.

He had only brought one bag with him. His publicist had taken his other bag home with him and would have it sent back to him.

The Uber driver tried to chat with him on the way home, but Walt quickly ended any chatting. He was glad to be home and just wanted some quiet time. The quiet time had started in his mind as soon as he got on the plane heading home, and the driver would not snap him out of it.

The Uber pulled up to his front gate.

"Thanks," Walt said as he got out, grabbing his bag.

He punched in his code to the front gate, and it slid open. It seemed to open like a glacier moving. Once the gap was big enough, he walked through it and down the path to his house.

The house was large. That was what most people told him when they saw it. It had far too many rooms for him, but he loved it. It had a rustic look and was surrounded by trees. There was a stone wall surrounding it, with a front gate. In the backyard, he had a stone pool with a hot tub located at one end, several feet above the pool. The warm water from the hot tub overflowed via a stone waterfall into the pool.

He opened his front door, walked in, and put down his bag. After taking off his shoes, he poured himself a glass of cognac and sat on the couch, sipping it for a few minutes. Then he put down the glass and walked over to a door with a padlock on it.

The padlock was the largest one he could find, and he had one key he carried with him and one hidden in the house in a fake power outlet.

He stared at the door for several minutes, building up his courage. He then opened the lock and went inside.

Walt walked down a flight of stairs and into a small room. The room light was dim. In the center of the room was a small wooden table. At the table was a single leather chair with locking wheels. To the right was a cabinet filled with reams of eight-and-a-half-by-eleven-inch paper.

Above the table was a single light that lit up the Wordsmith typewriter. It was an old gray typewriter, the kind that did not use electricity but required you to forcefully press the keys to type anything. It looked new. There were no scratches or discolorations anywhere on it. The return arm stood out and was a slick silver color.

Walt looked at it. Now that he was reassured it was still there, he left and went back up the stairs. He locked the door, changed his clothes, poured another cognac, and went to bed.

Walt stood staring down, watching waves crash over the rocks. He was naked and could feel the warm wind coming from behind him. He stood with his toes over the edge of the cliff. He thought he should move away before he fell, but he couldn't move. He was stuck standing at the edge of the cliff, and the wind picked up. He did not move. Eventually the wind knocked him off the edge of the cliff, into the rocks.

That was the point at which he always woke up. He felt his heart beating fast in his chest, ready to burst out. He was sweaty and after a few seconds felt cold. He got up.

The dream was always the same. He went and got a cognac to calm his nerves. After a few sips, he felt warm and safe again.

He went down to his kitchen with the cognac. It was still early, so no one had arrived yet. The cleaners or gardeners or someone was always there working, starting around ten in the morning. When you had a house as big as his, there was always something needing to be done.

He got out some eggs, a frying pan, and the spray olive oil. He knew that Marie would be there soon, so he made a couple of extra eggs for her. He added spinach and cheese to the eggs. He then put some toast in the toaster. He didn't eat the toast himself, but Marie seemed to be able to eat whatever she wanted and never gain any weight. So he made the toast for her.

There was a knock on the door right as the eggs were almost done. He knew she only knocked as a courtesy and would let herself in after waiting a minute or so.

He heard her coming before he saw her. Her footsteps didn't make a lot of noise, but it was enough that he knew she was coming.

He turned to look at her while turning off the heat on the stove.

She smiled as she saw him. Her smile was the first thing he had noticed about her when they met. It lit up the room. She had beautiful dark hair that touched her shoulders. She had been his personal trainer before they developed a relationship, and he spent most of the time as she trained him staring at her. He felt creepy just staring, so he asked her out before she could think he was a creep.

She ran up to him and hopped up into his arms, and he kissed her. The kiss was long, and he carried her out of the kitchen to the couch. They quickly undressed, throwing their clothes on the floor around them.

When they finished, he held her for a few minutes.

"How was the trip?" she asked.

"It was OK. As usual, I liked the TV appearances but hated the book signings," he said.

"I'll never understand why you hate your fans so much. They gave you all this," she said, looking around at the large house.

He was quiet. He never talked about his feelings for his fans.

"Did you hook up with any bimbos?" she asked.

They had an open relationship. When they had first started dating, he told her he had no interest in a relationship because he liked sleeping with different women. She said she did not mind as long as he didn't mind her sleeping with women as well. That had been fine with him. He had hoped she would be interested in threesomes, but she made it very clear that she would never bring another woman into their bed. That was theirs. But what he did on the road she didn't care about. It worked out well for him. He wanted her to tell him about her other women. The stories excited him.

He knew she was always a little jealous, but he was always honest with her about it. It was important that he kept to the agreement. He loved her, so he was honest with her.

"Unfortunately not," he said.

"Too bad for you," she said.

They both got up. He stayed naked, and she pulled on her underwear and shirt.

He went back into the kitchen. The eggs were cold, so he turned the burner back on and heated them up. He threw away the cold toast and made her another piece.

Once the eggs were warm, he plated them and buttered her toast and took both plates to the kitchen table, where she sat looking at her phone.

He knew she was reading e-mail. She had a lot of clients. She looked great, and she worked people hard.

So she was always reading and answering e-mails from her clients. He didn't mind. He was a quiet person, so it was good when she was occupied and he didn't have to think of things to say.

He started to eat. She put down her phone and grabbed the toast.

"I finished reading your book while you were away. It was excellent, as usual," she said.

He looked up at her. She knew he didn't like to talk about his books. He purposely never gave her a copy, but she always bought one.

"Thanks," he said.

One of the things she loved about him was how creative he was. His books were always about different things, and she often learned things about herself by reading them.

She had learned quickly that he did not like talking about them. When they first met, she had not read any of his books. When she realized she was attracted to him, she purchased one to read. She didn't want to date a man who wrote trashy books.

It was about Los Angeles gang members. It was very personal and human, which she loved. The ending made her cry.

When she tried to discuss it with him, he stopped her. "Sorry, I don't talk about my books unless I have to," Walt said.

That was that. He had been honest about that. He never talked about any of the stories in his books.

He would talk about publishing the books, the book tours, and every damn thing else, but he never discussed the stories in the books.

She thought it odd, but since he would not change, she learned to live with it. She couldn't help, though, telling him how much she liked them after she read them. That was all she would do. She wouldn't ask about the characters, even though she had so many questions.

She was interviewed about him once or twice. Aside from their relationship, though, she didn't have much to say—no great insights into his characters, since he never shared them with her.

Even when he did public interviews, he was often vague about his characters, only giving the most basic details. He told her this let people develop their own thoughts about the characters. It made the books better if he didn't ruin things for the readers.

Most of the time, he seemed to have disdain for his readers. But in this one area, he was adamant about not ruining it for them. She had always thought he was odd this way. She blamed it on his being a writer.

He finished his breakfast.

"Want some coffee?" he asked.

"Sure," she said.

He got up, grabbed both their plates, and went to the kitchen to put the plates in the sink. He started a cup of coffee for her.

"What time is your first client?" he asked.

"Ten a.m. It's your friend Jake. Last time he worked out with me, he said it was a piece of cake. So I'm going to kick his butt today," she said.

"Tell him hi for me, and please don't kill him," Walt said, bringing the cup of coffee to her.

"When are you going to start on your next book?" she asked.

"Not for a few weeks," he said.

She was relieved. When he was writing, he never wanted her around. While writing he would keep anyone from coming around, including the cleaners and gardeners.

They would occasionally meet at her place or go to dinner while he was writing, but most of the time he liked to be alone.

"It should be a busy couple of weeks. They have finally finished the expansion to the cancer wing at the children's hospital," he said.

He had given several million dollars to them to help build the expansion. This put his name on the wing. The Walt Erickson Children's Cancer Center had a nice ring to it, Walt thought. He went down frequently while they were building it. The construction had interested him much more than reading or writing had.

He also like talking to the kids. It was a little depressing, but most of them were upbeat, and since they were facing death, they lived the best they could. For some reason he didn't understand, their perseverance inspired him. He knew that was selfish, but he couldn't help it.

While he was on his book tour, the final pieces of the cancer center came together, and they were ready to open it. He was excited just thinking of it.

"The kids should be able to start using the rooms and facilities in two weeks," Walt said. "The ceremony to open it will be Friday. Are you going to be there?"

The joy in his voice came through, and his love of the kids made her smile.

"Of course," she said. "Shit, I'm going to be late," she added. She kissed him on the lips and rushed out the door.

As she closed the door behind her, Walt stared at it. He thought about what she would think of him if she knew. He always lived with the fear of her finding out. The guilt of what he was doing washed over him. He hated it. But he couldn't quit. He liked the money too much. So he would continue. He had a few weeks before he had to worry about it. One book per year was what he tried to write. Writing more sometimes crossed his mind, but no. He could barely stomach what he had to do for one per year.

He poured a glass of cognac, drank it down like water, and then poured a second one immediately. That one he drank without rushing.

He went out to his backyard. The sound of the waterfall from the Jacuzzi relaxed him. He sat at the edge of the pool, listening to it. The pool water was cool and felt good on his feet as he dipped them into the water.

He had been taking meditation classes, which helped him to not think about what he would be doing in two weeks. He focused on the sound of the waterfall. After a while he forgot about the typewriter and relaxed. Two weeks, he thought.

The sound of the lawn mower in the front yard snapped him out of his meditation. The gardener was there. Most likely the gardener would not want to see him sitting naked by his pool. Walt stood up and went inside. He tracked wet footprints across the kitchen floor, and by the time he got to the living room, his feet were dry. He went upstairs and showered and dressed. He knew the opening ceremony wasn't until Friday, but he wanted to take a look at the finished construction.

Mitch had come to him almost a year ago, asking if he would contribute some money to help expand the Cancer Center at the Children's Hospital. Mitch had a friend whose son had gone through chemotherapy there. During the process of chemo, someone found out that Mitch knew Walt, so the hospital had asked if he would speak to Walt about perhaps donating some money for the new expansion.

Mitch had asked Walt, hoping Walt would give something. He knew that in the past Walt had donated to several charities. Walt surprised him by agreeing to be the major funder for the wing. The only request Walt had was that he wanted his name on the wing.

He said he would like to be there at the opening ceremony, but he wanted the kids to be the ones to cut the ribbon. They were the ones it was for, and they were the ones who would be using it. It seemed to Walt like the right thing to do.

The fact that he was the major contributor got him a few extra privileges. Walt was interested in the construction and visited the area frequently. The kids rarely knew who he was. Occasionally the parents would recognize him. His picture was on the backs of his books. Everyone knew his name, but not everyone knew what he looked like.

Some of his books had been made into movies— some good, some not so good. The good ones had won awards and had made him a lot of money. Mitch was a great agent and publicist, and he negotiated great deals. Walt still received checks from the first movie made from his first book.

He donated any money from his early books to various charities.

He wanted to take a look at the new cancer wing before the opening ceremony. He called for an Uber and went to say hi to the gardener. His gardener's name was Juan, and he and his wife had just had a baby.

"Hey, Juan, how's the boy?" Walt asked.

"He's doing great. He's almost sleeping through the night," Juan said.

Walt knew that for the past few months, Juan had been exhausted all the time. Andrew would sleep only a few hours at a time, and then he would wake up crying. Juan and his wife would take turns getting up with Andrew, but it had been hard on them.

Walt could never remember Juan's wife's name. He had met her once, and she seemed nice, but Walt had never been good with names.

"That's good. I wasn't sure you were going to make it there for a minute. I thought your son was kicking your ass," Walt said.

Juan smiled. "Hey, man, no way. No son of mine is going to kick my ass," he said.

Walt smiled. "My Uber's here. I'll see you later."

Juan waved and got back to work on the garden.

Now that he had gotten some rest, Walt was feeling much better. He made small talk with the Uber driver.

The traffic was bad as usual, and what should have been a twenty-minute ride ended up taking almost an hour. He watched the cars next to him as they crawled along in traffic. Two guys whom he guessed were in their early twenties were passing a joint back and forth as they drove. He had seen that frequently and always wondered how people could do that and drive. The weed was so strong lately, and every time he had smoked, he just wanted to sit. Someone had told him once it depended on the kind of weed you smoked, but Walt thought that guy was full of shit. Weed was weed.

A lot of people were texting as they drove. They were not going fast, so it wasn't that dangerous, but he watched as someone looked down to text and almost rear-ended the car in front of her. She looked up at the last second and slammed on the brakes. The car screeched to a halt and stopped a hair's distance from the car in front of her.

Walt smiled. Fast reflexes, he thought.

It seemed as if time had slowed, but they eventually arrived at the hospital.

Getting out of the Uber, Walt looked over the hospital. He walked along the outside and looked at the new wing. They had matched the color with the rest of the hospital. It blended in, and you could not tell that it was a new wing.

He went inside and waved at the lady sitting at the front desk. He knew she recognized him. He was a frequent visitor, so she no longer spoke to him. But out of courtesy, he always waved. He walked down the corridor to the administration wing of the hospital. There, he went to the hospital president's office.

"Hey, Jess," he said.

"Hi, Walt. Let me see if he's available," Jessica said, picking up the phone. "Hi, Mike. Walt is here. Yeah. OK," she said, hanging up the phone. "Go ahead and go in," she said.

"Thanks, Jess," he said. He walked into Mike's office.

"Hey, Mike, how goes it?" Walt asked.

"Same old shit. It never stops," Mike said.

"Yeah. No crap. If you don't mind, I'd like to take a look at the new wing," Walt said.

"You know I can never say no to you," Mike said. He stood up and walked around his desk. Walt had always admired Mike's office and how nice it was. The only thing Walt really didn't like was the view of the parking lot the office had.

Walt followed Mike out of the office.

"I'm taking Walt to see the new wing. It shouldn't take more than thirty minutes," Mike said to Jessica as they left.

Walt knew Mike was a little irritated with him. He had shown up unannounced and expected a tour of the facility. Walt didn't care. He had put up a lot of money and wanted to see what it was making.

When they got to the wing, Mike started going over what they had done. Walt knew most of it already, but he let Mike go on with his canned tour. By now Mike had done this so much, he had it down.

"We have made everything state-of-the-art," Mike said. "All the rooms are equipped with the latest equipment. We have gone out of our way to make everything as comfortable as possible for the young patients. This is a hospital, but as much as possible we want to relax the kids, and we want to help comfort the parents as well."

Walt was looking at some kind of robotic device. He knew that more and more surgeries were being performed by robots controlled by surgeons. He wondered how long it would be before the robots would be performing surgeries on their own.

"The tools we have installed are the latest of their kind. We have robots for surgery. The best testing equipment and research labs," Mike said. "The idea is that if we have the best equipment and research labs, we can attract some of the best doctors and scientists in the world. We think we can really make a difference. I hope you see we have put your donation to good use."

"Everything looks great. How soon will the kids be able to start using the new rooms?" Walt asked.

"The idea is as soon as the ribbon-cutting ceremony is over, we will start moving people in. We are finishing the testing of the equipment and training the staff on how to use it," Mike said.

Walt thanked Mike for the tour. Mike said it was no problem, shook Walt's hand, and left.

Walt watched Mike as he walked down the hall away from him. He had enjoyed the tour and was happy his money was going somewhere that would help kids.

He needed a drink. This had helped for a little while, but now there was the weight of the next novel and what that meant. A drink should help with that.

Taking out his phone, he called for another Uber. Standing outside the hospital as he waited, he enjoyed the fresh air and the slight breeze. He debated canceling the Uber and going back inside to visit with the sick kids, but he didn't think he could handle that today.

The closer it got to the start of his next book, the worse this feeling would get. He was aware of it creeping up on him.

Walt thought of the typewriter sitting on the table. The typewriter had its own personality. It did not move or talk, but Walt knew that in its own way it was alive.

A honk from the Uber driver snapped him out of his thoughts. The car had pulled up as close as it could, but it was still about fifty feet away from where Walt was standing.

Walt walked over to the car. Looking at the Uber *U* in the front window, he smiled at the driver and got in. No reason to be a jerk to the driver. Besides, they rated you, and he didn't want too many bad ratings. He knew he'd gotten a few. He could be a jerk at times.

The driver confirmed the address with him, and off they went. Walt stared out the window, and the driver turned on the radio. Walt didn't mind. He liked the music and didn't feel like talking. Traffic wasn't bad, so they made pretty good time to the steakhouse. Walt's favorite place was a steakhouse called the Whole Cow. Steak and cognac sounded good to him.

The place was dark, with wood everywhere. It was made to look like an old saloon. The only things missing were the double doors cowboys would walk through in Old West movies.

Walt sat at the bar. Markus, the bartender, knew Walt well. He got Walt a cognac without his even having to ask.

"Hey, man, been a while," Markus said.

"Yeah, I've been on a book tour."

"I know. I watched you on TV. Why do you sometimes seem annoyed to be on TV?" Markus asked.

"I get asked the same questions a lot of the time," Walt said.

"Shit, man, if I was on TV, I'd be lovin' it," Markus said.

Walt smiled at that. Markus was a big man. He wore a tight shirt that showed off his large muscles. Walt thought of him as a big teddy bear. He was friendly and always wore a smile. Walt guessed that when you were that big, you had no reason to be an asshole.

Walt always thought the drink glasses looked like little miniature glasses in Markus's hands.

Walt ordered a rib-eye steak, medium rare. The drink felt warm going down. As Walt finished the first one, Markus brought the second. Walt drank half of it quickly and then sipped the rest. He let the alcohol do its job, and his mind and body went numb.

Perfect.

"Hey, Markus, can you turn on the TV? Something mindless," Walt said.

Markus turned on the TV to a daytime courtroom show. Walt thanked Markus and watched the show. He watched as the judge presided over a man who claimed a woman had smashed out all the windows in his car after they broke up. The judge was chastising the woman when Walt's steak arrived. The judge seemed annoyed with both the man and the woman. It was amusing to watch. It came out that the man had been having sex with the woman's sister before they broke up.

The judge told the man he was an idiot but told the woman the law was clear that she was liable for the damages.

On the way out of court, both of them were interviewed. The woman was upset and crying, and the man was gloating. Walt guessed the judge's words had not changed him at all, and he was happy to have the money for his windows.

By the time Walt finished his steak, he was on his third drink. He'd had Markus make it a double. When he got up to leave, he wobbled a little. He steadied himself on the counter and walked carefully to the door. He sat down on the bench out front and called Marie.

"Hey, babe. You free now?" Walt asked.

"I just finished with a client and am wide open the rest of the afternoon," she said.

"I'm sitting outside the Whole Cow. Any chance you're around here?" he asked.

"I can be there in twenty minutes," she said.

"Cool. I'll be here," he said and hung up.

Walt watched the lunch crowd start to come in: a lot of people in suits. He knew the steaks were expensive and that most of the crowd would expense their lunch. It was a popular place for people to take their clients or have meetings. He knew they just didn't want to pay for their own steak. Cheap bastards, he thought.

Marie pulled up in fifteen minutes. She tended to drive like a maniac. It sometimes scared Walt, but she had a perfect driving record. She loved scaring people with her driving. He'd caught her looking at him out of the corner of her eye as she'd taken a turn fast or pushed the car over one hundred miles an hour on empty roads.

He'd nearly shit his pants, but she'd loved it. He was glad she was driving normally today. It was hard to drive crazy in the middle of the day. There was too much traffic.

As they drove, she asked how the hospital looked.

"It looks great. They will start letting people use it right after the opening ceremony," he said.

"You, sir, are slurring your words. Drinking at lunch. Tsk-tsk," she said, with a slight note of judgment in her voice.

"Yes, ma'am. Maybe you can punish me. I've been bad," he said.

She put her hand on his thigh and lightly stroked. He wished she would go higher. Eventually she did.

They pulled off the road on the way home and found a secluded spot. The sex was fast, the car rocked, and the windows were fogged up by the time they finished.

Sitting in the car, he wiped off the fog from the area in front of him. He could see outside, but it was blurry.

She had to look around in the backseat for her panties. He had taken them off her and tossed them into the back when they started. As she leaned into the backseat, he watched her ass peek out from her skirt.

She turned and sat back down in the driver's seat. She was small enough that she could bring both her legs up in the driver's seat and pull on her panties, lifting her butt off the seat when they were up high enough. Her movements were graceful and sexual without her consciously making them that way.

She turned on the car and the AC. He cracked the windows. They were both covered in sweat and would need a shower. For right now, he didn't care.

The air flow began to clear off the windows, and they both sat looking at the trees. She held his hand.

He fell asleep after a few minutes.

Walt woke up as they were pulling into his driveway. Marie punched in the code to his gate, and they drove up to the house. She hopped out of the car and went inside to take a shower.

He was still a little drunk and groggy from the sleep, so he got out much more slowly. As he came into the house, he heard the shower running, and he stripped down when he got to the bathroom. She liked the shower hot. The steam came out like smoke when he opened the door. He would have liked a colder shower, considering how hot he was, but she never took cool showers. Heat never bothered her.

When they were first dating and going through the cursory first-date checklist, she had told him she had lived the first eight years of her life in Arizona. She loved the dry desert air. After college she briefly lived in San Francisco, but the cold and fog all year long drove her nuts, and she had eventually been driven from the city by it. Her carefree attitude fit in but not her love of heat, which she found out was the stronger of the two.

"Weather: one. Free spirit: zero," she'd said to him.

He was glad she had not stayed in San Francisco.

He joined her in the shower, and the soaping and cleaning turned to round two.

Afterward they both sat on the couch. The TV was on but more for noise than anything else. He poured himself another drink. Sipping the drink, he listened as she talked.

She told him about her day. The clients seemed to always want to be pushed harder. She knew the young men she trained were trying to show off for her. She enjoyed pushing them to their limits, punishing them for thinking with their cocks instead of focusing on the workout. They did not seem to mind. She had only lost clients on a few occasions.

Walt thought about Ian. He doubted Ian was his real name, but when he had first met him that was the name given, and Walt had never bothered to find out his real name.

It was closer now. He could feel the tension building up inside as it got closer. He knew he would feel the way he had the first time he was required to speak in public, with his insides knotted up and that constant sick feeling.

As it got closer, he knew he would drink more and eat less. He could count on at least ten pounds of weight loss. He was already skinny, and this would make his bones show up more clearly under his skin.

Marie saw the worry in his face and asked him if he was OK.

"Oh yeah, I'm fine. Just thinking about the next book. You know how it is," he said.

She smiled, trying to be positive. She worried the writing would one day kill him. He seemed to stress himself so much to write.

"Are you sure you're OK?" she asked.

"I'm fine. Don't worry," he said.

"You have any ideas for the new book?" she said.

"Just a basic outline," he said.

She reminded herself that he didn't like talking about his books and changed the topic. "We got invited to an event for the new Rich Harrison movie. His new movie, *AI Awakening*, is coming out soon, and they are doing the screening and an after party on Saturday," she said.

Walt always enjoyed movie screenings. He like to meet the celebrities, and the parties could be fun.

"What's the movie about?" he asked. He thought he could guess, based on the title. Probably something about computers and world domination.

"Something about computers taking over the world," she said.

Nailed it, he thought.

"Sounds fun," he said.

She moved closer and snuggled up next to him. She smelled like fresh flowers.

For dinner they ordered pizza. He was sober and was trying not to drink any more tonight. He had seen the look in Marie's eyes. She was worried about his drinking. He could go one night without a drink. Couldn't he?

They watched a show on Netflix about chicks in prison. The show was funny and dramatic. They were hooked by the fifth episode and watched the whole first season before falling asleep on the couch.

At some point during the night, they went up to bed. She got up and went first, and he turned off the TV and checked all the doors.

He unlocked the padlock and went down to look at the typewriter. From inside the cabinet sitting in the back of the top shelf, behind all the papers, he pulled out a phone. It was a burner phone. It had been bought for one purpose. There was a single number programmed into it. Next week he would turn it on and send one text message. Then, a week later, Ian would show up.

He felt cold, and his stomach knotted. He put the phone back and went upstairs. He didn't pour a drink, which he badly wanted, and he went to bed sober and with clear thoughts. He hoped he would be able to sleep.

Walt stood at the edge of a cliff over an ocean. He knew this was a dream, but he felt cold. The waves below were large, and he could feel the mist from them as they slammed into the rock face of the cliff. He was barefoot and could feel the cold, wet grass beneath his feet. He began to shiver as the mist soaked his clothes. His toes curled over the edge of the cliff. As the strong wind picked up from behind him, he sat down in the grass. He felt the water soak him where he sat, and his feet dangled over the cliff. The wind grew stronger, and he lay down and rolled onto his stomach. He dug his hands into the grass and held on. The ground underneath him slowly angled down. Walt tried to hold on, but he felt his hands slipping through the grass. The wind and gravity were too much for him to fight, and he fell.

2

A scream welled in his throat, and he woke up shivering under the blanket as though he had a fever. Marie was still asleep next to him.

Walt stood and went to the kitchen, being careful not to wake Marie. He poured a glass of cognac and sipped it. The alcohol warmed him. Somewhere in the back of his mind, he knew it really wasn't warming him. Its warmth was as fake as the cold from his dream.

He sat on the couch, sipping his drink. There would be no more sleep tonight.

The first week passed quickly. He had enjoyed the movie's release party. There had been celebrities there, and he spoke to most of them. They had read his books and as usual had questions he did not want to answer—not that he could even if he wanted to. But he didn't want to. It was hard not to answer someone like

Tom Cruise when he asked, but he had gotten good at deflecting the questions.

He had gone to see several psychologists in his life, and they almost never answered a question directly. "What do you think it means?" That was the common way they would speak to you. He had perfected it as well. By now he thought he would make a good psychologist.

He'd learned after his first party with celebrities that if you had something to say that they liked, they would spend time talking with you. If you just gushed on how great you thought they were, they would almost never engage with you. His books were a good way to break the ice with them. Several times he had made sure they got advance copies of his new books. This made them feel as if they owed him something, which got him invited to more parties and other events than almost anything else he had done. So he would keep doing it. He promised Tom Cruise that he would send him a copy of his next book early. Tom gave him his publicist's contact information, explaining to him that he almost never gave out his personal number. He didn't want any wackos calling him. Better to be safe.

Walt had said he understood, and Tom went on to the next person looking to speak with him.

The suit was uncomfortable. Walt never liked wearing suits. He had tried to figure out how to get out of wearing them to events like this, but Marie quickly put a stop to that.

"What are you, a hobo?" she had asked him.

After that he never brought it up again.

He saw her talking to two men. He was not the jealous type, so he watched with amusement. They were both hitting on her, and she mentioned that they both looked a little scrawny. She mentioned her gym. She had a way of doing it that never seemed to piss the men off. They would often take a card and show up at her gym sometime in the future.

Marie had great business sense. She did a lot of the personal training herself and had hired someone to manage the finances of the gym. She also made sure to hire only attractive trainers. It worked well. A lot of the time, the men she met at these parties would go to her gym, and she would get them signed up with other trainers. She had a pretty full schedule already.

"You're Walt Erickson, aren't you?" a voice asked.

Walt turned and looked. The man was dressed immaculately. He was wearing a dark Prada suit with a beautiful blue tie. His hair was trimmed neatly, and he was lean. Even under the suit, Walt could tell he was fit.

"I am," Walt said smiling. He had learned long ago that when someone approached you at one of these parties, it was always better to be friendly. You never knew who the person approaching you might be.

He had been at a party once, and someone in what looked like hand-me-down clothes had approached him. Walt had been a little bit of a jerk, and a few months later, someone passed on optioning one of his books for a movie. It turned out that the underdressed man had been a major financier. After that Walt was always friendly.

"Hi," the man said, reaching out his hand. Walt shook it.

"I'm Mark Vance. I loved your last book. The ending had me thinking for several days afterward. That poor lady. Absolutely wonderful."

Mark Vance. Walt thought for a second. Where did he know that name from? Oh shit, this man ran the biggest movie studio in Hollywood. They had just optioned one of his books.

"Thank you so much. I think the ending is one of the most important parts of the books, and I'm glad you liked it," Walt said, not believing it as he said it, but he knew people loved things like that.

"Has anyone approached you about it yet?" Mark said.

"Not yet," Walt said.

Mark smiled, handing him a card. "Have your manager give me a call. I'd like first crack at a deal," Mark said.

Walt took the card and looked at it. Mark Vance, CEO, Lightshow Media.

"I'll do that," Walt said.

"Very nice meeting you," Mark said, shaking his hand and then moving on to the next person.

This was turning into a great party, Walt thought.

Marie came up behind him and pinched his ass.

"Hey, you. Having fun?" she asked.

"Oh yeah. That was Mark Vance, the head of Lightshow. He wants to option *Lonely Nights*," Walt said.

"Wow. I also saw you talking to Tom Cruise. You are just on a roll tonight, aren't you?" she asked with a smile.

Walt returned the smile. "You know me. Mr. Friendly," he said. He kissed her and asked, "You ready to go?"

"Yeah. I think I got a few potential clients, and I've had enough free drinks," she said.

"We should go say our good-byes to Charles," Walt said.

Charles Smyth was the director, and he was the one who had extended the invitation to the release party. Walt had known him since he had directed one of his films. They had been friends since the movie. They both liked to drink and both hated talking about their work.

Walt and Marie found Charles talking to Mark.

"Hi, Charles, Mark," Walt said.

"You two know each other?" Charles asked.

"We just met a few minutes ago," Mark said.

"Ah. Then I don't need to introduce you again," Charles said.

"Wonderful party, Charles. But we are going to head out. I really appreciate your having us," Walt said.

"You know you are always welcome. Thank you so much for coming. We should have dinner soon. My husband has been asking why we haven't seen you in such a long time," Charles said.

"If you have some time, we can work something out this week. Otherwise, it will have to wait a few months. I'm going to start work on my next book," Walt said.

Charles had known Walt long enough to know he did not like to be disturbed while he worked on his novels.

"Let me see what my schedule is for this week, and I'll give you a call," Charles said.

"Give Vince a hug for us, and tell him we look forward to the dinner," Walt said. Vince was Charles's husband and also one of Marie's clients.

"Hey, he sees me every week and never asks about dinner," Marie said.

"Yeah, but you are trying to kill him," Charles said with a smile.

"I keep him in great shape for you," Marie said.

"That you do," Charles said.

Marie and Walt both hugged Charles and shook Mark's hand and left.

They were quiet on the way home. Marie knew Walt was thinking about his next novel. She was prepared not to see much of him for the next few months—and for him to be upset when she did see him.

Marie dropped off Walt at home and left. Walt stood outside and watched her headlights fade and disappear. Then he went inside and changed, poured himself a drink, and sat on the couch.

3

His brother's voice sounded in his head.

Walt had been in his early twenties and was struggling with money. His brother, Paul, had saved up some money and had an idea.

"We should bid on some storage units," Paul had said.

"Huh?" Walt said.

"You know—when people don't pay for their storage at one of those storage places, they sell the contents sight unseen to people at auction," Paul said.

"So we would buy the storage unit?" Walt said.

"Just the contents. We bid, and if we win, we get the contents of the unit. Then if we're lucky, we can sell the contents for more than we paid for the unit," Paul said.

Walt stared at Paul. Paul always had some kind of scheme he was working on. But Walt thought it might be fun to bid on a unit.

"How much do they usually go for?" Walt said.

"Not sure. I know it's not much. Most of the time people just leave junk in them, so it's risky. I think we could get a unit for a few hundred if we are lucky," Paul said.

"OK. Let's try it," Walt said.

It took them a few months to figure out all the logistics. First they had to figure out where and when the auctions were. It turned out most storage places had the auctions a few times a year. It was straightforward to sign up.

Paul had always been better with people than Walt had been. He had spoken to several people who owned storage centers and had arranged for them to be at their first auction.

They stood outside the storage unit that was about to be auctioned. It was a warm and sunny day. Paul had brought a flashlight and was shining it inside the storage locker. What they saw was a wall of boxes. The boxes were labeled: kitchen, bedroom, master bedroom, and so on.

Walt was guessing that someone had moved from their house and had placed all the items in storage. For some reason, they had never come back to pick up their items and had stopped paying.

The bidding started at fifty dollars. Walt waited until the third bid, seventy-five dollars, before he made a bid.

"One hundred," Walt said, raising his hand to indicate his bid.

Walt had been hopeful that the man handling the bidding would speak like the auctioneers he had seen on TV as a kid. The fast-paced talking had always amused Walt. But this man spoke like the turtle in the race between the turtle and the rabbit. Walt had wanted the rabbit but got a slow turtle.

But they won the bid for $300. He hugged Paul and paid the auctioneer with the cash they had brought.

Walt had been right about the boxes. It was items from rooms. Most of the items were used and would not get them a lot of money. Inside the box marked "kitchen," they had found some silverware that looked expensive. The other boxes contained old electronic equipment, including a stereo with speakers and an early VCR. Those items would not be worth a lot.

The clothes were nothing special, and they figured they would just donate those. They found some jewelry in the box marked "master bedroom." Walt was not sure if it was real gold, but if it was, it should be worth something.

It took them half a day to go through everything, and then they borrowed a truck from one of their friends and hauled everything away.

The silverware and jewelry they took to a pawnshop. The pawnshop owner looked over everything and offered them $500. Walt asked for $600, and they agreed on $550. Minus the cost of gas, they had walked away with a little over $200.

Not bad. Not great but not bad. They would use this money to bid on another unit.

For the next six months, they improved their skills and went to more auctions.

They got good at looking inside a bin and making a decision about whether they would find valuable items. Most of the time, they made a few hundred dollars.

Once they bid on a unit that was full of boxes. After winning the bid for $200, they had found the boxes to contain newspapers. Old newspapers might have been worth something, but the person who had collected them had marked them up. Whoever they were, they had edited the newspapers like a teacher grading papers. They had crossed out misspellings, placed commas, or just made notes in the borders of the paper about what was written, making all the papers worthless.

Walt was discouraged by that. Paul had said that was bound to happen, and in the next unit they made almost $1,000. Someone had left some nice jewelry in a jewelry box, and they pawned that off for a nice profit.

In the seventh month, they found the typewriter.

It was a cool day, with cloud cover blocking the sun. Looking back on that day, Walt remembered a sense of foreboding. He had a bad feeling about the locker and didn't want to bid on it, but Paul insisted, telling Walt he had a good feeling about it.

After winning the auction for just under $200, they stood inside, looking around. This locker was full of antique items. There were several old handheld mirrors. Walt never understood the need for handheld mirrors. His brother said people used them to look at the back of their head. Walt's hair was short, so it had never occurred to him to look at the back of his head.

There was old jewelry that needed to be cleaned. It had grown dull sitting in the storage unit.

Sitting in the back right corner on the floor and covered in a protective cloth cover was an old typewriter. Paul pulled the cover off and stood looking at it.

"I think this might be worth something. Maybe a couple of hundred dollars. It looks to be in great condition," Paul said.

There was an envelope stuffed down in the space in front of the carriage. Paul pulled it out. The paper was faded from white to yellow and was starting to dry. Paul opened the envelope, and there was a small handwritten note: "DO NOT USE!"

Whoever wrote the note had used all caps and wrote only the single sentence. Walt took the note from Paul.

Weird, he thought.

The typewriter looked almost new and was labeled Wordsmith on a small metal plate on the front. Aside from that and the letters on the keys, there were no other marks.

Paul put the cover back on it, and they finished packing up the storage locker. Paul put the typewriter in the front seat of the truck, between himself and Walt.

Paul dropped off Walt at his house.

"I'll come by in the morning, and we can go pawn everything," Walt said. "Looks like we might get a few hundred dollars."

"Hopefully more. I think some of this stuff might be worth a lot," Paul said.

Walt went up to his small apartment and opened a beer. He sipped at the beer and watched some TV. He thought about antique collectors. Maybe they would get a good amount for these items. He knew there were a lot of people who collected antiques.

He remembered going antiquing with his grandma when he was little. They had spent half the day going to odd-smelling stores filled with old items. Walt had thought most of it looked like junk, but his grandma was excited by several of the items she had found. At that age he hadn't understood.

In reality he still didn't really understand, but if it was worth money, he was all for it.

Go on, you old ladies, collect your items, he thought. Make me some money.

Walt watched Jay Leno on TV and then poured out the little bit of his beer that remained and went to bed.

Walt woke up at 6:00 a.m. He knew Paul would be there at around eight, and he didn't want to rush.

He got ready and sat reading the paper and drinking coffee. He read the stock section. He was thinking maybe he should invest in some stocks now that he had a little bit of extra money. He would have to ask someone what he should invest in.

The understanding he had about the stock market was almost zero. He did know that companies offered stock so that anyone could own a piece of the company, but that was as far as his knowledge went. Maybe Paul knew something.

His brother knocked on his door at a little after eight.

"Hey, Walt," Paul said.

"Morning, Paul," Walt replied.

Paul had called one of the pawnshop owners he knew and had persuaded the guy to meet him early that morning. Brian was always fair in what he offered them, so Paul liked to give him first crack at the items. Paul had gone through the items once more the night before and removed anything he figured Brian might not want. Aside from the pawnshop, Brian sold antiques and collectibles. He had a good eye for the items.

When they were first getting started, Walt would often take items to a few different places to see which ones gave the best deals. That was how they had found Brian.

Brian was a slightly overweight middle-aged man with dark hair that was just starting to get gray. He wore a T-shirt for an old rock band and jeans.

"Morning, guys. What do you have for me?" Brian asked.

"We got a pretty good locker yesterday with some good antique items," Paul said.

"Nice," Brian said as he went to the back of the truck and started looking. He looked through everything.

"Very nice. I'll give you $700 for the lot," Brian said.

"I was thinking it was worth at least $900," Walt said. "I mean, the typewriter alone, I think, would be worth $150. Plus those old mirrors and the jewelry."

"Didn't see a typewriter. But everything else is worth $700," Brian said.

Walt looked at Paul, who said, "Done. We'll take it."

That's $350 apiece, Walt thought. He'd been hoping for $400 at the lowest. He wondered why Paul hadn't brought the typewriter. Still, he had a decent profit for two days' work.

They helped Brian unload the items and took them inside his shop. He gave them cash and a receipt. They shook hands and left.

On the ride home, Paul was quiet.

"Why the fuck didn't you bring the typewriter?" Walt asked.

"I want to keep it. There's something about it I like," Paul said.

"Fine, but I want fifty dollars from you if we aren't going to sell it," Walt said.

"I don't think we would have been able to sell it for one hundred. Maybe fifty. I'll give you twenty-five for your half," Paul said.

"Thirty," Walt said.

"Fine. Done. Shit, you drive a hard bargain," Paul said.

"What the hell are you going to do with a typewriter? I didn't know you could even write," Walt said.

"Ha. Funny. I don't know. I just think it's cool," Paul said.

"I'm hungry. You should stop at a McDonald's," Walt said.

Paul did just that.

Almost a week went by, and Walt didn't hear from his brother. He went by Paul's apartment and knocked. Paul didn't answer. His car was there, but he had several ladies he would often stay out with.

Walt didn't start to get worried until the second week. Paul had never been with any lady that long, and even if he was, he would call Walt after a few days.

They had missed opportunities for several auctions.

Walt was knocking on Paul's door when he thought he heard a noise from inside.

Clack clack clack.

Walt stopped knocking and pressed his ear to the door. The apartment was quiet except for the clacking sound. Was that typing? Walt wondered. Was Paul in there typing?

"Paul!" he shouted as loudly as he could, knocking hard at the same time.

The door next door to Paul's opened, and a man leaned out and looked at Walt. "Dude, I'm trying to sleep," the man said. "Can you please shut the fuck up?"

Walt nodded at the man, who closed his door.

Paul had given him a key but made him swear he would only use it with Paul's permission or in case of an emergency. "Don't fucking use this key unless I'm dying. I don't want you walking in on me banging some chick or with my dick in my hand," Paul had said.

This was beginning to feel like an emergency. Walt thought about Paul's words. Yes. This counted as an emergency.

He opened the door.

The first thing he noticed was the rotten smell. Paul was a clean person for a young single man. He never let dishes sit in the sink, and he didn't let old clothes pile up. But the apartment smelled as if something had shit itself before dying and was lying there rotting in a pile of its own last shit.

Walt put his shirt up over his nose and held it there with his hand. He didn't want to breathe in whatever he was smelling.

The second thing he noticed was the clacking. It was loud and consistent. The pace never slowed. He pictured one of those wobbling birds that continually bobs down to drink water. The clacking moved faster than that, but the pace stayed exactly the same.

Clack clack clack clack clack.

The sound was coming from Paul's bedroom.

Walt walked cautiously to Paul's room. He was not sure what he would find, but he could feel something wasn't right.

The door was closed most of the way, with just a small crack. Walt pushed it open. His brother sat at his desk. The typewriter had been placed on his desk, and Paul sat there typing. Paul didn't acknowledge his brother. He just kept typing, with no change in pace at all.

Paul looked as if he had lost about twenty pounds. He was drastically thinner. He wore a pair of shorts and a T-shirt. His skin had a yellow color, like paper that had been sitting out in the sun too long.

Walt grabbed Paul's shoulders and called his name. "Paul! It's me! Hello!" Walt said, shaking Paul by the shoulders.

Nothing. Paul kept typing. Walt put his hand in front of Paul's face. Paul's typing never slowed. Walt looked at what Paul was typing. It was a story of some kind. It was not nonsense. He was writing something.

Walt grabbed Paul and pulled him out of the chair, away from the typewriter, and they fell to the floor. For a second Paul turned and looked at Walt. It was the first time since Walt had entered the room that Paul had acknowledged his presence. Then Paul stood and went back to the chair and sat down and started typing again.

What was going on here? Walt wondered. He was starting to freak out. He again grabbed Paul by the shoulders, wrapping his arms around him from behind and pulling him away from the typewriter. Once again they both fell to the floor.

This time Walt did not let him go. He held Paul tightly. Paul struggled to get up. For a few seconds, he tried to pull himself away. When that failed, he leaned his head forward and brought it up hard into Walt's nose.

Pain exploded in Walt as the cartilage in his nose snapped with an odd popping noise. Blood and tears covered his face. He put his hands on his nose, and when he brought one of them away to look at it, it was covered in blood. Fuck! That was his only thought. He got up and went into the bathroom and Paul stood and went back to the chair. Walt's face was a mess, and his nose was bent at a weird angle. Great, he thought. The pain wasn't so bad now, but there was still blood flowing from his nose. He ran a towel under warm water and put it on his nose. Touching his nose caused pain to shoot out across his face.

Fuck. Be gentle, he told himself.

After cleaning up his face the best he could, he went back to Paul.

Clack clack clack.

Paul was sitting back at the typewriter and once again typing. Same speed as before. Nothing had changed.

Jesus, what the fuck is going on? Walt wondered.

He had a couple of options. The first was just to leave. Let his brother do whatever he was going to do.

That was not really an option. Something was wrong with Paul, and doing nothing would not help him.

Judging by how Paul looked, Walt figured he had not eaten in a few days. He needed to get him to a hospital and get him some help. Great, he thought. My brother has gone crazy over a stupid typewriter. Walt wondered if it would be a good story. Then he pushed that thought from his head. What was he thinking?

He decided he would call for help. His nose was beginning to throb. Each time blood pulsed, he felt a pain in his nose. He needed to get medical attention.

He pulled out his cell phone and flipped it open.

"911, what's your emergency?" a female voice on the other end of the phone said.

"Hi, yes. My brother just assaulted me, and I think my nose is broken. I think he needs some kind of help too," Walt said.

"Is he injured as well?" the lady asked.

"No, I don't think so. But he hasn't eaten in a while, and he's typing," Walt said.

"Sir? Typing, you said?"

"Yes. He's been typing without stopping for I guess a few days. When I tried to stop him, that's when he attacked me and broke my nose."

"OK, sir. I'm going to send an ambulance and the police. Do you want me to stay on the line?"

"No. I think it's fine as long as I don't try to get him to stop typing," Walt said.

"Very good, sir. Have a nice day," the lady said, and before he could say anything else, she hung up.

Walt sat and watched his brother while he waited for the police to show up. The clacking of the old typewriter was kind of soothing. It had an almost hypnotic effect on Walt.

The loud banging on his door snapped him out of it.

Walt got up and answered the door.

"Sir, are you OK? We have been knocking for a while," the police officer said, fixating on Walt's nose, which had stopped bleeding but had blood rings around the nostrils and was crooked on his face.

"I'm fine. No ambulance with you?" Walt asked.

"No. Should be here soon, sir," the officer said.

"I'm Officer Koch, and this is my partner, Officer Sanchez," he said.

Officer Koch was neatly dressed, with well-trimmed hair. He looked as if he had stepped straight out of a military uniform into a police uniform. His partner was a dark-skinned lady. Her hair was in a neat bun on the back of her head.

"May we come in?" she asked.

Walt moved out of the way and welcomed them in.

"Where is your brother at, sir?" Koch asked.

"He's in his office. You can hear him typing," Walt said.

All three of them were quiet for a second, and they heard the clacking sound.

Walt led them to Paul.

"Hey, Paul. The police are here," Walt said.

Clack clack clack.

Paul's typing did not slow down. He stayed focused on the typewriter.

The officers went to Paul and stood on either side. Most people would have felt unnerved having two police officers standing over them. Paul paid no attention and kept typing.

"Sir, we would like to have a few words with you," Officer Sanchez said.

Paul kept typing.

"Sir! Please stop typing," Officer Koch said in a firm voice that Walt guessed made his kids crap their pants.

Paul kept typing.

The officers both looked confused. They were not sure what the next step should be here.

"Maybe we should wait for the ambulance?" Walt said.

"Sir?" the lady said, snapping her fingers and waving her hand in front of Paul.

Paul kept typing.

"Yeah. Something isn't right with him. We should take him in for a medical evaluation," Officer Koch said.

"Would you guys like something to drink?" Walt asked.

"No, thank you, sir," Sanchez answered for both of them.

They asked Walt what had happened, and he explained, starting with not seeing his brother for a few days and ending with the head butt.

As he finished the story, the paramedics knocked on the door.

Walt let them in and explained what was happening.

"I think he needs to be taken in for a psych eval," Sanchez said to the paramedics.

"The problem is I don't think we will be able to move him without force. He attacked his brother when he tried to move him," Koch said.

"First, we should take a look at his nose," one of the paramedics said, gesturing at Walt.

"Yeah. It is throbbing pretty bad," Walt said.

They cleaned up the blood and put a bandage across his nose.

"You should have a doctor take a look at it," the paramedic said.

"OK," Walt said.

Now that Walt's nose was fixed up, they debated on how best to subdue Paul.

"When I tried to move him earlier, that's when he attacked me. So please be careful," Walt said.

"I think we are going to take him to the floor and cuff him. We will take him down to the hospital in the police car," Koch said.

Walt didn't like the idea of seeing his brother in handcuffs, but he couldn't think of anything else to do.

The two police officers went and stood on either side of Paul.

"Sir, we are going to ask you one more time to stop typing and speak with us, or we are going to have to cuff you," Koch said.

Paul kept typing.

Officer Koch snapped a cuff onto Paul's right hand. He then swung his arm down and around in one single, fast motion. Officer Sanchez placed one hand on Paul's shoulder and grabbed Paul's left wrist and swung it back behind him. Officer Koch then snapped the cuff onto his other wrist.

In its entirety the action took less than two seconds and seemed like something these two officers had done many times in the past.

For the first couple of seconds, Paul sat there not moving. Then all hell broke loose.

Paul stood and began to struggle in the handcuffs. Using his left hand, he wrapped his thumb and forefinger around the cuff on his right hand and began to pull his hand out of the handcuff.

"Hey, wait!" Officer Sanchez shouted.

Skin on Paul's right hand started to come off at the thumb as he pulled it through the handcuff. Blood poured out of the gash, covering the handcuff. It acted as a lubricant, allowing him to completely free his hand from the cuff. For a second before blood covered it, Walt saw the bone on the knuckle of Paul's thumb.

"Jesus, what the fuck are you doing?" Walt screamed at his brother.

Ignoring Walt, Paul sat back down and began to type again. Blood covered the keys and a flap of skin hung from his thumb, flapping with each press of the space bar. Paul's hand was half covered in blood, and Walt noticed there were abrasions on all his knuckles where the cuff had scraped them.

Paul's left hand still had the cuff wrapped around the wrist, and the blood-covered cuff that was supposed to be holding Paul's right hand rested on the table right where the typewriter ended.

Clack clack clack.

All five of them stared at Paul, who ignored them and continued to type.

"I—I've—Jesus," Officer Koch said.

Officer Sanchez looked at the paramedics and asked, "Do you guys have any sedatives?"

"Yeah. Yeah, we do. I'll go get it," the first paramedic said.

All of them were fixated on Paul's hand.

"Bring some bandages too. We have to stop that bleeding," Walt said.

"Way ahead of you," the paramedic said as he left.

"Paul?" Walt whispered. Then he repeated it with more force.

Nothing. His brother was not answering, and he had almost pulled his thumb off to be able to continue writing.

A few minutes later, the paramedic returned with a bandage and a shot. He had preloaded whatever it was that they were going to use to sedate his brother.

"Hi, Paul, I'm going to give you a shot in your arm," the paramedic said.

Paul kept typing during the administration of the shot.

After a few minutes, the typing for the first time began to slow down.

Clack. After a few seconds came another *clack*.

The paramedics stood on either side of Paul, and when he finally slumped over, they caught him and moved him to the floor.

The silence of the room was strange. They were all so used to the typing that the quiet was uncomfortable.

One of the paramedics knelt down by Paul and began to bandage his hand. The other one went out with Officer Sanchez and then came back, pushing one of the paramedic cots. When they got it lined up next to Paul, the paramedic lowered it down.

Walt watched them load Paul onto the cot, and then they raised it back up.

"Have you guys ever seen anything like this before?" Walt asked.

"I haven't. But you never know. We will take him down for a psych eval. Is he on any kind of medication?" the first paramedic asked.

"Shouldn't you have asked that before giving him the shot?" Walt asked.

The paramedic didn't say anything.

"No, he isn't that I know of," Walt said. "Where will you take him?"

"Mercy General. They have a psychiatrist on hand for emergencies. He'll need to be evaluated," the paramedic said.

"OK. I'll meet you guys down there," Walt said.

Everyone left, leaving Walt alone in the apartment. He turned to look at the typewriter. The table was covered in blood from Paul's hand. There was no blood on the typewriter. Walt at first thought he had just missed it. So he went and got a washcloth and put some warm water on it. He rubbed it on the keys, and it came up clean. The typewriter looked exactly as it did when they had found it in the storage locker: clean and new.

What the fuck? Walt thought.

He then felt a chill and got the same feeling he would often get as a kid when he was alone in the dark and heard an unknown noise. He needed to get to the hospital. He turned and left, not running—but wanting to.

The hospital was crowded. It took him almost ten minutes to find parking, and once inside it took him another few minutes to find where they had taken Paul.

For the psychiatric evaluation, Paul would be checked in to emergency and then placed in a room until a doctor could come evaluate him. It was a busy evening, and it seemed the wait would be a while.

Walt sat with his brother. They had restrained his arms and legs with leather bands that would prevent the kind of injury he had gotten when pulling free of the handcuffs.

As far as Walt knew, his brother had never done any drugs, aside from some pot they sometimes smoked. And he drank a few nights a week—usually just a couple of beers, nothing that would explain this.

At some point Paul had woken up and started struggling against the restraints. Nothing anyone did got him to stop, so they had sedated him again to prevent him from further hurting himself.

After what felt like forever to Walt but was really only two hours, a doctor came in with a nurse. He was an older man, thin with graying hair. The nurse was a younger man but much larger.

Walt figured they wanted someone who could help restrain his brother if they needed to.

"Hi, I'm Dr. Holland," the doctor said, putting out his hand. "Would you tell me what happened?"

Walt shook his hand and told the story from when he got to Paul's place.

"Has he taken any drugs that you know of?"

"No. As far as I know, the only thing he ever does is pot and beer," Walt said.

"Has he ever exhibited any psychotic issues before, or does your family have any history of psychotic events?" the doctor asked.

"My grandma had Alzheimer's. But that's the only thing I know of," Walt said.

"The fixation on the typewriter is unique. Also, he is a danger to himself. We are worried about what will happen when the sedation wears off. Pulling his hand from the handcuff caused some damage to the bones in his hand, and it had to be extremely painful. Our main goal will be to keep him from hurting himself or anyone else. We also want to run some tests," the doctor said. Then he continued. "You will need to get him checked in to the hospital. Also, the damage to his hand is extensive, and we will need to operate to repair it. You will need to sign the approval for that as well. I think the police will want to talk to him if we can figure out what is wrong and get him well enough."

Walt thought for a second. He was worried about Paul's insurance. No time to think about that now. His brother was having a psychotic episode, and nothing else mattered. Walt needed to focus only on Paul getting better.

"OK. I'll get him checked in. You go ahead and run the tests, and I'll sign the approval for you to operate. I'll come back by tomorrow morning," Walt said.

Walt shook the doctor's hand and went to get Paul admitted.

There were tons of forms to fill out. Filling out as many forms as he could and signing all the approvals for the surgery and for the tests they wanted to run took him almost an hour.

Walt was tired. He needed to go home and get some rest. First, though, he thought about the typewriter. It had been clean. Walt had expected there to be blood on the keys, but it had been shiny and new. What did that mean?

Not worth thinking about now. Focus on your brother, he thought. He's what matters now. Don't worry about the typewriter.

Pushing the typewriter from his mind was harder than it should have been. He went home and had a couple of beers, which he badly needed. Lying in bed, he thought of Paul pulling his hand from the handcuff. It had happened so fast, and there had been so much blood. Paul had not hesitated to do it—no pause to build up courage. Just one quick, deliberate act that had mangled his hand. Blood had been on everything—everything but the keys of the typewriter.

Walt found himself thinking about the clacking of the keys as his brother typed whatever story he was writing.

After a little while, he fell asleep.

He stood in a big grass meadow. In the distance, he heard waves. He couldn't see anything in the dark, but he felt the wind blowing in the direction of the waves. The wind was strong, almost pushing him. He wanted to go see the waves. Besides, he didn't think he could fight the wind, so he walked toward the sound with the wind edging him, making him walk faster.

Noise from the alarm woke him up, breaking him out of his dream. He hit the snooze button and nine minutes later forced himself out of bed.

He wanted to go to the hospital this morning to check on his brother. But first he would go by his brother's place. Telling himself that he wanted to go clean up the blood mess but knowing subconsciously that he really just wanted to see the typewriter, he got dressed and drove over to his brother's place.

He let himself in, went into the bedroom, and looked at the typewriter. The blood on the table had dried into a dark brownish color. It circled the typewriter like a weird moat. Walt picked up the typewriter and set it on the floor.

Cleaning up the blood took a little time. He found some cleaner under the kitchen sink and first sprayed the blood to let it soak. He then got a bowl, filled it with warm water, and grabbed a sponge and some paper towels. Using the rough side of the sponge, he started cleaning. The water in the bowl turned red as he cleaned.

Most of the blood came up, but it left a stain on the table. Paul would have to repaint the table to get rid of the stain—or replace the table.

He saw a couple of other spots of blood on the floor and repeated the cleaning on them.

He picked up the typewriter and placed it back on the table. As he lifted it, he checked the bottom for any bloodstains. Nothing. Clean as a whistle.

No blood.

Walt took a few steps back from the table and typewriter as one would from a growling dog. Give it some distance, or you'll get bitten. Had the typewriter bitten his brother, so to speak?

Don't be a fucking idiot, he thought. Paul is sick. Go see him.

Walt was being crazy, and he was a little scared. He wasn't sure why he was scared, but something caused him to get goose bumps, and he felt the chill run over his body.

He went to the kitchen and poured his brother's blood that had mixed with the water down the drain. He then cleaned the bowl and put it in the dish rack. The sponge now had a red tint. He tossed it in the trash because nobody wanted a blood sponge and then went back in Paul's room. On the dresser, next to the table with the typewriter, he noticed two stacks of paper. One stack was still wrapped and was the fresh typing paper Paul had been using. The second stack was whatever he had been writing. Paul had laid each page facedown as he finished it.

Walt picked up the stack of paper and read the title.

Forgotten Boy.

Interesting title, he thought, and he started reading.

Growing up, Paul had never expressed any interest in writing. His grades had been passable but not great. But this story was engrossing.

It started with a bang: a child being killed. After that it began to tell the story of the dead boy's family dealing with the loss of their child. Walt could not stop reading it.

After an hour he forced himself to stop. He needed to go to the hospital. Paul needed him. He was able to stop reading after another fifteen minutes.

He left the book, split now into two piles. He left the pages he had read facedown where he had found the book. Next to that he left the rest of the book face up. He did not want to lose his place. He would go help Paul, and then he would go to work, and then he would come back here to finish the book—the book that wasn't finished because he had stopped his brother from writing it.

Holy shit, the book would never be finished! What had he done?

He'd helped his brother was what he had done. The book wasn't important, he told himself, more to make himself believe it than because it was a fact. He wanted to read the end of the book, and not being able to was going to be like not being able to scratch an itch in the middle of his back.

Walt left Paul's apartment and headed to the hospital.

He thought about his brother. Had Paul really gone crazy over writing, or was there something more to this? There was no blood on the typewriter. Walt didn't want to believe it was the typewriter. That did not make any sense. This was not a Stephen King book with evil cars or insane rabid dogs.

Paul had never had any psychological issues before. He had been as sane as Walt was. No one he knew of in his family had ever had any problems like this. No drugs, either. So what could make a perfectly sane man pull his hand from a handcuff without a second thought? Paul had yanked his hand from the cuff as if he were popping the tab on a soda.

Walt thought again of Paul's hand with the skin pulled off his thumb—the skin torn and flapping, blood streaming from his hand in pulses and covering the table in the red liquid, yet none at all on the typewriter. The Wordsmith typewriter was as clean as when they had found it. Was there something with the typewriter? How the fuck would he prove it was the damn typewriter?

There was no way he was going to try typing on that thing. If it was the typewriter, he had seen what it had done to his brother.

Walt parked at the hospital and went up to Paul's room. The room was empty. He went to the nurses' station and asked about his brother. There was a thin Filipino lady sitting at the desk.

"We had to move him. He woke up during the night and hurt his arm trying to get out of the restraints," she said.

"How did he hurt his arm?" Walt asked, the concern and aggravation coming through in his voice.

The nurse spoke to him as if he were a child. "Sir, sometime during the night he woke up, and before we could get him sedated again, he'd managed to pull his already injured hands from one of the restraints. His hand started bleeding again, and we managed to get him sedated before he was able to hurt himself further. During the process he struck one of the nurses who was trying to restrain him and gave her a black eye."

"Jesus. Is she OK?" Walt asked.

"Aside from the black eye, she's fine," the nurse said.

"Where is my brother now?"

"We moved him to psych, where we keep the violent patients."

The nurse gave Walt instructions on how to find Paul.

When he got to the psych ward, he found a nurse and asked about his brother.

"Let me get the doctor," she said.

Walt sat down in the waiting area and picked up an *Us* magazine. The doctor arrived in a few minutes.

"Hi, I'm Dr. Kanade," the doctor said.

The doctor was Indian, Walt guessed by his name and dark skin. He had no accent and was lean with neatly cut hair.

"We had to sedate your brother again. Anytime he wakes up, he struggles to get out of the restraints. He will not speak to anyone and does not respond to anything we say. To be honest, we are not really sure what's wrong. We have run all the tests we are able to run with him sedated. Blood is clean. No drugs or anything that would explain this behavior. Everything looks normal. Is there anything at all you can tell us that might help?"

Walt thought about the typewriter but pushed it from his mind.

"No. I've told you guys everything I know. I hadn't seen my brother in a few days, and when I went to see him, I found him sitting at the typewriter. Anytime someone moved him, he freaked out trying to get back to it," Walt said.

"OK. We need to keep him here until we figure out what's wrong. He is a danger to himself and others, so we cannot release him. I also think the police want to speak with him once he is well," Dr. Kanade said.

"Can I see him?" Walt asked.

"Yes. He is in room 122A."

Walt walked down the hall and found Paul. His hand had a fresh bandage on it, and he was motionless on the bed except for the rising and falling of his stomach as he slept. His arms and legs were restrained.

"Hey, bro," Walt said, touching Paul's leg.

They had put an IV into his unbandaged hand. He looked very thin.

Walt went and found a nurse.

"How is my brother getting food? He looks so thin. Also, his lips look really dry. Is there anything we can do?" Walt asked.

"He is getting nutrition through the IV. We can't get him to stop trying to escape when he is awake. So we don't have any other choice. I can give you some Vaseline for his lips," the nurse said.

Walt took the Vaseline from the nurse and went back to Paul's room.

"Hey, bro, I'm going to put some Vaseline on your lips," Walt said. Paul was asleep, but Walt had heard people say that even unconscious patients needed to hear voices. So Walt spoke to him.

"That's better, right?" Walt said, putting a small amount of Vaseline on Paul's lips. Then Walt put the lid on the Vaseline and set it on the table next to Paul's bed.

Looking at Paul's unbandaged hand, Walt noticed for the first time that the tips of all of the fingers had a dark tint from bruising, and the skin was raw. The index finger had a Band-Aid on it. He figured that one had been bad enough that a nurse had cleaned and dressed it.

Walt peeled back the Band-Aid to take a look. The skin had worn down at the tip where it had been striking the typewriter keys. A thick scab had formed on it. Walt put the Band-Aid back in place.

How long had his brother been sitting at the typewriter, typing through the pain?

Walt felt guilt rush over him for wanting Paul to finish the story. But he still wanted it. He ached to find out how the story ended.

The question was whether the story even belonged to his brother. Paul had never written anything in his life. He'd had no interest in it, Walt knew.

"So if you didn't write this, then maybe it was the typewriter," Walt said out loud.

Walt was tempted to unhook the restraints. He had a feeling that if he did that, Paul would go back to the typewriter and finish the story. He resisted that impulse.

How could he test whether it was the typewriter or his brother? If he let someone else type on it, how long would that person sit there typing? Would he or she stop when the story was finished or keep going?

Looking at his brother, he figured the outcome would not be good. Paul was thin and looked skeletal. His eyes had sunken in and looked black. His cheeks looked like thin pieces of meat barely holding on to his face.

Sitting there looking at his brother, Walt thought about the beautiful story Paul had created. Then Paul opened his eyes.

4

For a second nothing happened. Paul stared at Walt, his eyes focusing for a moment.

"Paul?" Walt said.

Paul stiffened and began to thrash against the restraints. Walt watched him pull the restraints tight—and then keep pulling, the muscles on his arms tightening as he pulled. His back arched, and he looked as if he were being electrocuted. There was a loud sound like a cork popping from a bottle of wine. His brother's right arm had pulled from its socket and drooped down.

Walt screamed for help, and several nurses rushed into the room. Two of them pushed his brother down before he could do further damage. A third nurse injected him with something Walt figured was another sedative.

After a few seconds, Paul stopped moving.

"Why the fuck would you let him wake up?" Walt yelled at the nurses.

"He—he shouldn't have woken up. We have him on an IV that should keep him unconscious," one of the nurses said.

A few minutes later, a doctor came in. Walt and the nurses explained what had happened.

The doctor pulled up Paul's record on the computer screen in the room and read through it. He looked at one of the nurses and asked, "Are these numbers accurate?"

"Yes," the nurse answered.

"He seems to be resistant to some of the medication. We will need to up the dosage. Make sure to keep track of his vital signs and notify me of any changes. You are his brother?" the doctor asked, turning to Walt.

"Yes. Doc, what's going on?"

"We have him on some medication that should keep him sedated. The dosage we had him on should have kept him sedated without any issues, but he woke up. Now we will need to give him a higher dosage. We are very concerned that every time he wakes up, he hurts himself. The next step will be to medically induce a coma. We are hoping to avoid that."

Walt didn't know what to say to that.

Feeling Paul's shoulder, the doctor told the nurse that the shoulder had been dislocated and would need to be placed back in the socket.

Walt did not feel like watching that, so he went out to get a soda. He went down the hall and asked one of the nurses where the cafeteria was. She told him, and he went down and got a drink and a bag of Doritos and sat at an empty table by a window.

Looking out the window, he thought about his brother. There did not seem to be anything he could do for him. If Paul hurt himself every time he was awake, they had to keep him asleep. That was no way for anyone to live.

If he could, he would tell them to let his brother out of the straps and let him go, but Walt knew they wouldn't do that. If Paul left the hospital, he would have to go to the police station. The police would want to know that he wasn't a danger to himself or others before they released him. Walt didn't know what the policy was for something like this, but he knew for certain they would not let him just leave.

Two ideas came to Walt. First, he thought about destroying the typewriter: grab a large hammer and smash it to pieces. Then he could tell his brother it was gone. But what if he destroyed it, and the only way to stop his brother's madness was by letting him finish the story? His brother would be forever mad.

Second, he thought about having someone else try typing on the typewriter to see if that person could stop typing or if the typewriter would affect him or her the same way. If it did, he wondered how long that person would type.

From the looks of his brother, he believed a person would at least type until the story was finished. Maybe after the story was finished, the person would snap out of whatever it was that was making him or her type in the first place.

Walt knew this was a crazy thought. A typewriter did not make you type. But if it did, he could find that out with a simple test: just have some other damn fool type on it. But after what the Wordsmith had done to his brother, he couldn't just have anyone type on it.

Maybe a homeless person? The city was full of them. Drugs or money would get one to come type one sentence. That was all he needed: one sentence. *The quick brown fox jumps over the lazy dog.* He had been told that sentence had every letter in the alphabet. That would cover the entire keyboard, and if it was just a crazy thought, the homeless person could type the sentence, and then he would pay him or her, and off the person would go. Easy money—and he would get rid of the crazy thought that a typewriter had somehow made his brother write the best story he had every read.

Simple. Except it really wasn't. Even knowing that not too many people would look for a missing homeless person, he didn't relish the idea of bringing someone who had been living on the street into his car and then into his brother's apartment.

He had often given dollars to homeless people when they asked, putting them into hands that were dirty and black with long, yellow fingernails. If you stood too long, the smell would wash over you like fog rolling over the mountains. You'd be doing your best not to wince, trying to say something but being grossed out. For most of them, it was not their fault. They needed to be on medication but either refused or didn't know.

Still, he did not want to bring that smell or dirt into his car. He needed to know, though. Find one that was semiclean, maybe. He had seen homeless people in bathrooms occasionally around the city, cleaning themselves. So maybe not all of them didn't shower.

Deciding that he would get a homeless person to try out the typewriter, he also decided he would use Paul's truck, since this was to help Paul. Well, mostly to help his brother—only a little to see if he would ever get to read the end of the story Paul had started.

Not wanting to use drugs as a bribe, he would use cash. He figured he would use $200 to bribe them. One hundred up front and a hundred after should be enough.

Asking someone to come with him just to type a single sentence seemed like an odd request. He would need to come up with some other reason. He could offer someone dinner and help the person get cleaned up. That might work. At least he hoped that would work—a dinner, a shower, and some cash because he felt sorry for the person and wanted to help.

Walt finished the soda and never opened the bag of chips. He left the chips on the table and went to check on Paul before he left.

By the time he got back to Paul's room, the doctors had reseated Paul's shoulder in its socket and bandaged it into place. It was an odd look, since Paul still had the restraints on his wrists.

There was no one in the room. Walt gave his brother a kiss on the forehead and left.

Once he got behind the wheel of his car, tears filled his eyes. Worry about his brother and the fear of what he was about to do came down on him like a sledgehammer. It would not stop him. No matter the guilt, he had to know.

Taking Paul's car instead of his, he went downtown. The city was as dark as it ever got, which wasn't that dark.

People stood on the street outside of bars, smoking and talking. After working all day, they needed to unwind, and alcohol fueled all kinds of fun. So all the educated, hardworking people stood at bars, talking about stocks or housing prices or whatever the fuck it was they talked about. But this wasn't the kind of crowd he was looking for.

Walt figured he would need to go to one of the areas where drugs were being sold—not by some guy in a suit at the back of a club. No, he needed to go where cars pulled up and the transaction happened quickly. He thought he might be more likely to run into police there, but it was also much more likely he would find someone who would take him up on his offer.

He parked his car at a cheap lot and shoved a five-dollar bill into a slot that allowed him to park for the evening. Then he picked a direction and walked. He wore an old T-shirt and some faded jeans with an old pair of running shoes. He wanted to fit in with the area and not draw attention to himself. He hoped he would not stand out.

He approached a man sitting on the street with a cup out in front of him and asked if he'd like to make some easy money.

The man looked at Walt. His mouth had a white crust on the outside edges of his lips, and he was caked in a thin layer of dirt.

"S'muh munny?" he said to Walt, trying to focus his eyes but failing.

"Never mind," Walt said, dropping a dollar into the cup. This guy was already way too wasted to be helpful.

Walt didn't want to stay in the area too long. By the fourth person he spoke to, he started to worry that this might not have been a good idea.

At the fifth person, he got lucky.

The man was sitting in front of a liquor store with a sign in front of him that said, "Need money for life. 'Cause life sucks, and I want to buy drugs." Walt guessed he was about his own age. He was white but had dreadlocks. He wore an old tie-dyed shirt and faded jeans that looked blue-brown, but Walt guessed they had started out light blue.

"Does that sign work?" Walt asked.

The man eyed Walt cautiously for a few seconds. Walt passed whatever test he had just taken.

"Yeah. People like honesty," the man said.

Pulling out his wallet, Walt placed a dollar into the baseball hat the man had turned over in front of him. There were a few dollars already in the hat, so the man must have been onto something.

"Thanks, man," the man said.

Slowly. Take this slowly, Walt thought.

"You make a lot of money sitting here?" Walt asked.

"I make enough. I'm not trying to get fuckin' rich. I'm just trying to get wasted. You know how it is," the man said.

"Yeah," Walt said, not really sure how it was. But agreeing was easier than not.

"Where're you from?" Walt asked.

"I live all over, man. I'm from the road," the man said.

"You don't live here?" Walt asked.

"Man, I'm a traveler. I'm just here for a while. Then I think I might head north. You know, I got to keep movin'," the man said.

"Want to make some extra money?" Walt asked.

"I ain't no fuckin prostitute, dude."

"What? Oh, no, no! Not like that. I need some help with something," Walt said.

"What the fuck can I help you with?" the man asked.

"I need some help at home, moving something. I'd pay you to help you with your travels," Walt said.

First lie.

"Why not get one of the Mexicans that hangs out in front of Home Depot?"

"You remind me of my brother. I haven't spoken to him in a long time. I'd like to help you," Walt said.

Second lie.

"So I move something for you, and you give me some money?"

"Yeah. Plus I'll get you a meal, and you can use my shower if you want," Walt said.

Standing, the man introduced himself as Stones.

"Stones?" Walt said.

"Yeah, man. Because I got some big ol' stones."

Walt smiled at that.

Stones gathered up his belongings. He had been sitting on a blanket, which he rolled up and put in his backpack. He also took the money out of his hat, put it in his pocket, and stuffed the hat into the backpack with the blanket. The dreads made wearing the hat impossible.

Stones talked the whole way back to the car. Walt learned that Stones's real name was Stan, but at some point, in high school, someone had started calling him Stones, and it had stuck. Stones liked the name better than Stan. Any name his bullshit parents had given him he didn't want, Stones explained.

Stones had left home at sixteen and had been living on the road ever since. He didn't mind begging and got enough money for food and drugs. He liked heroin and spent most of his time trying to find some.

Walt didn't really care. Stones seemed nice enough, but Walt was trying not to like him. If he found himself liking Stones, it would make what he had to do a lot harder.

The problem was that Stones would not shut up. Walt could not do anything to piss off Stones, so he had to listen. Listening led to liking. Stones was really a nice guy.

When they got to Paul's apartment, Walt found he liked Stones. Jesus, how the fuck could you like this junky? Pushing forward, Walt and Stones walked into the apartment.

"Nice place, man," Stones said.

"Thanks. I want to carry the couch out of here," Walt said.

Stones looked at the couch. It was big, and he figured it was heavy.

"How much you paying me?" Stones asked.

Walt had expected the question earlier.

"One hundred enough?" Walt said.

Stones nodded. More than enough, he thought, thinking about the heroin he would be injecting into his arm in a few hours.

"Can you type?" Walt asked.

"Huh?"

"I have this old typewriter, and I had this guy fix it, but I think some of the keys are still off. He says I'm imagining it and that the keys are fine. I wonder if you could type on it real quick and let me know if you think it feels off—or if the repair guy is right, and I'm just full of shit."

"Sure. I can type a little," Stones said.

"Awesome. It's in my room at my desk," Walt said, pointing into the bedroom.

Stones hesitated for a second and walked to the door of the bedroom.

There was an old typewriter sitting on a desk. It looked new but was one of the old typewriters with the manual-return carriage.

"Just type 'the quick brown fox jumps over the lazy dog.' That hits all the letters, and you can tell me what you think," Walt said.

Stones sat at the desk and pressed the *T* key. After that he began to type quickly. Walt watched as he typed and kept going.

Clack clack clack.

It was the same pace Paul had been typing at, the same clacking sound. Walt found himself smiling at the sound. He went up behind Stones and leaned over his shoulder. The *T* was followed by a space. Then the writing began in midsentence of something else.

Walt went to the pile of papers that he had stacked up earlier. From the bottom of the face-up pile, he picked up the last paper. The last sentence started with "Winter had" and then abruptly stopped. That was when the police had pulled Paul from the typewriter for the last time.

After the *T* there was a space, and the first sentence was "come early that year." Stones had picked up the story exactly where Paul had stopped: "Winter had come early that year."

Holy shit. That was the only thought Walt had.

This was not possible. Somewhere deep inside, Walt must have known that would happen. He had gone through all the trouble of finding Stones and bringing him back to Paul's place.

Stones kept on typing, not noticing that Walt had backed out of Paul's room and gone to sit on the couch.

Clack clack clack.

The sound was soothing. Walt thought about the sound of the clacking, about Paul in the hospital, and about what he had just done to poor Stones. Maybe he would stop typing once the story was finished. Somewhere deep inside, where you are always honest with yourself, Walt knew the truth. After a while Walt fell asleep on the couch to the sound of the typewriter.

Clack clack clack.

Walt woke up to the sound of the typewriter. The pace had not changed. He looked at the clock, and it was five in the morning. He stood, stretched out his legs and back, and went into Paul's room.

The ream of paper was about half gone now. Stones's eyes were bloodshot, and Walt could see that the tips of his fingers had turned red—and, he guessed, sore—from the large amount of time he had been typing.

Walt thought of Paul's hands, red and bruised, parts of them worn through so much that when Paul had stopped typing, scabs had formed.

Walt did not try to stop Stones. There was plenty of paper left, and Walt figured he needed to go visit Paul and go to work. He knew Stones was not going anywhere.

Walt left and double-checked to make sure the door was locked behind him. If he pressed his ear to the door, he could hear the clacking, but just standing at the door, he could not hear anything.

Walt drove home and showered and changed his clothes. As he showered he thought he should stop and buy some more paper. He didn't know what would happen if Stones ran out of paper, but he didn't want to find out.

Going on about his day, he visited Paul and went to work. The storage-locker business had been Paul's idea, and Walt had no interest in continuing it unless Paul was with him. No brother, no bidding.

He had brought some clothes with him, along with his toothbrush and shower supplies. He didn't know how long Stones would be typing, and he thought it would be easier to just stay at Paul's place.

Nothing had changed with his brother. By figuring out the right dosage, the doctors had kept him from waking up any further. Everything else stayed the same. No one had any idea of what to do, so they seemed to just be biding their time. They would keep him asleep until they either figured out what was wrong or there was a medical reason not to.

Work went slowly, and Walt kept checking his watch. He knew that the more he checked his watch, the slower the day would go, but he couldn't stop himself.

Walt worked in a warehouse and drove a forklift. Up until this point, he'd liked the job. He had the afternoon shift most days, and it allowed him to sleep in. Listening to music was allowed, so he always brought his MP3 player, and that made the days fun. The pay was good as well. Combined with what he and Paul made with their storage-locker business, he was doing pretty well.

Today, though, it just dragged. Like sand through the hourglass, he thought, thinking of the beginning of a soap opera he had watched with his mom on daytime TV when he was young. *Days of Our Lives* was the name, and it was a dumb show, but he had enjoyed watching it with his mother.

He looked at his watch again. Five more minutes had ticked by. One slow grain of sand at a time.

His break came, and he went to McDonald's and got a Big Mac, fries, and a Coke. Even his lunch seemed to be taking forever. Any other day he would have loved his lunch to feel like forever. He often would eat and go for a walk—that is, when one of the other guys he worked with didn't want to go to lunch with him.

After what felt like forever, lunch was over and then finally the day. He had never been so happy for the workday to be done.

He checked out of his work and stopped and got something from Taco Bell on the way home. He got some cheap meal that had way too much food.

When he got to Paul's place, he put the Taco Bell bag on the coffee table and went to check on Stones. He heard the *clack clack clack* as soon as he opened the door, so he knew everything was still humming along, but he wanted to see.

When he walked into Paul's room, the smell of piss and shit hit him. Stones had crapped himself. He had not moved from the chair, and the pee had absorbed into the leather chair and had also run down the sides and pooled on the wood floor underneath the chair.

Fuck.

Stones was also a lot thinner than he should be after just one full day of typing. His face had taken on a skeletal look, and his eyes had sunken black shadows around them. His lips had dried and stuck to his teeth. Blood covered the tips of his fingers and dripped down into the typewriter.

Walt stood staring with his mouth dropped open. Stones was wasting away.

Walt turned and left the room.

Clack clack clack.

The pace hadn't changed. Stones kept typing at the same speed, with bloody fingers and covered in his own piss and shit.

Feeling sick, Walt went to the bathroom and grabbed a hand towel. He turned on the warm water in the sink and let it run for a minute to warm up. Then he added a little cold water so the hand towel was warm. He then soaped up the towel and grabbed a second one and repeated the action without adding soap.

Taking both towels into the bedroom, he cleaned up Stones's face and as much as he could of his hands, first using the soapy towel and then following up with the clean towel.

He debated with himself for a second. Then he slowly pulled the chair away from the typewriter in a steady motion. As the chair moved back, Stones leaned forward to keep typing. His pace never changed, and Walt managed to get the chair out from under him.

Now Stones was kneeling in front of the typewriter. Kneeling on the hard floor must be painful, Walt thought, but Stones did not move. Only his fingers and hands were moving as he typed.

Walt grabbed a pair of black sweats out of Paul's dresser. Next, he went to the kitchen, and, using a pair of scissors, he cut the sweat pants at the knees. This way, he figured, if he needed to do this again, it would be a lot easier.

Walt then grabbed a towel and a large plastic trash bag. Using the scissors, he cut first one side and then the other side of Stones's pants. The smell of the shit was strong, and Walt had to struggle to keep from throwing up. He thought about what homeless people ate, which he figured must not be that healthy.

Walt then pulled the pants forward and down, being careful not to touch Stones's waste. Wishing Paul had rubber gloves, Walt placed the pants in the trash bag. He had been worried about getting the pants from under Stones's knees and lower legs, but Stones was not resistant at all. When Walt pressed up on his leg to move it, Stones had moved it up.

Next, he did the same thing with Stones's underwear. Stones wore multicolored boxer shorts.

Anyone coming into the apartment at that moment would have laughed. Stones was bottomless and on his knees in front of the typewriter, clacking away. It was an odd sight.

Walt used the soapy towel and cleaned up Stones. He turned and looked away as he cleaned Stones's dick and balls. The last thing he did was run the soapy towel down the crack of Stones's ass. The towel was now a brown color.

Walt dropped the now-brown towel into the plastic trash bag with the boxers and pants.

He then used the other warm towel to clean up all the soap. Next, he put the sweat shorts onto Stones. He put the shorts over both his feet and then pulled them up to where his knees met the floor. At that point he lifted one leg and then the other and pulled up the shorts the rest of the way.

Now to clean the chair. Walt grabbed some paper towels and a spray cleaner with chlorine that Paul kept under his kitchen sink.

He soaked the chair with the spray and let it sit for a few minutes. This would ruin the chair, but he really hated the smell. After a few minutes, he wiped the chair, removing most of the piss and shit. He hadn't realized until now that shit could soak through pants, but it had.

Walt dried the chair as best he could and then pushed it up against Stones's back. He then gently nudged Stones up into the chair, pushing it forward as he got Stones up. It was difficult, and it took Walt at least ten minutes, but finally Stones was sitting back in the chair again, still typing.

Stones had never slowed down his pace.

Walt looked at Stones and made sure he had done everything he could. He didn't know how much of Stones was still in there, but he wanted him to be as comfortable as possible.

Now Walt did not feel so bad when he picked up the stack of typed paper.

Looking over the large stack of paper Stones had typed, he noticed there was a page that was half empty near the end of the stack.

In the middle of the page after the last sentence were the words *The End*.

On the very next page, Stones had started writing a new story.

The color drained from Walt's face. Stones had finished the first story and had gone right on to a second one.

Clack clack clack.

Walt backed up against the wall, the stack of paper hanging from his right hand. He stood looking at Stones.

"Stones, I—" Walt started and then stopped, knowing Stones would not hear him, and even if he could, it wouldn't matter.

If Stones could hear him and was still himself in there, nothing Walt could say would be enough. For the first time, he admitted to himself what he had known all along: Stones was going to type until he was dead. He wouldn't eat, wouldn't sleep, and wouldn't stop.

This was bad. Walt had murdered him—not with his own hands, but he had put the tool that would kill him in Stones's hands.

Surprising himself, he realized he had no strong emotions except for concern. Somewhere inside he had known what would happen, so the thought of Stones dying wasn't the problem.

How the fuck am I going to get rid of the body?

People would notice him carrying a body out of Paul's apartment. You couldn't just throw a body over your shoulder and walk it out to the Dumpster.

"Hey, neighbor, how's it going? Me? I'm just taking this guy to the trash." Nope. He would need to come up with something better.

No need to think about this now, but he needed to start figuring it out.

Walt took the finished story and went to the couch.

He sat down and started reading. The story was just as good as it had been when Paul had been the one writing it. There was a slight difference in the writing style, but the story was the same one it had been.

Walt fell asleep to the sound of the clacking typewriter, and he dropped the paper he'd had in his hands.

He woke up, and for the first time since he had heard the clacking of the typewriter from Paul, the typing was slowing down.

Clack. Pause. *Clack.* Pause.

The pace had gone to half of what it had been. Walt went in to take a look at Stones.

An odd odor came from Stones. It was not quite the smell of decay, but that was the way it was heading.

Stones's lips had dried to his teeth, and his head hung down. Stones fought to keep his head from completely falling. His eyes were looking up to compensate for the low angle of his head. The muscles in his arms and legs had melted away, leaving his skin drooped over his bones as though someone had deflated him.

Walt focused on his fingers. Skin had given way to bone on the tips of his fingers. Blood would stick to the keys as he pressed them. After a few seconds, the blood on the keys would disappear, only to be replaced a few seconds later by the next press of the key.

Walt felt sick and went to the bathroom. He did not throw up. Leaning over the sink, he splashed cold water on his face, which made him feel better.

Clack. Pause.

Not noticing what he was doing, Walt had started washing his hands. He rubbed the soap on and then let the cold water run across them. He stood there for several minutes, scrubbing his hands, before he realized what he was doing and stopped himself.

Walt grabbed his bag from the living room where he had slept, showered as fast as he could, and got dressed.

He took one last look at Stones and his disfigured hands, once again unconsciously rubbing his own hands, and then he left for the hospital.

At the hospital, he spoke to the nurse who was checking on Paul.

"Any change?" Walt asked, already knowing the answer.

"No. He's still being kept under," the nurse said.

"OK. I'm going to sit with him for a little while," Walt said.

The nurse nodded and left.

"Hey, bro. I had someone else try the typewriter," Walt said. "He finished the story you were writing and then started on another one. It doesn't seem to help you, though. I don't know. I had hoped it would help you."

Paul did not move.

Walt sat with Paul as long as he could before he needed to be at work. Walt thought about the typewriter and Paul, letting himself understand that his brother would never be the same again. Stones would be dead soon, and Paul would always try to get back to the type-writer if he was awake.

Tears filled Walt's eyes as he began to accept that Paul may as well be dead. Life was over for him. Walt would keep trying, but after seeing Stones typing with the bones showing on the tip of his fingers, he knew the truth.

Walt hugged his brother for a long time and then left.

Work once again dragged by as if someone were pur-posely slowing time for him. Walt checked his watch throughout the day until finally the day was over.

When he got back to Paul's apartment, there was no more clacking.

As he opened the door, he realized that the smell of decay had started to fill up the apartment.

In the bedroom, Stones had collapsed to the floor. He was motionless and smelled of death. There was a half-full page still in the typewriter. Stones had stopped midsentence.

Stones's body was thin, and Walt stripped him to his underwear. He picked up Stones's body, which was light. It had to weigh less than eighty pounds. Walt took the body to the bathroom and placed it in the bathtub.

He had heard a story once about a man named Roy DeMeo, who had been a Mafia hit man. Roy and his crew had a method for disposing of bodies that came to be known as the Gemini method.

They would shoot a person in the head, wrap the head in a towel, and then hang the person in a bathtub to drain the blood. They would then cut the person up and place the body into separate bags and dispose of the bags in Dumpsters around New York. The body parts would be taken to the dump and would never be found.

After placing the body in the bathtub, Walt got dressed and made a trip to Home Depot. He went over the list of items he would need: large trash bags, duct tape, some kind of saw for cutting up bones, and cleaning supplies.

Walt looked at the saws and decided upon a bow saw, figuring that bone was close to wood. He bought two saws. Having done some work with saws before, he was concerned about the blades going dull before he finished his grisly work.

Holding the duct tape and the heavy-duty trash bags, Walt stood looking at cleaning supplies. He needed something with bleach. The apartment was starting to stink, and he needed to get rid of any possible smell of rotting flesh.

He grabbed a bottle of bleach and then Clorox spray cleaners with bleach. He also got several packages of sponges—the ones with the hard-scrubbing side.

At the checkout stand, he made small talk with the clerk and felt he did well, not seeming to be freaked out.

On the way home, he stopped and picked up food from In-N-Out Burger. The double-double and the chocolate milk shake were delicious.

Walt took everything to Paul's apartment and placed it outside the bathroom. He then stripped down to his underwear and turned on Metallica. With "One" playing in the background, he began to cut up the body.

First he went for the easy parts. He threw up into the tub when he sliced through Stones's neck and spine, but removing the head was easy. He picked up Stones's head by the hair and placed it in a bag. He wrapped the bag in duct tape and then placed that bag in a second bag.

He repeated the process for his arms and legs. Each arm and leg went into a separate bag, which he closed with duct tape and then placed in another bag. When he finished, in total he had a bag for the head, each arm, each leg, and the torso. Then he placed the saw in a separate bag.

Walt poured bleach over the shower and scrubbed until he could not see any blood stuck anywhere. Several of the sponges had soaked through with the blood, and he placed those in the bag with the saw. He then ran the shower to finish washing away all the blood.

After he finished in the bathroom, he went to Paul's room and cleaned up the area around the typewriter.

He closed up the final bag, which contained all the cleaning supplies and the saw, sealed it with duct tape, and placed it inside another bag.

He had seven bags he would need to get rid of.

It was midnight, and most people were now asleep. He figured he could get everything into his car in three trips. The torso would be the heaviest, so he wanted to take that out first. He made it down to the car with the torso without anyone stopping him. He opened the trunk, lifted the bag into the back, and gently closed the lid.

On the second trip, he ran into a neighbor who was coming home from a bar. Walt smelled the alcohol on his breath.

"Hey, man, how's it going?" the neighbor asked Walt, dragging out the *s* when he spoke.

"Good. Not as good as you," Walt said, forcing a smile.

"Ladies' night at the bar. Woo!" the neighbor said, and, as if on cue, a lady who seemed to be equally shit faced came up.

"Who's your friend?" the lady asked with a smile. She also dragged out the *s* just a little too long.

"Hi," Walt said.

"You want to come have a drink with us?" she asked, with *us* coming out like *ussssss.*

The neighbor, whose name Walt could not remember, got the same look on his face Walt had when his mom had caught him climbing out his window when he was twelve. Three's a crowd, Walt thought.

"No, thanks. I have some work to do, but thanks for the offer. You two have a good night," Walt said, and he continued his walk to the car.

The final trip went without incident. He now had all of Stones's body in the trunk of his car. Now he needed to figure out where to dump it. Remembering how Roy DeMeo had spread the body parts out, he figured he would do the same. It was late enough that he was sure he could find several empty restaurants where he could stuff the bags.

He got in his car and turned the ignition. For a second the car made a long sound as it tried to start. Walt's heart rate sped up until the car finally started. Deep breath.

Walt drove downtown and parked in the first empty lot of a restaurant he found. He parked as close to the trash bin as he could. He then popped the trunk, got out, and picked up the first bag. The bag was wrapped tightly and looked like any other bag of trash.

He opened the lid on the Dumpster and shoved the bag down the side. The smell of rotting food from the restaurant would hide any smell from the decaying body.

Walt closed the lid of the Dumpster, got in his car, and continued his mission.

Two of the places he tried had locks on their Dumpsters, but after a few hours, he had all the bags disposed of.

Walt drove back to Paul's place. As he opened the door, he took a deep breath through his nose. All he could smell was the bleach.

He double-checked the bathroom for anything that looked like blood. Nothing.

Then he went into Paul's room and sat at the chair and looked at the typewriter.

Everything was clean and shiny. It still had the new look it had had from the storage locker.

Walt raised his hand. He moved slowly with caution.

The typewriter needs you to type on it for it to control you. You'll be fine if you just touch it, he thought.

With a pause and a deep breath, Walt touched the side. It felt warm, and there was a slight tingle at the tip of his finger where he touched it. But he did not have any urge to start typing, and he was able to remove his hand.

He had liked the feeling of touching it, though.

Grabbing the sides, he picked up the typewriter. It was light, as though it were hollow, but it felt like the metal it looked to be made of.

Walt put the typewriter down and took one last look at Paul's apartment. Knowing he would not be coming back, he gathered all his items and took them down to the car.

Next, he went back upstairs and grabbed the typewriter. He took it down to his car and placed it gently in the trunk.

On the last trip upstairs, he got the finished story, the new story Stones had started before he died, and the extra reams of paper.

He locked the door as he left. He never returned to Paul's apartment.

5

Over the next few months, nothing changed. His brother's condition stayed the same. They would periodically try some kind of different medicine, but when they woke him, he would immediately start struggling to get out of the restraints. They were always prepared and were able to sedate him before he could hurt himself.

Walt had placed the typewriter on his dresser. He felt calm when he saw it, but he never dared to type anything on it. He would lay his hand on the side and feel the warm tingle, but he never touched any of the keys. That would be death.

Selling the story that was a weird collaboration between Paul and Stones came on as a casual thought. He had gone to Barnes and Noble one weekend, and looking at the best sellers, he thought, maybe I could sell a book. Then he laughed it off and put it out of his mind.

The idea would not die, though, and over the next few weeks, it became something he had to do. It happened as these things do, starting with a simple idea and ending up becoming an obsession. It was all he could think about.

But how would he sell it? He did not have any clue about what to do.

Walt went back to Barnes and Noble. He took a notepad and, looking through the books, wrote down the names of some publishers. He chose them from the shelf with the best sellers.

It could not be that easy. You can't just go and take your story to a publishing company—and bam—they would publish the book.

He went to their websites. They pretty much all said the same thing. "We do not take submissions except through literary agents."

Literary agents. OK. Now he knew what he needed. But how do you get a literary agent? Without a doubt he knew if they read the book, they would like it. Mr. Wordsmith on his dresser had seen to that. Once someone started reading the story, that person would keep reading to the end.

He'd tried it out on some of his friends. Even if they didn't really like it, they would always finish it. That was the strangest part. Out of the four people he'd had read it, three had loved it, and one had thought it was just OK. But even the one friend who thought it was just OK had devoured the book in a weekend.

Walt looked up literary agents. He found there were a few big ones and a bunch of smaller ones. It also turned out the smaller ones were a lot easier to get in touch with.

Walt got the idea that he would send a few of them the first few chapters. If he could get some of them to read those chapters, he knew they would come to him for the rest of the book.

He got four large yellow envelopes and made copies of the first few chapters of his story. He then wrote a letter, explaining that he was a new author and was looking for an agent. He had included a copy of the first few chapters of his novel, and if they were interested, he would let them see the rest.

He then mailed out the envelopes to the agents and waited.

All they had to do was read the first few pages, and he knew he would have them. But did they even open the envelopes? If he didn't hear anything in a few weeks, he would try a different approach.

Walt was sitting in his apartment, watching Jerry Springer. A lady was yelling at her baby daddy, something about cheating on her after she was pregnant. Walt wasn't really paying attention, but the noise of the TV helped him to think.

It was almost time to send out the next batch of envelopes. He had decided that if he didn't hear from the first agents, he would try the next agents he found.

After mailing to everyone he could find, he would start at the beginning again, and this time he would find the locations and go down to the offices to drop them off.

That would be a harder sell, but he knew that if he could just get them to read the first few pages, they would be hooked. He wasn't sure how much an author would get for a first book, but this one was good enough that if he could get a couple hundred thousand, he would have time to figure out how to get someone to write a second book for him.

Homeless people seemed to be the best answer.

A ring from his phone brought him back from his daydreams.

Never wanting to seem desperate for someone to call, he always waited a few rings before answering.

"Hello?"

"Hi, I'm looking to speak with Walt Erickson," the voice said.

"Hi, I'm Walt."

"Hi, Walt. My name is Mitch, and I work for Laser Focus Agents. You sent your manuscript to us?"

"Yes. I did," Walt said, trying to contain his excitement.

"I have to say, for a first-time writer, that is an amazing first few chapters. I was wondering if it would be possible for me to get the rest of it?"

Walt smiled to himself. "Yes, of course. Are you interested?"

"Straight to the point. Good," Mitch said. "Yes, we are interested in representing you if the rest of your novel is as good as that was. I have to ask, did you write it? It's not plagiarized, is it?"

"You mean did I steal the story?" Walt asked.

"Any of it—the story idea, passages, characters," Mitch said. "Is anything in the book not your own? The reason I ask is because we have never heard of you and couldn't find anything you have ever written, and this is very good. We are frankly confused about how a writer of your caliber could never have been published anywhere. So before we move forward, we want to make sure nothing is not yours."

Not mine? Walt thought. Wow. He guessed that was a compliment in a weird kind of way.

"No, I wrote it all myself," Walt said, lying.

"OK. Go ahead and send the rest of the book to the same address. Just put 'Attention: Mitch Conner' on the envelope. Are you talking to any other agents?" Mitch asked.

"No. I mailed copies to four others, but you are the only one to get back to me so far."

"Good. If the rest of the novel is just as good, we will want to take you on as a client. We have great contacts at several publishing houses, and we can get you a great deal. Just keep us in mind if anyone else calls," Mitch said.

This seemed unreal to Walt. It had been far easier than he thought. He had been expecting to have to send out at least a few more groups of envelopes to agents.

"You still there?" Mitch asked.

"Yeah, I'm here. I'm just a little surprised by this," Walt said.

"Well, you've written something really good. I think we can make some money off this," Mitch said.

Walt got Mitch's contact information, thanked him, and they hung up. Walt started wondering how much money Mitch could get him for this book. Not wanting to delay anything, Walt went out and got another envelope and made a few more copies of the novel.

He then placed one of the copies inside the envelope and filled out the address, adding "Attention: Mitch Conner." He put on more stamps than he thought it needed. He then went to mail the envelope.

Outside it was warm, and the air felt good. This all seemed surreal to Walt. Thinking about Paul brought him down a little. Paul had been corrupted by the typewriter and would never recover.

It still didn't make sense. Somehow Walt guessed it had corrupted him too. He felt no guilt at all over Stones and had grown to accept what had happened to Paul, even though it was not as easy to get over as Stones's death was.

Dropping the envelope into a blue mailbox, he listened to the thud as it landed inside. The door of the mailbox squeaked as it closed.

A liquor store was on the same corner as the mailbox, so he went in and got a six-pack of cheap beer. The clerk was an old, gray-haired man. His face was wrinkled more than it should have been, and Walt guessed he was a lifelong smoker.

"Can I have a small bag?" Walt asked.

The man nodded and handed him a bag, not saying anything.

Outside, Walt pulled one of the beers out of the plastic rings that held the six-pack together. He placed the beer in the small bag, popped the tab, and took a long drag off the beer. He used the open ring on the six-pack as a handle.

He felt a little better. Walking home, he finished off the first beer and tossed it onto the street. Then he opened a second one.

By the time he had gotten home, he had finished off most of the second one. The alcohol had done its job, and he was starting to feel better. Inside, he sat on the couch and turned on the TV. He fell asleep on the fifth beer when some cop show was on TV.

Walt woke up on the couch to the sound of morning news. He had a slight headache from the beer and from sleeping on the couch. He let the hot water spray his body for a long time. Standing in the shower loosened his muscles and made him feel much better.

By the time he left, it was too late to stop by and visit Paul. Not being much of a drinker, five beers had hit him hard. The jarring of the forklift as he operated it did not make his head feel any better.

He was almost late coming back from lunch. He had gone to sit in his car and had fallen asleep with his head leaning to one side, drooling onto his shoulder. The wet spot of saliva soaked into his shirt and darkened the area.

Walt went into the bathroom and cleaned the drool from his shirt. Using water made the wet area bigger, but it was better than being covered by his own spit.

"Dude, your shirt's wet," one of his coworkers pointed out.

"Thanks, I hadn't noticed," Walt said, irritated.

"I'm here to help," the coworker said and walked off.

Walt took a few aspirin, and by the end of the day, his headache was gone.

On the way home, Walt stopped and got another six-pack and then drove to the hospital to visit Paul. When he got to the hospital, he drank half a beer and went upstairs to see his brother.

"So, an agent called me about the novel you wrote. I told him I wrote it. Hopefully you don't mind," Walt said to his brother.

Silence.

"Yeah, I didn't think you'd have any problem with it."

A nurse came in to check on Paul.

"How's he doing?" Walt asked.

"Same. He's fine until we wake him up. That's really all I know. Do you want me to have a doctor come talk with you?"

"No," Walt said.

Walt knew nothing would help. He wasn't sure how this was going to be paid for. He didn't think they could charge him, but he knew at some point the subject would come up. Paul had insurance, but now that he wasn't working, Walt didn't know how that would work.

"Bro, I think I'm going to stop visiting as much," Walt said. "I hate seeing you like this. It's odd, you know? Things seem to be going great for me, but it's at your expense, sort of. So anyway, I think I'll visit less. This is just not good for me."

He bent over and hugged his brother. He held the hug for a while, and tears welled up in his eyes. Then he stood, wiped his eyes, and left.

Nothing exciting happened for the next month. Walt was sitting on his couch, three beers into another six-pack, when the phone rang.

"Hello?" Walt said.

"Hey, Walt. It's me—Mitch. How ya doing?"

"Hey, Mitch. I thought you had changed your mind."

"No, no, I showed a bunch of people your novel. They all loved it. So we reached out to a couple of publishing houses, and I let a few of them read it. First, I want to say I think we can get you a great deal. I'd like you to sign with us. Once you do, I think I can get you somewhere between half a million and a million for this."

"Holy shit!" Walt said.

"I want to move quickly on this, so I was wondering if you could meet tomorrow to sign a deal."

"What kind of deal?"

"Well, I think ten percent of anything we secure for you. Standard is ten to twenty percent, so we are giving you the low end. We are very confident we can sell your novel."

Walt thought for a second and then asked, "Where do you want to meet?"

On the other end of the phone, Mitch smiled. Gotcha.

Mitch gave him the address, and they said their good-byes and hung up.

Walt danced around his living room.

Time to celebrate. He walked outside and went to a bar.

The closest bar was a small, dark place that was never very busy, but he didn't care. After what had happened to Paul and what he had done to Stones, he was glad to finally get something out of it.

For a brief moment, he thought about what he was doing, and as quickly as he could, he pushed the thought out of his head.

Only focus on the good. Don't be a fucking bummer.

He ordered a glass of the most expensive cognac they had, which was not anything great. They were a small, shitty corner bar, after all.

There was a couple sitting next to him at the bar. The man had skinny arms and legs and the beginnings of a beer belly. Next to him was a very attractive woman with long, dark hair and dark eyes. She wore a short black skirt that had pulled up a little too far when she sat on the barstool.

When the drink was brought out to him, he turned to the couple and raised his glass. The man was a little apprehensive about cheering him, but the woman quickly raised her pink martini and clinked his glass.

"To life," Walt said.

"To life," she repeated. "Petey, don't be rude. Pick up your dang glass," she said to the man sitting next to her.

Petey reluctantly picked up his glass and tapped Walt's glass.

"I'm Walt," Walt said, holding his hand out.

"I'm Kim, and this party pooper is Peter," Kim said.

"Hi," Peter said, shaking Walt's hand.

"Nice to meet you both. I think I may have just sold my novel, so this round is on me," Walt said.

"Oh, congratulations! What's it about?" Kim asked.

What is it about? Walt wondered. It was the first time he was asked a question that he would grow to hate.

"Life and its trials," Walt said. Vague but accurate.

"Isn't that what most books are about?" Kim asked.

"I wouldn't know. I don't usually read," Walt said.

"You write, but you don't read?" Kim asked.

Walt, now realizing he had fucked up his answers, changed his tactics a little. "I based the story on something that happened to me. I just hope it's interesting," Walt said.

Kim smiled, but Walt could tell she now thought he was full of shit.

Walt, having finished his cognac, ordered a beer. He had to be up and out early tomorrow and didn't want to get too drunk.

Kim and Peter went back to talking to each other, and Walt sat there thinking.

He knew he would have to be able to answer these kinds of questions in the future. Kim had gone quickly from being impressed with him for writing a novel to thinking he was some asshole who was lying to her about being an author to try to get into her pants.

He would have to read the story a few more times. It should be ingrained in him, and he should know what it's about in detail.

Walt finished his beer and went home.

At home he got out the manuscript and started reading it from the beginning again. He read until he fell asleep.

He woke up early, got up, and made some coffee. He mixed cream and sugar into the coffee, sat at his table, and continued reading.

Three times, he thought. I need to read this at least three times, and I need to focus on the story.

Knowing that he might be able to get one time done before his meeting with Mitch, he pushed through.

The first time he had read the book, he had just pushed through it, eager to find out what was going to happen. He hadn't tried to understand anything about it. This time he really tried to take something away from it.

He read until it was time to leave and go meet Mitch.

During the car ride, he worked out what he would say the story was about if asked. Of course, he should have told Kim it was about loss. That was essentially what it was about—how a family deals with the loss of someone important in the family.

Walt thought about his brother lying there in a forced coma to keep him from killing himself to get to the typewriter.

Walt guessed he was also somehow being controlled by the typewriter himself. Why else would he be sad about Paul but not either tell someone about the typewriter or smash it to bits?

Maybe he should smash that thing to bits. Take a sledgehammer and hit it until it's smashed and its keys are no longer able to drink blood. As he thought about the blood absorbing into the keys, a chill ran down his spine.

He arrived at Laser Focus and walked up to the lobby. The offices were in a six-story building with dark-glass windows. Inside, the floors were marble, and the security officer sat behind a tall oak desk in front of the elevators.

Walt walked up to the security desk. He could hear the sound of his own footsteps on the marble floor as he walked.

"Hi, my name is Walt Erickson, and I'm here to see Mitch Conner," Walt said to the security guard.

"I'll need to see an ID," the security guard said, holding out his hand to Walt.

Walt pulled his driver's license out and handed it to the security guard.

The security guard took down some information and then printed up a badge. It had Walt's name on it, and it said, "Guest of Mitch Conner."

"Please stick that to your chest. You'll take the elevator up to the sixth floor. Someone will be there to greet you."

Walt thanked the security guard and got on the elevator. That was a guy bored with his job, he thought.

As he got out on the sixth floor, an attractive blond woman stood up from behind her desk, which faced the elevator. She came around the desk and held out her hand. "Hi, Walt, I'm Kathy. Follow me, and I'll take you to Mitch's office," she said with a smile.

"I hope Marcus didn't give you too much trouble. He's a bit of a grump but a teddy bear once you get to know him. Don't tell him I called him a teddy bear," Kathy said.

"It's fine. This place is really nice," Walt said.

Mitch's office was large. There was a couch with two chairs facing it. In the middle of the couch and chairs was a small table. The furniture was a dark-brown leather, and the table was glass with a dark metal base.

Mitch got up from behind his large oak desk and walked around it to meet Walt. He held out his hand, which Walt took. The handshake was firm and brief. Mitch was lean, with broad shoulders and a formfitting dark-gray suit with a light-blue tie.

"So nice to meet you. Please have a seat," he said, gesturing toward the couch and chairs. Walt sat on one of the chairs.

"Would you like something to drink?" Mitch asked.

"I'll have a coffee with lots of cream and sugar, if it's no trouble," Walt said.

"Of course. No trouble at all. Bring me a black coffee as well, please," Mitch said.

Kathy nodded and turned to go get the coffees.

"I get a lot of stories in the mail. Most of them are absolute crap. Just awful. No focus, way too wordy, or just plain boring. Yours was wonderful. Stories like yours are the reason I still like to read some of the submissions that come by mail."

"Thanks," Walt said.

"I'm thinking we should easily be able to sell this. I've drawn up a contract that is amicable for both of us. Ten percent across the board for anything we bring in, if we sell to a publisher, plus any movies or other media we manage to sell. How does that sound?" Mitch said.

"That does sound good," Walt said.

Kathy returned with the coffees. She brought them on a tray, and it had a small bowl with creamers and sweeteners. After setting the tray down on the small table, she went to Mitch's desk and brought the contract and handed it to Walt.

"Thanks. I'm pretty new to all this. I think I want to get a lawyer to look at it before I sign anything, if that's OK," Walt said.

"Of course. It's all very standard. So please have anyone you want check it out. If the contract matches what I've said, would you go forward with us? I'd like to at least get the story into some publishers' hands to start reading. With something this good, we may be able to get a little bit of a bidding war going. That would get us a much better price."

Walt couldn't believe this. Mitch seemed very excited to work with him. Of course he loved the story himself, but it seemed Mitch loved it just as much as he did.

"Yes. If everything is as you say, then we should be good," Walt said. This was all happening so fast. He sipped the coffee, trying to stay calm. "How much do you think we can get for it?" Walt asked.

"To be honest, I'd like to get half a million, but if we can get a bidding war going, it will be closer to one million. You already have the story written and not just a treatment, so they will be buying a full product. I'll have an editor take a pass at it and then get it out to some publishers. This might take a few weeks.

"If you'd like, we can have dinner tonight. My treat," Mitch said. "I know a place if you like authentic Italian. Then tomorrow you can run the deal by a lawyer and sign. I'm really interested in getting this going. No delay. I don't want to let the grass grow under us."

The enthusiasm was contagious, and Walt wanted to get it going. "Sure, I'd love to go to dinner."

"Great. I know you have a little bit of a drive to get here, so if you want, we can book you a room and you can stay the night in this area. That way we can have a few drinks," Mitch said.

"That sounds great," Walt said.

Someone else paying for him to stay at a hotel was exciting. Up until now, he had had to pay for everything himself.

I'm being wined and dined like he's trying to get into my pants, Walt thought. I'm going to make him work for it. He enjoyed the thought.

Mitch got up and dialed the phone on his desk. "Kathy? Yeah, we need to get Mr. Erickson a room for the night here in the area. Something nice. No, not that place. That's a dump. Something nice, I said. Yeah. Uh-huh. OK. Better." Mitch hung up.

"We will put you up at the Plaza. A suite. It's a beautiful room," Mitch said.

They arranged a time to meet up. Mitch gave him the name of the place and said they would send a car to get him. Walt got up, and they shook hands.

"I'll see you tonight. If you talk to Kathy on the way out, she can arrange a car to take you to the hotel," Mitch said.

Walt went up front and told Kathy that he needed a car to the Plaza. She told him to wait out front and a car would be by in a little while to pick him up.

He thanked her and went downstairs. This kind of treatment was something he could get used to. They were taking care of everything for him, and he loved it.

After a few minutes, a black sedan pulled up. A man in a black suit got out of the car and came around. "Are you Walt?"

"Yes. Hi—and you are?"

"I'm Terry. I'll be driving you to the Plaza."

Terry was a large man with dark skin and short hair. He looked as if he might also double as a bodyguard.

Walt got in the car. The interior was black leather and was neat and clean.

"You a writer?" Terry asked. Without waiting for an answer, he continued. "Most of the time, if someone gets a ride to the Plaza, they are a writer. Mitch—you met with Mitch, right? Yeah, I bet it was Mitch. Mitch likes to give writers the Plaza. He hates the Holiday Inn. Not sure why—it's a nice hotel. Not as nice as the Plaza, mind you, but not bad."

When Terry paused for a second, Walt said, "Yeah, the Plaza and Mitch. You are right about both."

"I knew it. Mitch is very good to the writers. You going to be staying there long?" Terry asked.

"Nah. Just overnight. Mitch wants to have dinner."

"Walt Erickson? That's your name?" Terry said. It sounded like a question, but before Walt could answer, Terry went on. "I don't recognize the name. You new as a writer? I try to learn the names of most of the writers we work with. Mitch likes to give the extra touch, so I try to learn their names and maybe read one of their books. Since I haven't heard your name before, I assume you have to be new."

"Yes. They are going to represent me on my first book. Try to sell it," Walt said.

"You couldn't be in better hands. Not just the company, but Mitch. He treats the writers really well. At least I think so, anyway. Where are you going for dinner?"

"Some Italian place," Walt said.

"I bet he's taking you to Papa's. That food is amazing. If you go there, you have to try the stuffed mushrooms. Those are so good. You like Italian?"

"Yes," Walt said.

"Of course, you can't go wrong with anything there, but for me the mushrooms are it. I always get two orders when I go there. It's expensive, but man, it's worth it. They told me I'll be picking you up tonight. Did you have a time in mind?"

"I'm meeting Mitch at Papa's at seven, so what time should we leave?" Walt said.

"I'll pick you up at six thirty. That will give us plenty of time to get there. Don't want to be late on your first dinner with Mitch. If you become a famous author, then you can be late for Mitch, but for now you should be on time. It will show Mitch you care and are serious about this. I know you are evaluating his offer, but keep in mind that he is also evaluating you. So best to make a good impression, you know?" Terry said.

"Yeah," Walt said.

Interesting that he was also being evaluated. He'd thought from the way Mitch was behaving that it was a sure thing. But just in case, he would listen to Terry and would be sure not to be late.

"Hey, Terry, I don't have any dress clothes. Is what I'm wearing OK for Papa's?" Walt asked.

Terry took a quick glance back at Walt, giving him an up-and-down look.

"You're fine. It's not a dressy place, but you shouldn't go looking like a bum. You look fine. I had a friend once who got kicked out of a restaurant for taking his shoes off while they were eating. Not at Papa's, but this place called American Diner. I guess someone complained about his feet smelling, and it turned into a whole thing and ended with him getting kicked out. Dumbass left his shoes. He got so angry at being asked to leave that he left his shoes. I love that guy, but he can be a dumbass. Well, here we are," Terry said as they pulled in to the Plaza.

Terry dropped him off at the front lobby.

"Just meet me here at six thirty," Terry said as he let Walt out of the car. Terry said good-bye and closed the door and left.

Walt went into the lobby. It was a busy place. There were people hustling all over, and several people in red bellhop suits moved by him quickly.

The lobby was bright and big. There were big pillars along the sides and a white marble floor with dark-gold trim. In the center were chairs with tables where people sat. There were drinks and laptops on the tables. There was a hum of conversation in the background.

Walt walked up to the check-in desk.

"How can we help you, sir?" the lady behind the desk asked.

"I'm checking in for a room for tonight."

"Name, sir?"

"Walt Erickson."

Walt heard her typing into a computer, and after a few moments, she said, "You are staying in the executive suit. Everything is taken care of. We just need a credit card for incidentals."

Hoping that his thousand-dollar limit would be enough, he handed her the credit card. He was nervous for a few seconds as she ran the card. Everything was OK, and she handed back the card and thanked him.

After another minute, she handed him a paper to sign and explained that check-out time was noon the next day. She then handed him a key and explained where everything in the hotel was located and gave him his room number.

Walt thanked her, grabbed his room key, and went to the bar.

Sitting at the bar, Walt asked the bartender what they had on tap.

The bartender was a young woman who looked just barely twenty-one. She smiled and had a sweet-sounding voice. Her long blond hair had a red streak down the right side. A small diamond chip was in her nose. Dyed hair and a nose ring—Walt liked her already.

Walt settled on some beer he had never heard the name of but the bartender had recommended.

The beer was hoppy, which Walt knew just meant bitter, but he didn't want to seem as if he didn't like her recommendation, so he drank it anyway.

"Good beer. Thanks. This is a nice hotel," Walt said.

"Thanks. Not about the hotel, about the beer. The hotel is nice, I guess. I've never stayed here. I just work the bar," she said.

"Ah. You like working here?" Walt said.

She was quiet for a second. He figured in that moment that she didn't like working there but didn't want to say that.

"It's fine. Just a lot of horny dudes have a few drinks and hit on me," she said.

Walt couldn't decide whether that was a hint for him to stop chatting with her or not. So he kept going. "Yeah. Drunk dudes are a pain," he said. Although he didn't really know. Usually if he was drunk, he was with a group of drunk dudes, and they always seemed OK to him.

"I just work here to pay for school. I'm studying to be a nurse," she said.

"What kind of nurse?" Walt asked.

"Well, I really want to help people, so I'm thinking an ER nurse or maybe a pediatric nurse. You know, so I can help kids. I just want to feel like I'm making a difference," she said.

Straight from looking as if she didn't want to talk with him to spilling her guts. Maybe *she* was drunk.

"That's awesome. More people should try to help people," Walt said, not sure he believed it, but it did seem like a good idea.

"What do you do? You seem underdressed to be at the Plaza," she said.

Zing. A dig at his clothes.

"I'm a writer. I'm here meeting with Laser Focus Agents," Walt said, trying to sound as if it weren't a big deal to him.

Narrowing her eyes at him, she said, "Seriously?"

"Yeah. I wrote a novel, and they want to sell it for me," Walt said.

"What's the novel about?" she said.

That's it. If he could answer this question so that it made some kind of sense, he knew she'd be interested in him.

"It's about how a family deals with the loss of one of their kids," Walt said.

"Oh, how sad. My brother committed suicide a few years ago. It was hard for all of us," she said, and Walt saw tears well up in her eyes. She took a second and wiped her face and took a couple of deep breaths.

"That must have been hard," Walt said. He couldn't catch a break.

"Yeah. But we had to learn that sometimes, no matter what you do, you can't help someone. He hid his depression really well," she said.

Walt sipped his beer, not sure what to say.

"We are doing a lot better now. There are counseling groups you can go to—people who have had the same thing happen to them. It's actually pretty comforting. How does the family in the book handle it?" she asked.

"Poorly. You'll have to read the book to find out, but they do not handle it well in the beginning," Walt said.

"Neither did we. It was very hard for us at first. If we hadn't found help, I'm not sure where we would be. Talking about it with other people who understood what we were going through really helped us," she said.

One of the other people sitting at the bar called for the bartender.

"Nice talking with you. I'll look for your novel. What's your name?"

"I'm Walt Erickson. And you are?"

"Rebecca—not Becky."

"Nice talking with you, Rebecca," Walt said.

She went to help the other customer.

Walt finished his beer that he didn't like and went up to his room.

The beer had made him tired, so he turned on the TV and took a nap.

He stood in the middle of an open field of grass. Wind blew at his back, and he could hear waves crashing in the distance. It was warm, and he thought it would be nice to go see the ocean. It was odd that the wind was blowing toward the ocean. He thought it always blew in from the ocean. He walked toward the sound of the crashing waves.

Beeping from the alarm he had set woke him when the ocean was in sight. Too bad. He would have liked to see the water.

His mouth was dry from the beer, and he opened one of the bottles of water in the room and drank it half down.

He had managed to sleep a couple of hours, and it was close to six thirty.

Washing his face, he wished he had a toothbrush. He knew hotels like this would be able to bring you a toothbrush, but he didn't have time to wait. Hoping his breath wasn't that bad, he went downstairs.

The lobby of the hotel was filled with people, and the bar was buzzing. The bartender he had spoken to was gone, and there were now two men serving drinks.

As instructed, he went out front to wait. The car arrived promptly at six thirty, and Terry hopped out.

"Hey, Walt." he said, opening the back door of the car to let Walt in.

Walt was still a little out of it from the nap, but that didn't stop Terry. He talked the entire ride over—first about the best routes, not just to the restaurant he was going to, but how to get around the city.

"The trick is to never take the main roads. I take a lot of back streets. Most of the time, this is much faster. The speed limit is slower, and there are more stop signs, but it's better than a dead stop, you know?"

Walt knew that was a rhetorical question and did not say anything.

Terry kept going, switching between topics as if there were a buzzer going off every few minutes that required it.

"None of the plays this year have been any good. I like to go to a lot of shows, and this season they have just all pretty much sucked."

Buzz.

"My sister won a trip to Hawaii by calling in to a radio show. She had to be the tenth caller or some such. She is always lucky."

Buzz.

"Make sure to try the stuffed mushrooms tonight. Best thing they have. A little greasy but good."

Buzz.

"Did you know dogs have a gland on their butt that causes them to scoot their butt along on the floor?"

And game. They arrived at the restaurant, and Terry jumped out of the car again to go open Walt's door. Terry's energy just made Walt tired.

"I'll wait here for you. Just come find my car when you are ready. I'll park over there," Terry said, gesturing to an empty part of the parking lot. "This place can get busy. Have a good dinner."

Walt thanked Terry and went inside.

The restaurant was bright and decorated with pictures of Italy and Italian decor. There was picture of the Leaning Tower of Pisa and a painting of a boat on a canal in Venice with a man rowing from the back.

Red-and-white-checkered tablecloths covered the tables.

"Hi. Welcome to Papa's," the maître d' said with a practiced smile.

"Hi. I'm meeting someone here. Mitch Conner," Walt said.

Looking at the check-in log, the maître d' nodded and said, "This way, sir."

He escorted Walt back to a two-person table. Mitch was already there. On the table was a stack of paper, and Mitch was reading one of the pages from the stack when Walt arrived.

Mitch looked up, stood, and shook Walt's hand. "Good to see you again," Mitch said. He sat down and added the page he was reading back to the stack and then placed the stack in a large yellow envelope.

"Just reading another manuscript someone sent us. I don't think I'll finish this one. Pretty boring," Mitch said.

"What's it about?" Walt asked.

"Nothing at all. It just seems to be a rambling mess. How's the hotel?"

"I love it. I've never stayed anywhere so nice."

"If you sign with us, it will be like that anytime we send you anywhere. We want you to know we appreciate you. I've already ordered us some appetizers to get us started."

"Terry insists I try the mushrooms," Walt said.

"Don't worry. I knew he'd say that, so I got those and the calamari. Both are excellent," Mitch said.

"This is all happening very fast. I thought it would take me a lot longer to find an agent. Is this normal?" Walt said.

"Well, to be honest, no. It was pure dumb luck that I read your book. I was bored and just decided to look through a couple of manuscripts. Rarely do we get anything so good by mail. Most of the time, we look for authors who have several things published already—mostly short stories, and they are ready to go to the next level. So we take them on and then help them move forward. But when an author is good, we will do what we are trying to do with you. We think we can really get a good deal for this, so we don't want to wait. It's just like any other product. Selling you is our job, and all you need to do is come up with good stories."

Walt liked his honesty. It made him trust Mitch, and he felt he was making the right choice.

When the waiter arrived with the appetizers, Walt order a cognac. He wanted something besides beer, and he liked the big round glasses the cognac came in. He also ordered spaghetti and meatballs—a Papa's specialty.

Terry was right: the mushrooms were delicious.

Ending the dinner with a tiramisu, Walt felt as if his stomach was going to burst. He had ordered a second order of mushrooms and had eaten all the spaghetti, and he stopped halfway through the tiramisu, unable to eat another bite.

He had also had several glasses of cognac and was feeling really good.

Mitch had also had several glasses of whiskey, but he seemed fine, as though the whiskey had not affected him at all.

Standing after the meal, Walt was a little wobbly on his feet, and Mitch laughed. "Looks like you enjoyed the meal," Mitch said, helping Walt steady himself.

Walt got his balance and was able to walk out of the restaurant on his own. When he got outside, he started walking toward where Terry had said he would park.

"Whoa, hold on. You can have a seat. I'll go get Terry."

Walt thought that sounded like a great idea. He sat on a bench in front of the restaurant. He closed his eyes and fell asleep in the few minutes it took for Mitch to have Terry drive over.

Terry jumped out of the car with as much energy as ever and came over to Walt.

"Aw, he fell asleep," Terry said, lightly touching Walt's shoulder to wake him.

"Oh heyyyy, Terry."

"Hey, Walt. How you doing?"

"I'm fine. Just a little tired," Walt said, adding an *s* to *just* after the *j*, so that it came out *jsust*.

Walt didn't remember the ride back to the hotel. He woke up with Terry gently shaking his shoulder to get him out of the car. "We're here. We need to get you up to your room," Terry said.

Walt looked at him until he came into focus, which took longer than it should have.

Leaning forward and to the right, he attempted to get out, but the seatbelt stopped his movement. At that point Terry reached across in front of Walt and un-buckled the seat belt.

"Thanks. Stupid thing," Walt said, still slurring his words.

"Thank you for not throwing up in the car," Terry said.

As though the words were a trigger like in an old Russian spy movie, Walt vomited on the street in front of the hotel.

Garlic was the first smell Terry noticed. Then the sickening vomit smell took over. Terry almost lost it, but he managed to hold it in. One of the valets was not so lucky, and he leaned over and puked into the plants behind the valet podium.

Terry tipped the valet fifty bucks.

"I'm going to help him to his room, and then I'll be right back down," Terry said to a valet who hadn't puked.

"Sure, no problem. Let me just have your keys, in case I need to move your car."

Terry handed the valet his keys and walked Walt to the elevator.

Managing not to puke on the ride up to the room, they found themselves standing in the hallway outside of Walt's room.

"Hey, man, I need your room key," Terry said.

It seemed as if Walt was getting less sober as they went. He leaned back against the wall in front of his door and patted down his front pockets. Then he reached into his back pocket and pulled out his wallet.

"Check in here. I might have put it in my wallet," Walt said.

Terry grabbed the wallet and looked through it. No card key.

Walt slid down the wall and was now sitting on the floor. His head leaned forward, and he was out cold.

"Shit," Terry said.

Thinking for a second, he figured Walt wasn't going anywhere, so he decided to go down to the lobby.

"Walt! Hey, man, I'm going down to the lobby to get them to let you into your room. I'll be right back," Terry said.

Nothing. Walt didn't move at all.

Downstairs, it took a few minutes for Terry to persuade the front desk to give him a key. He explained what had happened. He told them he was the driver and that Walt had had a little too much to drink and couldn't find his room key. The person at the front desk made a duplicate key and called one of the bellhops over.

"Please take this card and help this gentleman get our guest out of the hallway and into his bed. Then bring the card back here."

Terry rolled his eyes. Whatever. He didn't need an escort, but this was the safer way to go about it, he guessed.

The bellhop grabbed the key from the front-desk manager and went back up the elevator with Terry.

When they exited the elevator, the hallway was empty.

"Let's check his room. Maybe he found his key," Terry said.

Opening the door to Walt's room, they found Walt lying on his back on his bed.

"I'm going to turn him over on his stomach. Then we can head out," Terry said.

"OK," the bellhop said.

Walt smelled like vomit, and Terry wanted a shower after rolling him over. He washed his hands and face and then left with the bellhop.

Standing at the edge of a cliff and feeling the wind at his back, Walt enjoyed the view of the ocean and the waves rolling in. Somehow he knew this was a dream, but he still fought back against the wind, which got faster and harder every few seconds. Walt sat to keep from being pushed forward. He heard the sound of a large wave hitting the cliff below him, and the water sprayed over the top of the cliff, hitting him.

Lying on his belly, he low-crawled to the edge of the cliff and looked down. He was at least one hundred feet from the rocks below. He watched as a large wave built up in the distance and headed toward the cliff. Cresting at over fifty feet, the wave smashed into the cliff with a force that Walt felt from the top. Water came up and splashed his face. It felt great to his drunk mind, even in the dream.

After a few seconds, another wave formed in the distance and raced to the cliff. This time Walt welcomed the wave and the splash of water to his face.

As he lay there, several more waves hit him, and he was feeling great. He had forgotten about the wind pushing him and now enjoyed the force each wave generated as it hit the cliff.

In the distance a small wave began to grow larger. As it got closer to the cliff, the wave's crest passed fifty feet and then seventy-five feet—and then the wave was over one hundred feet and higher than the cliff. Walt got nervous and wanted to run, but as he stood, the wind pushed him back down, and he couldn't move.

"Oh no," he mumbled as he realized the wave was going to hit him.

The wave slammed down on him like a hammer.

He woke up covered in sweat and felt as though he'd had the air knocked out of him. It seemed so real that for a moment he thought the sweat was the ocean water. His mind cleared, and he began to convince himself it had been a dream.

Not sure what to do, he turned on the TV. He did not want to go back to sleep, and it was only two o'clock in the morning. He got up, walked to the window, and looked outside. As he expected, it was dark and quiet. No one was there, and nothing was moving.

Looking around the room, he thought back to the wonderful dinner. He'd had a driver for the night. This was exciting. Knowing he hadn't written the book didn't bother him. Even the dead hobo didn't bother him. He feared losing all this, even though he had had only the tiniest taste of this life.

He resolved that he would do what it took to help sell the book, and a calm came over him. Yes, he would do whatever it took. After all, he had already caused the death of someone.

With the TV on, he closed his eyes and soon fell asleep. This time there were no dreams to wake him.

The alarm woke him at seven in the morning. Nursing a hangover, he showered, letting the hot water run over him for a long time. It did not help.

He went down to the lobby at eleven to check out. The hotel clerk asked him if he had enjoyed his stay. Walt wanted to scream, "Yes! I loved it!" But he politely just said he had and went to find Terry.

Terry was leaning against his car and reading a book. It was a paperback with a car on the cover. Walt walked up to him, and Terry folded over a top corner of one of the pages and closed the book.

"You survived. I was worried for a minute," Terry said, smiling.

"Sorry about that. I don't usually get that drunk," Walt said.

"No worries, my friend," Terry said, opening the door to let Walt into the car.

They drove back to Laser Focus Agents, where Terry dropped Walt off at his car.

Walt thanked Terry for everything, and Terry left.

Walt opened his car door and got in. After a couple of seconds, he got back out, figuring he should go thank Mitch for everything.

At the front desk, the receptionist told him that Mitch was in a meeting. She told him Mitch had said he would be in touch in a few days to let Walt know what all the next steps would be.

Walt felt depressed as he left: back to his boring job and boring life. This had been an escape from his mundane, average life, and he did not want to go back. As he drove home, he told himself he would focus on his job and just wait for time to pass.

Back in his apartment, he stared at the typewriter. Putting a hand on the side, he noticed that it still had that warm, electric feel. The room was cool, and the typewriter was warm. He was not sure how that was possible. Nothing about any of this made any sense.

He would need to stop thinking about these kinds of things. If the book sold and he made a little money, he wanted to buy a house, a small two-bedroom house, with a nice trimmed lawn and a brick path to the door. Inside, there'd be a big TV with a large leather couch, and in the bedroom, he'd have a big king-size bed with high-thread-count sheets. High-thread-count sheets were expensive. He'd have a big oak desk in his office.

Walt went on with his life. He didn't hear from Mitch in a few days as promised, but one day later.

As Walt sat on the couch and drank a beer, the phone rang, startling him.

"We sold the book," the voice on the phone said.

"Mitch?" Walt said.

"Yes. We sold the book to the second publisher we spoke to. We sent a courier, and he read the book overnight. Over fucking night. I've never seen that shit. Anyway, they want to buy it," Mitch said.

Silence.

"You there, Walt?"

"Yeah," Walt said.

More silence.

"Hey, buddy, you OK?" Mitch said.

"How much?" Walt said.

"I've been waiting for you to ask that. It's the largest offer I've ever received for a first-time writer. You should be proud of yourself."

"How much?" Walt said, getting excited.

Mitch told him, and Walt dropped the phone.

"Hello?" Mitch said.

"Sorry about that. I dropped the phone," Walt said.

"The good news is you have the completed novel already. So they will give you 1.5 million for the book. We can work out the rest of the deal, and this is just a starting point. I will take care of you. Don't worry. I've never had an unhappy author I've represented. Congratulations. Again, I've never seen anything sell this fast," Mitch said.

"Thank you. How long before I see the money?"

"Probably a few months, while we work out the deal and get everything signed and have the lawyers look over it. Just remember, you will be taxed, and you have to pay us our percentage, so you will not be getting the full 1.5 million. But it will still be a very large sum of money. Also, we will work out something so that you get a percentage of sales," Mitch said.

"That means I will have to keep my job for a while," Walt said.

"Yeah. Don't go all crazy. Wait until you have the first check before you do anything. Nothing is guaranteed, so until you have the check, be ready for it to fall through at any time. I only say this because I have seen people quit their jobs when they heard they sold their book, only to be very disappointed when the deal fell through—or with how much they got. So don't be an idiot," Mitch said.

"OK," Walt said, nodding. Knowing that he would have to keep working when he was expecting a big amount of money would not be easy.

Everything took even longer than he thought it would. It was six months before he received any money, and the book was published around the same time. Walt put on a ball cap and went to a bookstore. Sitting there on a shelf under the new fiction releases was his book. It was a strange feeling to see his name on a novel.

As of now he had read the book multiple times and had forged his ideas on the story. For a second the guilt about Paul and Stones crossed his mind.

His brother was still in a medicated coma. Nothing had worked, and the doctors had decided it was the best course of treatment. Walt had checked with a lawyer to make sure he wouldn't be responsible for the large medical bills that were building up.

They had moved Paul to a long-term-care facility. Walt had not visited him at the new facility. He still checked on his brother weekly by phone, but as nothing ever changed, it was more out of habit than anything else.

Stones's death had caused him some guilt, and at moments like this, it bubbled to the surface. Walt's stomach would knot, and he would get a sick feeling. Pushing the feeling down and focusing on the book, he felt better. Thinking of something else—in this case, his book—always helped.

Looking at the cover in the bookstore, he liked how it had come out. Four people stood with their backs facing you, holding hands. A little girl was fading away from the group. It was exactly how the book made you feel. A strong family bond crushed by the death of one of the members.

How much of Paul and how much of Stones was in the book was something that Walt often thought about. In the end the story had a happy ending, but it was very emotional overall.

Mitch had told Walt that he would be starting a book tour soon. Walt asked a lot of questions, but in the end Mitch had convinced him that he just needed to relax and try to enjoy it. A lot of authors never got the chance to do this.

"You have talent and are a nice guy. So don't worry about it. Just talk about the story. It'll be fun," Mitch had told him.

Walt wanted to scream, "It's not my book! I didn't write it!" But he kept quiet. He liked the check he had received and did not want to lose out.

The bookstore he was in had a café section. Walt got a coffee and a newspaper and sat down at a table where he could see his book. Maybe someone would buy it while he was there.

Not focusing much on the newspaper, Walt watched as people came up to check out the newly released books.

An older man with gray hair and a slow walk picked up Walt's book. Flipping open the back cover, he read the description. The man then started reading it. After a few minutes he turned and left, taking the book with him.

Holy shit, Walt thought, that man just bought my book. He wanted to jump up and yell, but he restrained himself. He finished his coffee and took the empty cup and placed it in the trash. Someone else would read the paper, he thought, so he left it on the table.

I'm an author was all he could think. Not really, but as far as the world was concerned, he was an author.

By the time Walt started the book tour, the book had moved up to the top ten of the *New York Times* best sellers. All the reviews had been good except for one. Walt wasn't sure what the guy hated about the book, but he was pretty scathing. It had not done anything to the sales of the book, but it stung Walt a little bit. He wasn't sure why, since he had not really written the book, but for some reason it still annoyed him.

At the first book signing, he was surprised that over one hundred people showed up. He sat at a Border's bookstore in New York as people came up, and he signed books over and over. By the time he was done, his hand was sore, and he was tired of answering questions. Mitch had someone there to help the crowd move quickly, and if anyone tried to engage in too long a conversation, the guy would move them along.

Two of the women in the line were very beautiful, and he started talking to them. "Holding up the line," the guy interrupted, and he moved them on. Walt was angry for a second, but the line wasn't even half done, so he had to keep signing. What he needed was a card he could hand out to people if he wanted to talk to them later.

Riding back to the hotel after the signing, he told the driver to stop at a bar. He wanted a drink and did not want to sit alone, back in his room, drinking.

"I know a nice place. Old style with a good crowd," the driver said.

At the bar Walt ordered a cognac. After the bartender brought him the drink, Walt looked around. The driver was right. This was a good neighborhood bar. People sat drinking and talking. There was enough light that it was easy to see, but it wasn't so bright that it didn't have that bar feel to it.

Taking a sip from the cognac, Walt looked around. He had done a book signing and was a writer. Keeping that in mind, he started up a conversation with the lady sitting next to him.

She was dark-haired with blue eyes, wearing tight-fitting jeans and a cropped top that showed off her thin stomach. She was drinking something that looked like lemonade in a martini glass. When she turned back from talking to her friend, he took a chance and spoke to her.

"Hi, are you from around here?" Walt asked.

One thing he had noticed about women was that whenever you approached to talk to them, they always looked you over before talking to you. This lady was no different, and she gave him a quick look.

As usual for him, he passed the looks test. He assumed that meant he didn't have a creepy vibe. He knew he was thin—but not too thin—and good-looking. Now he had to get past the part that he failed the majority of the time.

"Yeah, why?" she asked.

"I'm just visiting on my book tour and was wondering what I should not miss doing while I'm here," Walt said.

"You're on a book tour?"

"Yeah. I just got my first book published, and this is the start of the tour," Walt said.

"What's the name of the book?" she asked.

She said it with a tone that dripped with disbelief. Walt knew she was thinking, "Bullshit, you lying asshole." He was glad she hadn't said that, but the message came through anyway.

"*Forgotten Boy*," Walt said.

"You wrote that? Holy shit, I love that book! Did you really write it?" she asked.

"I did," Walt said.

"Wow. I've never met an author before. I have some friends writing books, but none of them have ever published any. You aren't bullshitting me, are you?"

"Nope. I wrote it." At least I took credit for writing it, Walt thought.

"You brought out the feeling of losing the sister so well. And when the son who lived confronted his parents for acting like both of their children had died, I burst into tears."

Walt didn't know what to say. "Thank you. I'm glad you enjoyed it." That was all he could come up with. He finished the rest of his cognac and called the bartender over.

"Next drink is on me," the lady told the bartender as he approached.

"Uh, thanks. Another cognac," Walt said.

"You aren't weirded out by having a lady buy you a drink, are you?" she asked.

"Not really, but I'm a little weirded out because I don't even know your name."

When the bartender set the new drink in front of Walt, the lady picked up her drink and held it out to him.

Walt picked up his drink and tapped the edge of his glass to hers.

"Cheers, Walt. I'm Chloe. Very nice to meet you."

"Cheers. How did you know my name? Oh, never mind," Walt said.

They continued talking about his book, and after a while they just talked.

In the morning, he woke up, and Chloe was lying there topless. He had gotten laid because of his book. She was smart and beautiful. Knowing she would only be a one-night stand, he had still had a great time. The sex had been great. They had both been drunk, which helped with any inhibitions they might have had otherwise.

Chloe did not have any issues with her body, and when she woke up, she smiled at him. She got out of bed and went into the bathroom. After a second she came back and, still topless, said they should order some breakfast.

Walt called room service and ordered them each bacon, eggs, and fruit with waffles.

The person who took the order told him it would be about thirty minutes.

After he ordered, they both got into the shower and went for round two. They did not hear the knock at the door, and a few minutes afterward, the phone to their room rang.

Walt opened the shower door, grabbed a towel, and ran dripping wet to the phone next to the bed.

"Hello?" Walt said.

"Hi. Yes, sir, the bellhop just came to your door with the room service. We need a signature, so you need to answer the door."

"Shit. Sorry. Please have him come back," Walt said.

"Thank you, sir," the voice said and hung up.

Answering the door in his towel, Walt signed for the food and wheeled the cart inside. He tipped the man ten dollars for his trouble. Then he closed the door and got back in the shower.

The food was cold by the time they ate it.

Two weeks later, Walt sat on the couch of a morning show he had never heard of. Three women sat and asked him questions about his book. Walt had done this at least five times already and was starting to get bored with it. Mitch had called him after the fourth show and told him to remember he was selling not only the books but himself.

"Try not to sound irritated with the hosts," Mitch told him.

"It's so boring," Walt said.

"I know. But we need them to invite you back for the next book. You like money, don't you?" Mitch said.

"Yes, very much," Walt said.

"Good. Then perk up and be nice," Mitch said.

"OK. I will try," Walt said.

"There is no *try*," Mitch said.

"Huh?"

"*The Empire Strikes Back*? Yoda?" Mitch said.

"Never saw it," Walt said.

"On that sad note, I'll talk to you later," Mitch said and hung up.

Yes, he wanted to sell books, and he wanted to make more money, so he would do as he was told.

"So, have you ever lost anyone?" one of the three hosts asked him.

Walt thought about lying to her for a second and saying yes, but it occurred to him that if he wanted to come back here, he had to be as truthful as possible. Then after a moment, he realized he *had* lost someone. Why had he never thought of it before?

"My brother. Well, he's actually still alive, but they have him in a medically induced coma. He had…some kind of episode and kept hurting himself. Now every time they wake him up, he ends up hurting himself, so they keep him in a coma. It is…very hard. We were very close."

"That's so sad. Sometimes it takes great pain to come up with great art," another of the hosts said.

"It helped me to get through it by writing. I think for me that's what my writing is for. It helps me to deal with things I might not otherwise be able to confront," Walt said.

"I think we all wish we had a way to do that. For me, I try to meditate," host two said.

"For me, it's a few glasses of wine," host three said with a tone that made the audience laugh.

"Thank you so much for joining us today, Walt. After this commercial break, we will have some tips on making traveling easier," host one said. They signaled they were at commercial. They thanked him for coming, and he was escorted offstage.

On the car ride back to his hotel, he thought of Paul again. He had been very close to him, and now he rarely thought of him. He figured it was mentally healthier not to focus too much on Paul. There was nothing he could do for him. It was Paul's own fault, anyway. Why had he typed on the stup—on the typewriter? He almost called the typewriter stupid, but he couldn't. Something had stopped him. Not stupid, he thought. It had been responsible for all this that was happening to him.

As they pulled into the drop-off area for the hotel, Walt told the driver he wanted to go to a bar instead—someplace with a lot of people.

The driver was a little irritated. Walt could tell from the way he answered. "Fine. Where?" the driver asked.

Walt didn't mind the attitude. He just wanted a drink—and maybe, if he could work it, some company.

"Somewhere with a lot of people and good cognac," Walt said.

"Not too sure about the cognac, but I know a place with a lot of people," the driver said.

In about ten minutes, the driver had him at a place called the Half Note. The logo was a single large musical note behind the words *Half Note.*

"This place is pretty good, and they have live music."

"Thanks," Walt said to the driver as he got out of the car. He gave the driver a ten-dollar tip and told him thank you but that he didn't have to stay. Walt would get himself back to the hotel. That perked the driver back up, and his attitude changed. He was friendly again as he said good-bye.

As usual, Walt sat at the bar and ordered a cognac. He started up conversations with several women at the bar before he got lucky on the fifth one. She knew his name and was currently reading his book. Bingo.

He bought her a drink. Then she returned the favor and bought him a shot.

After a few drinks, she put her hand on his leg and smiled at him. He smiled back and ordered another cognac. Everything went hazy after that.

Everything came back into focus when the sunlight hit his face in the morning. Opening his eyes, he winced as the headache hit him. He felt sick, but looking at the naked woman next to him cheered him up. He had spent too much time at the bar drinking cognacs. The lady had done several shots of tequila, which Walt had passed on. They had drunkenly made out at the bar until the bartender had asked them to leave.

After a drunken cab ride with lots of kissing and touching in the backseat, they had made it back to the hotel. Walt thought back to paying the cabdriver and realized he had given him one hundred dollars on a ten-dollar cab ride by mistake. Crap.

More kissing and fondling in the elevator, and at some point her hand had ended up in his pants. When the door opened, an older gentleman stood staring. The older man was in a white T-shirt and boxer shorts, and he held a container for ice.

"Oh my," he said, looking at her hand inside Walt's pants. She pulled her hand out and turned red, embarrassed.

"Don't mind me," the older man said as he changed places with them, getting into the elevator while they got out.

"Sorry," she said, with a slur on the *s*.

As the elevator doors closed, she turned and started kissing Walt again. They made their way to his room and went inside.

Now Walt was lying on his side with a headache, admiring her body. He could not remember her name.

Her eyes opened, and she winced.

"Oh my god, my head hurts," she said. Then, in a quick motion, she jumped out of the bed and ran to the bathroom. Walt watched her ass as she went.

He heard her throw up, which killed the erection he'd had.

When the sound of her throwing up stopped, he heard the water running. The water stopped, and she came out of the bathroom. As she walked back, he stared at her breasts as they gently bounced with her steps.

She lay down facing him. He could smell the vomit on her breath.

"I feel like shit," she said, the vomit smell coming at him with each word.

He winced at the smell.

Her eyes got big, and she put her hand over her mouth. "Does my breath stink?" she asked through her hand.

"A little," Walt said, being nice. It smelled like the trash outside a bar, but he didn't want to hurt her feelings.

She got back up and went back to the bathroom.

"They don't have a fucking toothbrush in here. Can I use yours?" she asked.

Walt picked up the phone and called the front desk. "Hey, we need a toothbrush in here," he said.

"Certainly, sir. We will bring one up in a few minutes."

"Thanks," Walt said and hung up.

She came back out of the bathroom and sat on the chair that was at a small desk. "I am not coming near you until I can brush my teeth," she said.

"OK," Walt said. For that he was grateful.

Walt dozed off and was awakened by the sound of a knock on the door. The lady wrapped herself in a towel from the bathroom and opened the door. She took the toothbrush, thanked the bellhop, and closed the door.

Sorry—no tip for you, buddy, Walt thought.

The lady then went to the bathroom to brush her teeth.

Maggie? Mary? What the hell was her name? It started with an *M*, he thought.

When she came out of the bathroom, she joined him back on the bed.

"From what I can remember about last night, I had a great time," the no-named woman said.

"Me too," Walt said. He didn't really want to talk more than necessary, since each word made his head throb.

Looking around the room, he saw her purse sitting on the floor by the door. A trail of their clothes continued from the purse to the bed. Shirts, then pants, and finally underwear and a bra.

Fuck, he thought, I didn't have any condoms. Next time he needed to use a condom. If this was going to become a regular occurrence, he would need to start traveling with a box of condoms.

In a few minutes, she was snoring.

Walt stood and walked over to the purse. He moved as quietly as he could, not wanting to wake her—but also because every step caused pain to shoot through his head.

While watching her and listening to her snoring, he carefully opened the mouth of her purse. Her wallet was tan with black trim. The tan area had the letters *L* and *V* in rows. A Louis Vuitton, he thought. From what he remembered, that was an expensive brand.

He popped the snap on the wallet and froze. It sounded like an explosion to him. He stared at the bed, and she continued to snore. It couldn't have been that loud. It's only a snap, he told himself.

Opening the wallet, he saw her driver's license. In her driver's license photo, she had a big smile, and her long black hair surrounded her head. Her bright-blue eyes popped out in the otherwise dark photo, giving them a very mysterious look.

Marie Moreau. She was French. At least he had been right about the *M*.

Walt closed the wallet, stood, and went to the bathroom. He washed his face with cold water and rinsed out his mouth, which was dry and tasted like cotton.

Lying back down on the bed, he looked at Marie's body. She had a firm, flat stomach, and her arms had just a touch of definition.

Her eyes opened, and she smiled when she saw him staring at her.

"I need some water," she said.

Walt stood and got her some water.

Downing the bottle quickly, she said, "Much better. Nothing helps a hangover like some water. We should also order some breakfast."

Marie looked around the room until her eyes found the information book for the hotel. She got up as though she were a spring. One moment she was on the bed, and the next moment she was standing.

Walt felt like an old man as he stood. His headache was still going strong.

"I'm going to get bacon and eggs and some fruit. You want me to order you anything? It will help if you eat something," she said.

"Sure. I'll just have whatever you have. Add some sourdough toast to mine if you aren't getting toast," Walt said and sat back down on the bed.

Marie ordered and sat back in the chair she had been in earlier, still naked. She was very confident in her body, Walt realized.

"You know I'm a writer. So what do you do?" Walt asked.

"You must have been pretty drunk," Marie said with a smile, "since we talked about this last night. But like I said, I'm studying to be a personal trainer. I love working with people, and I love working out. It seems like a natural fit for me."

Walt felt a little embarrassed that he didn't remember.

"You do look like you work out," Walt said.

She smiled at that and stood and went over to the bed.

Standing in front of him, she asked, "You like my body?"

Walt nodded and felt himself start to get hard.

Her breasts were at his mouth, and as he went to kiss them, she pushed him back onto the bed. She was forceful and grabbed his wrists as she climbed on top of him. She rubbed herself on him until he was ready and then slid him inside her.

Again, he thought, no condom. But he didn't really care.

When they finished she went to the bathroom to clean up, and he answered the door for the room service. Together they ate breakfast. She was warm and smart and beautiful. The time passed quickly, and it was time for him to get ready to check out.

Marie got dressed and gave him a hug and a very long kiss.

"Will I see you again? Maybe next time I'm here?" Walt asked.

"Probably not. I'm moving out to California next week."

Walt grabbed a hotel pen and wrote his name and phone number on the hotel stationery. He folded it and handed it to her.

She opened it and looked at the phone number. She folded it back up and put it in her purse.

As she walked out of the room, she smiled at him.

"See ya around," she said.

With that, she was gone. He would not see her again for ten years.

6

The rest of the book tour went smoothly, and in what seemed like a flash of lightning, Walt was back home in his apartment. He had a number one best-selling book now, and he knew he would need to move. This little apartment would not cut it. Also, he had always wanted to move to Southern California. Something about the warm weather and beach life had always appealed to him.

Mitch told him that more checks would be coming. They had not expected the book to do this well, and Walt had met some numbers that would get him some bonuses. Mitch called him a few days after the book tour ended.

"So, are you thinking about when you will start to write your next book?" Mitch asked, getting right to the point of the call.

Walt was quiet at the question. He did not relish the idea of what he needed to do to write another book. Mitch, of course, thought of this as a business, and when you had a good thing, you needed to keep it going.

Walt looked at the Wordsmith. It looked clean and neat and new.

"I'll probably take a little break from everything and then get to work on a new book," Walt said.

Walt heard Mitch take a breath on the other end of the line.

"Listen, don't wait too long. Right now you have a good reputation, and it would be easy for us to sell a new book. If you wait, you will still get a good price, most likely, but it's always good to strike while the iron is hot. After your second book, you can take a little longer break. But I'd like to get you a reputation as an author you have to read. So if there is any way you could get another book out in a year, that would really be great," Mitch said.

"OK. I won't take too long. Don't worry. Maybe a few weeks' break, and then I'll start."

"That's great. A month even wouldn't be so bad. Also, if you want to move, now would be a good time. I know a good real estate agent, and I could set you up with a trip out to SoCal. Just let me know," Mitch said.

"Please set it up. I don't want to stay in this apartment," Walt said.

"Will do. You should get a call from her in a few days," Mitch said, and then they said their good-byes and hung up.

Walt had been staring at the typewriter as he talked to Mitch. The idea of having someone use the typewriter again gave him a sick feeling. He knew he would do it. There was no doubt in his mind about that. He liked what it had brought him so far.

Going out again and picking up a homeless person seemed risky. The first time he'd taken longer than he had wanted to find someone and had almost given up. To go out and do the same thing now that he was sort of recognizable could be bad. He'd been on talk shows recently, and it was possible that someone would recognize him. He would need to figure out a way to find someone without risking being recognized.

Time was something he had. Do not rush, he told himself. You need to be careful how you do this.

He poured himself a cognac and sat in the dark on his couch.

"I'm not sure how to find someone," he said to himself in the dark.

He set down the cognac, stood, and went into the bedroom and looked at the typewriter. He picked it up and brought it to the living room and set it on the coffee table. Then he sat back down on the couch, picked up his cognac, and took a drink.

As always, the typewriter had been warm when he'd picked it up. No matter how cold the room was, the typewriter was always warm. In the dark he stared at the outline of the typewriter sitting on the coffee table. Thoughts of his brother and Stones typing away as though they were possessed crossed his mind.

"What are you?" he asked, looking at the typewriter. There was no answer.

After I move, I will figure this out, he thought.

Walt finished his drink and fell asleep on the couch.

In the morning the sunlight came in through the front window and woke him up. He'd slept wrong, and he woke up with a sore neck. If he was going to move, he wanted a new couch also. It seemed lately that he fell asleep frequently on the couch. A more comfortable couch to sleep on was not a bad idea.

He showered and got dressed.

The phone rang, and the real estate agent was on the other end. They worked out a time for him to go look at some places in the Los Angeles area.

Walt called Mitch and asked him to arrange a flight out to Los Angeles for him.

"I think you are getting to the point where you might need an assistant—someone to free you up for other, more important things," Mitch said.

An assistant was something Walt had never thought about.

"How's that work?" Walt asked.

"What do you mean? You pay them, and they do things for you. Nothing to it," Mitch said.

"I guess. How do I find one?" Walt said.

"Once you move to LA, I'll help you find one. Doing it now is probably not a good idea since you are moving. I'll get the flight set up for you. You been thinking about ideas for the new book?" Mitch asked.

"Yeah. I've got some things rattling around." Walt was getting pretty good at lying. It was pretty simple. Most of the lies he told just ended up with him agreeing with what people were saying. Keep the lies simple so you can remember them. Don't elaborate unless you have too. As long as he followed those rules, he seemed to be doing pretty well with them.

"Great. That's good to hear," Mitch said, obvious happiness in his voice.

Walt hung up and looked at the Wordsmith sitting there on the coffee table.

"I hope you are hungry," Walt said to it. He was starting to think of it as a living thing that liked the taste of blood.

For the first time in what seemed like a long time, although in reality it had been less than six months, he had nothing to do. He looked at the clock. It was ten in the morning.

Was this too early for a drink? he wondered. No, of course not.

He poured himself a cognac, sat back down on the couch, and turned on the TV.

Mitch had recorded his appearances, and Walt put the tape in the VCR and watched himself on TV. In the first few interviews, he could see how nervous he had been. His answers were stiff, and his voice was shaky.

As he went along, though, he got much better. His story about how he came up with the book idea got refined, and he had what he considered a pretty good story. Also, he got comfortable enough that he joked with some of the hosts.

By the time he finished watching the tapes, he was on his fourth cognac and was feeling pretty good.

Most authors, he assumed, had to figure out an idea for the story. But he needed to figure out how to get someone to type the story for him. An assistant. Someone to do things for him. But not just any kind of assistant. He needed someone who could find writers for him. Finding someone to bring in writers for him would not be an easy task. He couldn't just ask people that.

"Hey, can you kidnap someone for me so they can write a story? Oh, how? Well, the typewriter keeps them typing until they die." That would not work.

But what if he told Mitch he was thinking of writing a book about mercenaries? He could then ask around and get help in talking to mercenaries. This was not a bad idea. He knew that a lot of writers would do a ride-along with police or interview criminals for books they were writing. It was not too farfetched for him to want to talk to mercenaries to get a feel for them.

A weight lifted off his shoulders. He felt as if this might work. First, he needed to move, and then he needed to talk to some mercenaries.

Walt sipped his cognac and spoke to the typewriter.

"I think I figured out the way to get you your next meal—and for me to get my next novel."

The Wordsmith did nothing. It remained motionless on the coffee table.

Walt smiled and sipped his drink.

Southern California was warm and sunny.

Walt had made enough money and was looking for a place up in the Hollywood Hills. He wanted to have a pool and look down on the LA valley from his backyard.

Looking at the houses, he kept a few things in mind. He would need a place for the typewriter. It would have to be a place where he could keep it locked up. The last thing he needed was for someone to come over and accidentally start typing on it.

He wanted a lot of space. All his life he had lived in small places where his family had been on top of one another. After he left his home, he had moved into a small apartment that was always confining to him, so he wanted a big open place.

Finally, he wanted a pool. He had never been much of a swimmer, but the idea of sitting out by a pool was an idea he'd always liked.

Most of the houses he looked at were boring. They were big but not open.

On the first house of the second day of looking, he found the one he wanted. The front-yard access was controlled by a gate. Trees and bushes were laid out to give it a natural look, but there weren't so many that it looked like a forest. In the backyard was a large rectangular pool with a hot tub attached in such a way that the runoff created a waterfall into the pool. It was made using natural stones that blended with the bushes and trees.

Inside, the house was big and open. There were hardwood floors and big windows that opened into the living room and dining room. Right outside the kitchen in the hallway was a door that went downstairs into a basement.

She was an attractive blond lady with perfect teeth. Walt thought her breasts might be fake, but he did not ask. They were large, and she had on a tight shirt with a low neckline that showed them off. She was skinny, which added to the idea that her breasts were probably fake.

Her name was Aileen, and she was very friendly. She had a large diamond on her left ring finger, so he did not try to hit on her.

"I love this place. It has everything I want," Walt said.

Aileen nodded and smiled. "The price is very reasonable. The owner had to move suddenly due to a family issue, and he is willing to take the first good offer, even if it is below asking price," she said.

Walt nodded. "Let me take one more look through the house, but I think I want to make an offer."

Knowing he already wanted the house, Walt walked through it again. He went down into the basement and stood. The room was not large, and the lightbulb in the center of the room gave off just enough light to keep the room from being dark but not enough that it was bright. There were shelves built into the wall that looked worn. The floor was cement, and there was a slight noise from his shoes as he walked.

Walt heard Aileen coming down the stairs.

"What a dark room," she said as she came into the room.

"I like it," Walt said.

"Maybe with a brighter bulb it would look better," Aileen said.

Nodding yes but knowing he would leave the dark bulb, Walt turned and walked past Aileen and back up the stairs.

Out by the pool, Walt took off his shoes and sat and put his feet in the water. The heater for the pool had been turned off by the current owner, and the water was very cold. Walt didn't mind. It felt good.

Aileen came outside after a few minutes.

"I want to make an offer, and I really want this place," Walt said.

"How much do you want to offer?" Aileen said.

"Offer asking price. I don't want to haggle. I just want to move from where I'm at," Walt said.

"We could probably get it for less," Aileen said.

"Yeah, but I don't want to lose it by being cheap," Walt said.

"OK. I'll get the offer ready," Aileen said.

"I'm going to sit here for a while," Walt said.

"OK. I'm going to head out to get the offer ready," Aileen said.

Walt turned and said good-bye. He did not stand to say good-bye.

Lying back and looking up at the sky, Walt felt relaxed. After thirty minutes, he stood, dried off his feet, put his shoes on, and left.

Flying home the next day was uneventful. The offer for the house was made and accepted, and a week later the house went into escrow.

A little over a year after finding the typewriter, Walt was a homeowner.

He made arrangements to donate most of his current furniture. The only items he was keeping from his current apartment were the pictures he'd had on the walls and the typewriter. Along with the furniture, he donated most of the clothes he owned. There were a few items he'd bought over the last six months that he kept, but everything else was going.

On the day he left, he took one bag with his few pieces of clothing that he was keeping and the typewriter. He had decided he wanted to drive across the country. Farmlands and open space were spread out over much of the country. He was surprised at the amount of open space as he drove.

On the first night, he stayed at a small, cheap motel a mile from the freeway exit. The bed was too soft, and there were only five channels on the TV. He heard the banging noises of sex in the room next to his, with low moans slowly building to loud screams—and then quiet.

Lying in bed, he listened to the sounds of the night. There were no further noises of sex, and infrequently he would hear doors open and close and people walking down the hallway outside his door, talking.

He thought about Paul lying in bed at a hospital in a forced coma. It still hurt him when he thought about his brother.

When he thought about Stones, he didn't feel bad. He hadn't known Stones, and what Stones's death had given him was worth his death.

After a little while, Walt fell asleep.

Walt stood on the edge of the cliff, looking down at the ocean. It was warm, and wind blew at his back.

Looking up, Walt saw stars and a bright, full moon.

Walt didn't hear the man come up from behind him.

The man put his hand on Walt's right shoulder and said, "Hello."

Walt turned and saw Paul and turned back away, ashamed.

"You left me," his brother said.

"I'm sorry. I couldn't stay. I—"

"*You left me!*"

Walt turned and looked at Paul, who was screaming. The bottom half of Paul's face had no skin, and the remaining skin on the top half was rotting. The skin was covered in dirt, and maggots crawled from his brother's face.

Walt screamed as Paul came in front of him and embraced him in a bear hug.

Screaming in Walt's ear, Paul said, "*The typewriter is mine! You stole it from me!*"

Walt struggled to get free, but Paul's grip was too strong. Paul leaned back and pulled Walt over the edge of the cliff and down onto the rocks below.

Walt woke up. He was breathing fast, and he sat up. He was alone in the dark. It was quiet inside and outside of the room.

"Hello?" Walt said to no one, and no one answered.

It was 3:00 a.m. Walt got up. He took a shower and got dressed. He went to the front desk and checked out.

"Heading out early?" the man at the front desk asked.

"Yeah. I want to beat traffic," Walt said.

"What traffic?" the man asked as Walt left.

Walt rolled the windows down in his car and blasted the radio. The noise and cold air provided little comfort from the dream.

His brother was still alive, but he was dead in the dream. Walt guessed that he was already dead here too. Nothing the doctors had done had helped him. No medication stopped him from trying to get back to the typewriter. Of course, they had no way of knowing that was what he was after. All they knew was that he would not stop trying to escape from them.

In a way, Walt guessed he was controlled by the typewriter as well—but only insofar as it was bringing him money that he did not want to give up. Driving that thought out of his mind, he drove on.

"I make my own choices," Walt said to himself.

After a while the darkness turned to light, as it always does, and Walt felt better. Something about the night turned his thoughts dark. After he drove a few more hours, Walt stopped at a Denny's and had breakfast.

Using a pay phone, he called Mitch to let him know he should be there in a few more days. Mitch asked how the drive was going, and Walt gave the standard answer: "Fine. Nothing eventful."

After some back and forth, Walt got to the question he had been waiting to ask.

"I have a good idea for a story, but it involves some mercenaries," he said.

"Are you talking about former soldiers?" Mitch said.

"Yeah, something like that. I guess they sell their services after they leave the army or whatever."

"Lot of stories about mercenaries," Mitch said.

"I know. But I think I have something that might be interesting. I'd like to talk to some mercenaries to hash out the idea. Problem is I don't know any," Walt said.

"Not sure I know any, either. But I can ask some people I know who might know some. I know some government contractors, and I know they employ ex-military from time to time," Mitch said.

"I am looking for some people who did some questionable work," Walt said.

"Questionable? What's that mean?" Mitch said.

"You know, snipers or people like that," Walt said.

"You want people that have killed people? Is that what you are looking for?" Mitch asked.

"Yeah. I want to get an idea of how it affected them," Walt said.

"OK. Not sure I'd want to talk to people like that, but I'll see what I can do," Mitch said.

"Thanks," Walt said.

Mitch hung up.

Walt held the phone in his hand for a second. In reality he had no desire to talk to a bunch of killers, but he needed the help.

Getting back in his car, Walt drove until it was dark. He stopped and went to a McDonald's drive-through and got a Big Mac and some fries for dinner. Not healthy, he thought, but it tasted great.

Walt pulled off the freeway and looked for a cheap motel. His only real requirement was that it be close to a bar or a liquor store. He found a Motel 6 that was across the street from a liquor store.

After he checked in, he walked over to the liquor store and bought a bottle of cognac. The clerk at the liquor store had a strong accent that Walt didn't recognize. The clerk tried to make conversation with Walt, but he couldn't understand him, so he just smiled and nodded.

Sitting alone in his motel room, Walt poured cognac into the one of the plastic cups the motel provided. Something about the plastic changed the taste of the cognac. Walt wondered if the chemicals in the cup leached into the cognac. At that thought, he quit drinking from the plastic cup and sipped the cognac straight from the bottle, and it tasted much better.

He stopped after finishing a third of the bottle.

Lying in bed, he felt his mind and body go numb. He let the feeling of being drunk overtake him, and he fell asleep. Exactly as he had hoped, he had no dreams. The only price he paid was a slight headache in the morning when he woke up.

Since the liquor store was closed when he was leaving, he stopped at a local grocery store. It was a little out of the way, but he needed some aspirin. He got the largest bottle they had, along with a couple of bottles of water. He took a few aspirin with one of the bottles of water and felt better after an hour. That to him was a small price to pay for the restful night's sleep.

For the next two days, he followed the same pattern: drive all day and drink enough at night to keep from dreaming.

When he finally arrived at his house in Southern California, he was relieved.

He did not yet have the key to his house, so he had to stop by the real estate office to pick it up.

"The place is empty and clean," Aileen said, handing him the keys.

"Thanks," Walt said.

"You having your furniture sent?"

"No. I'm getting all new furniture. I didn't like anything I had."

Walt said good-bye and shook her hand and left. He was tired and did not feel like talking.

On the way to his house, he stopped at a sporting goods store. He purchased an air mattress. He got the nicest one they had and made sure it included a pump.

Exactly as Aileen had said, the house was clean and empty. Walt walked the area outside the house and then sat down at the pool. He took off his shoes and put his feet in the pool. He immediately pulled his feet back out. The water was freezing.

Walt got up and went to the pool shed. Inside, he found the filter, but he did not see a control for the heater.

Frustrated, he went back outside. It turned out that the heater was next to the hot tub. There were two controls there: one for the hot tub and one for the pool. Walt turned on the hot tub first and then turned on the pool heat.

He had to guess at the temperature for both. He had never owned a pool and had not had one growing up. He put the hot tub at one hundred degrees and the pool at seventy-five degrees. He hoped that would be warm enough for both.

He went inside. His footsteps echoed in the empty house as he walked. He looked around the house and felt calm. This was his place. He would get to make it however he wanted. He thought about the small apartment and the small house he had lived in growing up. Never had he thought he would own a place like this. He had hated school, and his parents were just thrilled when he graduated from high school.

Walt went out to his car and got the air mattress. He pumped it up in the living room. No reason to put it in the bedroom. The whole house was his. After the mattress was pumped up, he went out and got the typewriter.

The temperature outside was warm, and the typewriter felt cool. Its temperature never seemed to change. In the heat it was cool, and in the cold it was warm. He took it downstairs to the basement and set it in the center of the room under the lightbulb. He needed to buy a table and chair. He also wanted to get a cabinet for the paper. Whoever was typing would need easy access to paper.

Walt went back upstairs, leaving the typewriter in the basement. He sat on the air mattress and thought about what he needed to do next. Furniture shopping was probably the best thing for him to do. He started to make a list in his mind of what he needed, starting with a real bed. He knew he'd be OK for a few nights on the air mattress, but after that he wanted a real bed.

He'd always wanted a leather couch—white leather. It would go well with the dark wood floors. Also, he needed a TV. He had never been much of a reader, so he was not sure what he would do for the next few nights. Sleep, probably. Drink and sleep.

It took Walt a few weeks to get everything ordered and delivered to his new house. The couch and TV came first. That was fine with him, since he found that even once the bed arrived, he still spent most nights on the couch. He would have a few drinks and watch TV until he fell asleep.

He was playing a waiting game. Mitch had told him that his friend was reaching out to some people he knew who did some military contracting and might know the kind of people Walt was looking for.

Checks for his novel continued to come in. It was an odd feeling to Walt to be making money for not working, but he enjoyed it. Some nights he would go out to a bar and pick up ladies. The "I'm a *New York Times* best-selling author" line worked more often than it didn't.

On the nights he had a woman over, he slept in the bed. This morning he was lying naked in bed when the phone rang.

"Hello?" Walt answered, trying to be quiet so he wouldn't wake his guest.

"Hey, Walt, it's Mitch. I've done it. I've got a few people for you to interview."

"Oh man, that's great," Walt said, no longer caring if he woke up his guest. He had been waiting for this for weeks.

"Now listen, these are some scary people, and there are some rules," Mitch said.

"OK," Walt said.

"The ones who agreed to be interviewed did so with the understanding that if they don't want to talk about something, you won't press it. So if they say they can't or don't want to talk about that, you will just drop it," Mitch said.

"OK," Walt said.

"I'm serious on that one. These guys don't want to be pressed on anything. You ask the question, and they will either answer it or they won't. If they won't, you drop it. Got it?" Mitch said.

"Yeah. I got it," Walt said. He didn't really care. He was looking for someone to help him kidnap people. He figured he needed shady people who liked money.

"Also, most of them will not use their real names. I don't know why, but don't expect them to be completely honest with you," Mitch said.

"OK. How soon can I meet them?" Walt said.

"One last thing. They all want to be armed. So you don't mind meeting with them if they are carrying a gun, do you?" Mitch asked.

"No. That's fine," Walt said.

"Great. Give me a few days. I'll arrange a time with them. Are you OK with meeting them at your house?" Mitch said.

Walt hadn't thought about that. Did he want a bunch of killers coming through his house? No, not really.

"How about I buy them dinner? I'll pay, and they can pick the place," Walt said.

"Sure. I think that will work. OK, let me set it up." Mitch hung up.

Walt got up and went into the bathroom. Mitch is awesome, he thought. If he knew what Walt was really doing, he would freak out, but with any luck, Mitch would never find out. These people seemed like exactly what Walt needed.

Walt peed and then looked at himself in the mirror. He was very lean. Before all this happened, he had been at least ten pounds heavier. Since all this began, he had switched from beer to cognac, which had fewer calories, and he wasn't eating as much.

Walt took in a breath and sucked in his stomach, and he could see the outline of his ribs. I need to be careful I don't get too skinny, he thought. He knew he was right on the edge of being unhealthy, and he didn't want to look like a skeleton. He washed his hands and went back to the bed and went to sleep.

After the first three interviews, Walt was worried. All three of them were nothing like what he was hoping for. It turned out that they considered themselves professionals and took pride in their work.

Each one looked serious. All of them were worried about protecting their clients' confidentiality more than they were worried about anything about themselves. Of the first three, two were ex-US Navy SEALS, and one was a former US Marine.

They explained that after getting out of the service, they found they could make more money as government contractors or by performing work for large companies that were working in hazardous areas. Protecting important people such as CEOs or other high-ranking corporate officials was common.

None of the first three did anything that Walt found out was called "black ops." Black ops meant things such as assassinations or kidnappings or other tasks like that. In the service most of them had gathered intel or helped train other countries' troops.

Walt was getting worried—and then he met the fourth person.

He identified himself as Ian White. He had a scar across his right eyebrow and wore a full beard. He had dark skin and eyes, and Walt thought he might be Hispanic.

When Walt shook his hand, the grip was strong, and Walt saw the veins in Ian's forearms.

Ian wore dark-blue jeans with boots and a black T-shirt that was formfitting. His hair was cut short but not shaved.

For the first part of the dinner, Ian said very little. He ordered a steak, salad, and Jack Daniels, neat.

Walt asked him what he'd done in the military.

"I started in the navy and eventually got into SEAL training. After finishing BUDS, which is the beginning SEAL training, I got assigned to work as a liaison with the CIA. I was on a team that performed special tasks," Ian said.

"Special tasks?" Walt asked.

"Yeah. Not to get into specifics, but it was mostly off-the-books work—things I can't talk about."

Now Walt was curious. He wanted more details but thought about what Mitch had said.

"Things like what?" Walt asked.

Ian focused his eyes on Walt and took a sip of his Jack Daniels. "The guy who set this up told me you wouldn't ask any questions I didn't want to answer. First thing you do is ask a question I don't want to answer. And then you fucking press it when I say I can't talk about it."

Oh fuck, Walt thought.

"You got some balls on you for such a skinny fuck," Ian said. Then he smiled. "Wet work. We fucking killed people for the love of country," he said, surprising Walt.

"Holy shit," Walt said.

"Yeah. It wasn't what I thought I'd be doing when I signed up. Now, I won't tell you any of the things I did, because if I did I'd have to kill you," Ian said.

Walt couldn't tell if he was joking or not. Most of the time when people said that, Walt knew it was a joke, but something about Ian made him not so sure.

"I will tell you this: I loved doing it. To me it was fun. I enjoyed hunting as a kid, and this kind of took it to the next level," Ian said.

"How long were you in for?" Walt asked.

"Total? About ten years. This includes the time before I was a SEAL. I was a SEAL about seven years. Got deployed to some fun places. I missed the work, which is why I do contracting work now. It's not the same, but it pays well, and the work for the most part is fucking easy."

"How much money do you make contracting?" Walt asked. This was important for Walt. He didn't want to go bankrupt asking Ian to help him.

"It depends on the work I can get. If I can get a long-term contract, I can make over two hundred K a year, depending on the work."

Perfect, Walt thought. I can exceed that, I think—provided the next book does just as well.

"Did it ever bother you, killing people?" Walt said.

"Why would it? I didn't know them," Ian said.

Walt nodded.

They talked and drank and got to know each other. Walt liked Ian, and he hoped Ian liked him.

Near the end of the night, when they were both several drinks in and feeling good, Walt brought up the typewriter.

"I'd like to show you something. It's going to sound crazy at first, but it's an offer for a job. First, I need to show you something."

Ian got quiet and looked at Walt. "What kind of job?"

"I need to show you something first and explain. It's going to sound crazy, but let me give you the story and show you something, and then we can discuss the offer," Walt said.

Ian was interested. He had always been up for anything, and the odd way Walt was acting after an evening of stories and joking made Ian think he was serious.

"OK," Ian said.

Walt paid the check, and they went outside. The cool air felt good, and Walt had the restaurant host call a cab for them.

They stood outside waiting, and neither one of them said anything. Even in the cab, they were both quiet. Ian's curiosity grew as they rode.

Before going out for dinner, Walt had cleaned out his freezer and placed the typewriter inside.

When they got inside the house, Ian said, "Nice place."

"Thanks. I'm going to tell you something you won't believe. But if you will listen to the whole story, it will make some kind of odd sense," Walt said.

"I'm all ears," Ian said.

Walt explained everything, starting with his work selling the contents of storage units. He then went into the story of how they had found the typewriter and how he had found Paul typing on it and how, no matter what they did, he still was trying to get back to it.

"So your brother is still in a forced coma?" Ian asked.

"Yes, but please let me finish," Walt said, and he continued the story.

He explained how the story Paul had been writing was amazing. Ian said nothing when Walt explained how he had picked up Stones and had him use the typewriter. Walt worried as he told Ian about Stones's death at the typewriter and how he had disposed of the body.

When he finished the story, Ian rubbed his hands over his face.

"Where is this typewriter?" Ian asked.

"Since I knew this story was going to be hard for you to believe, I put the typewriter in the freezer," Walt said.

"What the fuck will that do?" Ian asked.

Walt went into the kitchen, and Ian followed.

"Open it and take out the typewriter. Do not touch the keys. You can touch any part of it, but not the keys."

This fucking guy is crazy, Ian thought. He approached the door of the freezer as though someone with a gun were sitting inside. Putting his hand on the handle of his gun that he kept hidden in his back waistband, he cautiously opened the door. Sitting in the center of the empty freezer was an old-looking typewriter. It looked new.

Ian took his hand off his gun.

"Go on. Pick it up," Walt said.

"Is it going to fucking explode?" Ian asked.

"No, it isn't. If it was, would I be standing in here with you?" Walt asked.

Ian reached out a finger and touched the typewriter. He felt the cold air of the freezer on his hand, but when he touched the typewriter, it felt warm. He grabbed the typewriter with both hands now and picked it up. Not only was it warm to the touch, but it warmed him when he grabbed it. It gave an odd sensation over his body. He held it up over his head and looked inside. Everything looked normal. There was no heat source that he saw. He turned and set it down on the kitchen table.

"How the fuck is it warm?" Ian asked, not expecting an answer.

"Just remember not to touch the keys. Once you start typing, that's it," Walt said.

"Let's say I believe this story you are telling. Why the fuck are you telling it to me?" Ian said.

"My editor wants another novel. So I need to use the typewriter again."

"You've never used it," Ian said.

"Yeah, right. Well, I need to have someone else use it again," Walt said.

"Is this how you ask me to help you kidnap some-one?" Ian said.

Walt was now feeling ashamed to be asking this. "Yes. That's exactly what I'm asking. Listen, if you help me, I'll pay you one hundred K before we do anything. Then you can help me with the task, and if at any point anything I've said turns out to be a lie, you can keep the money and leave. But if it works as I say, I will give you a percentage of the book money."

"What's to stop me from killing you and taking the typewriter for myself?" Ian asked.

That thought had not occurred to Walt. It was a flaw in his plan. Ian was right. He could kill him and take the typewriter.

"I have no desire to be an author. But I'd want thir-ty percent of the profits," Ian said.

It would be easy work, and Ian figured he would only have to work once or twice a year at most, if what this crazy fuck was saying was true.

"Thirty percent will not be a problem," Walt said.

"First, though, I'll want the hundred K, and then we can figure out how to test out this typewriter so I can see if what you are saying is true," Ian said.

Ian felt the typewriter again, and the temperature was the same. He picked it up again and examined it, making sure to stay away from the keys. Better to be safe.

Walt called a cab for Ian and gave him money to pay for it.

Ian left, and Walt sat at the kitchen table with the typewriter.

"Well, he seems like he is interested," Walt said to the typewriter.

Walt turned off the light in the kitchen and went upstairs to bed.

In the kitchen the typewriter sat, and its warmth attracted a moth, which landed on the *D* key.

When Walt woke up in the morning and went into the kitchen, he noticed the moth on the key, and he tried to shoo it away. It did not move. Walt picked up the typewriter by the sides and shook it until the moth fell off the key and onto the table, motionless. It was dead and dry.

Walt picked up the dead moth and stared at it for a second before dropping it into the trash. He then picked up his phone and called his bank. Walt had no idea how in the hell to give someone $100,000.

It turned out it wasn't that difficult. Ian had him write out a check to his company, and they would book it as bodyguard services. Everything aboveboard. Walt did not want anyone looking into this to think it was odd.

Ian and Walt decided that Ian would charge him for a six-month retainer valued at $100,000. He would pay taxes on the earned money, which should make it all look legal.

Walt was sitting on the couch when the phone rang. He had been in deep thought, and it took a few rings before he heard it.

"Hello?" Walt said.

"It's Ian."

"I'm going to write you a check to your company for the hundred thousand," Walt said.

"OK. I'll come by tonight to pick it up, and we can discuss how we want to proceed with this. No more talking on the phone after this. I'll be there at eight tonight," Ian said. He hung up.

Walt held the phone for a second until there was a dial tone, and then he hung up.

Arriving promptly at eight, Ian knocked on the door. Walt had been sitting out by the pool. He had swum earlier and was still wearing his swimming trunks. The temperature of the pool had been perfect—a little cold at first, but once he was swimming, it felt good.

Now he wore a T-shirt and damp swim trunks. When he heard the knock, he got up and went to greet Ian.

"Hi, Ian. Here's the check," Walt said, after inviting Ian inside.

Ian took the check and then looked around. "Are we alone?" he asked.

"Yeah. Nobody here but us," Walt said.

"Once the check clears, I've got some ideas on how we can do this," Ian said. "The first time, you said you picked up a homeless guy. He came by choice, correct?"

"Yeah. It took a little bit to find someone, though. He was maybe the fifth or so person I spoke to. So now I'm nervous about doing that again."

"OK. First, just so you know, I did some research on you and on your brother. So far, everything you've said checked out. I called the hospital and asked to speak to your brother, and they told me he was not able to talk on the phone. They wouldn't give me any other information, but with what you said, it makes sense. Also, I was able to get ahold of the police report on when they arrested your brother. You know, if he ever comes out of the coma, he will probably go to jail for assaulting a police officer."

"Yeah, I know," Walt said.

"So until something you said ends up being false, I've decided to trust you. The hundred thousand helps. What we should do for this next...novel—" Ian seemed unsure about what to call it but seemed happy with *novel* once he said it. "What we should do for the next novel is take someone—not give them a choice. Homeless is not a bad idea. But we need someone who's not crazy. They need to be afraid of me. Crazy people tend to have no fear. So I'll do some recon to find someone who fits what we are looking for. With the number of homeless people in this city, it shouldn't be a problem."

"We are going to kidnap someone?"

"Not *we*. I'll kidnap them. You need to be as low profile about this as possible. If I get caught, I don't want you involved. The kidnapping and then the ride over here will be the dangerous parts. You have a nice secluded house here, so once we have them on the premises, it should not be a problem," Ian said.

Walt was nodding as Ian spoke. Ian was really going to help him do this. Walt was starting to understand the true power of money. Maybe it wasn't just the money. Ian had held the typewriter.

"You said the person doing the typing will die, correct?"

"Yes. They will literally type until they die."

"OK. That works for us. Getting rid of a body should not be a problem. I know a place we can dispose of the body. But what it seems like is that even if someone finds the body, it will not look like a homicide. They will have no injuries, and no other indicators of homicide will be found on the body."

"That's true, I guess. Honestly, I'm not sure what they would find," Walt said.

"If the body isn't found for a while, they will just find a decomposing body. But let's not worry about that now. So here's how it will go. First, the check has to clear. Next, I'll do recon on some homeless people until I find one who meets our needs. Once I have one in mind, I'll let you know. I'll call and just say, 'Walt, tonight,' and you just answer OK and hang up. Then be ready. I will arrive between midnight and one. Any questions?"

"If I need to reach you, what should I do?" Walt asked.

Ian wrote down a phone number. "Call this number and leave a message. I will get the message, but assume other people may hear it. So keep it concise. Do not mention anything that could come back later and bite us in the ass. Any other questions?"

Walt thought for a minute. He did not want to think about this too much, or he would start doubting what they were about to do. Better just to push forward.

"No," Walt said.

Ian left, and Walt poured himself a cognac and went back out to the pool. He set the drink on the table by the pool, took off his shirt, laid it on the back of a chair, and jumped in the water. The cool water of the pool felt good, and he swam laps until he was tired and no longer worried about what he was going to do.

Walt managed not to spend too much time thinking about Ian. The check had cleared after a few days, and now he was just waiting to hear from him. After a few weeks, he started to get nervous. If he had taken the money and run, there was nothing Walt could do. All Ian would need to say if Walt complained was that Walt had tried to pay Ian to kill someone. So Walt waited.

Near the end of the third week, Walt was getting to the point that he was about to call the number Ian had given him.

The phone rang, and Walt picked up.

"Hey, Walt, it's Mitch. Just checking up to see how you are doing."

"Hey, Mitch. I'm doing good. I've started on the book, and it's coming along great," Walt lied.

"Awesome, buddy. That's great. How's the new house working out?"

"I love it. The pool especially. I never had one before, and I spend a ton of time in it."

"Great. Well, I don't want to bug you too much, but I just wanted to make sure everything was going OK. See if there was anything you needed from me. The interviews with the special forces guys went well?"

"Yes. That went great. Better than expected."

"Super. OK, well, give me a call if you need anything. I'm glad everything is going well. Talk to you later," Mitch said.

"Thanks for checking in. Talk to you later," Walt said, and they hung up.

"Ian, hurry up and fucking call!" Walt yelled—not that yelling helped, but it made him feel a little better.

Typical of how things in life work, Walt picked up a lady one night when he was feeling anxious. His writer story and the fact that he was a number one best-selling author almost always worked in certain bars. The more upper class the bar was, the more likely he was to be able to pick someone up.

As he got her home and they got inside, the phone rang.

"Hello?" Walt said.

"Walt, tonight," the voice said.

Fuck, Walt thought. Of course.

Walt did not want to put this off any further, so he answered, "OK," and hung up.

He turned to the blond woman he had picked up. She was short and thin and wore cute cut-off shorts and a plain white shirt.

"I hate to do this, but something just came up, and I have to go. I'll call you a cab to get you home," Walt said.

"Um, OK. Everything OK?" the blonde asked.

"Yeah. Just a small family emergency," Walt said and picked up the phone.

It took what seemed like forever to Walt, but in reality it was only twenty minutes until the cab arrived. Walt paid the driver in advance and said good-bye. He watched until the taillights of the cab were gone.

When he was sure she was gone, Walt went back inside and waited. He was not sure how Ian would bring this person to the house. Sitting on the couch, Walt wanted a drink. He kept from having one and instead poured himself a glass of water. A clear head was needed. Whatever help Ian needed, Walt had to be ready. It wasn't an option to have a foggy head.

Sitting in the dark living room, Walt listened for the sound of a car. The wait wasn't long. An engine sound that was just barely louder than an idling car pulled up outside. Walt waited a few seconds, and he heard a car door open and close.

Walt went outside and walked over to the car.

Ian was standing by the trunk of the car. In the dark the car seemed to be a dark blue. It was a four-door car with what looked to be a large trunk.

Ian looked at Walt as he walked up to him but didn't say anything. Ian was listening for sound in the trunk. When he was happy that it was still quiet, he opened the trunk.

There was a thin man with long hair and a beard tied up with duct tape in the back. His hands and feet were wrapped up with the tape, and another piece covered the man's mouth.

"I've chloroformed him. We have a little bit before he will wake up. I'd like to get him in the house before he wakes up. Grab his feet," Ian said.

Walt did as he was told and picked up the man's feet. The jeans the he had on were ripped near the bottom, and Walt guessed they had not been washed in some time. His shoes seemed new compared to the jeans. He was heavier than Walt had expected and Walt had some trouble holding him as they hefted him out of the trunk and walked with him inside.

Ian led the way, walking backward, holding the man underneath his shoulders.

Once they had him inside, they laid him down on the floor.

"Watch him. Holler if he wakes up," Ian said and went back outside.

Walt heard the trunk slam, and then Ian came back in. They picked up the man again and carried him downstairs.

Walt had ordered a small table and an office chair. He had purchased a chair with wheels, making sure it had arms and that the wheels could be locked.

They sat the man in the chair, and Ian explained the next part of the plan.

"This next part will be dangerous. When he wakes up, we will explain to him that we just want him to type one sentence," Ian said, pulling a gun from the small of his back.

The gun was a Glock. That was about all Walt knew. It was black and seemed to have a big hole in the front.

"To be clear: if he starts typing, and it doesn't work like you said, I will kill him, and then I will kill you. If it works like you said, I will go upstairs, and you can watch him type," Ian said.

Ian cut the tape off the man's hands and feet. He put something under the man's nose, and he woke up. At first he blinked a lot and squeezed his eyelids tight together. He then looked at Walt and Ian standing over him.

He was about to say something when Ian pointed the gun at his face.

"Quiet. We just want you to do one thing, and then we will let you go. Nod if you understand."

The man nodded.

"Good. All we need you to do is type one sentence on this typewriter. If you don't do it, I will shoot you in the face."

Walt watched the man look at Ian for a second and then look at the typewriter. The man studied the typewriter for a second, and then he put his hands on it and pressed the first key.

Clack.

The sound startled Walt. It was loud in the small basement, but that was all it took. Immediately after the first key was pressed, the man began to type in earnest.

Ian watched the man start typing.

Clack clack clack.

Ian lowered the gun after a few minutes, and the man's typing did not slow down at all.

"Jesus," Ian said under his breath. He looked over the man's shoulder and read what he was writing.

"How is this possible?" Ian asked. From the tone of his voice, Walt knew he didn't want an answer.

Ian replaced the gun in the waistband of his pants at his back.

Walt watched as Ian grabbed the man from behind and threw him to the floor.

The man instantly climbed back into the chair and continued typing.

Clack clack clack.

Ian looked at Walt, shook his head, and walked back upstairs.

Walt watched the man for another minute and then joined Ian upstairs.

"That's incredible. I thought you were shitting me," Ian said.

"Yeah, I know. But now that man will type until he's dead," Walt said.

Ian went out to the backyard and sat in one of the chairs by the pool.

Walt knew they had nothing to worry about now that the man was typing, so he poured himself a double cognac. He then turned on the TV. He really didn't care what was on, but he wanted to get his mind off the man typing himself to death down in his basement.

Ian came inside after a while and poured himself a drink and then went back outside.

"We need to put him in a diaper. He won't move to use the bathroom," Walt said.

Ian looked at him with an angry stare. Walt went to the cabinet and pulled out some adult diapers.

It was a little tricky to get the pants and underwear off the man and get the diaper on him, but working together they accomplished it. First they cut away the pants and underwear. Walt laughed at the look of the man kneeling with no pants and typing. Ian put the diaper on him, and they got the man seated back in the chair.

Now they both waited.

Walt went upstairs to bed after a few hours, and Ian came inside and slept on the couch.

In the morning, Walt woke up to the smell of bacon and eggs. Looking at his clock, he saw it was 10:34 a.m. Ian had only slept four hours.

Walt got up and went downstairs. The first thing he did was go down into the basement. As soon as he opened the basement door and heard the clacking sound of the typewriter, he knew the man was still at work. He went downstairs anyway and watched the man type for a little while before going back upstairs.

Ian had made enough breakfast for both of them, so he ate some bacon and eggs with toast.

"How long does it take?" Ian asked.

"Maybe a week or so. He will start to look like a skeleton in the next day or so. I think the typewriter takes something from them. But maybe it's just that they don't eat or drink. But now there is nothing we could do to stop it, even if we wanted to," Walt said.

"I peeked over his shoulder for a while this morning. The odd thing is that now I really want to read the rest of it," Ian said.

"Yeah, that's how it works," Walt said. "I really wanted my brother to finish what he wrote before they stopped him, but he couldn't leave the hospital. So that was when I got Stones. He picked up the story right where my brother stopped. It was amazing. Thinking about it, I knew he would start at the same point. I'm not sure how I knew that."

"The odd thing is, I don't feel bad for this man at all. I'm just happy he's typing," Ian said.

"I know how you feel. It's...comforting to have him typing," Walt said.

Ian nodded in agreement.

They finished eating and cleaned up the dishes in silence.

"One of us should always be here," Ian said.

Walt nodded. "I have no plans for the week and was planning on staying anyway," he said.

"I've got some other work to do, but I'll be here whenever I'm not working," Ian said.

Walt opened the door to the basement and propped it open. The door had an arm on it that always pulled it closed when it was open, so Walt put a chair in front of it.

Clack clack clack.

Walt turned on the TV, sat on the couch, and sipped a cognac.

Ian left at some point, but Walt didn't notice.

In the afternoon Walt went swimming. He swam for around thirty minutes and then sat on the side of the pool.

They only needed to change the diapers on the first two days. By the third day, the man no longer went to the bathroom.

Walt didn't leave the house. He either swam or watched TV. A few times he stood behind the man as he typed and read what he was writing. At one point the man ran out of paper, and Walt watched as he stood and went to the shelf with the reams of paper.

The man picked up a ream, opened it, dropped the torn paper cover on the floor, and took the open ream back to the table. He then rolled a sheet of paper into the typewriter and continued typing.

Walt was surprised that the man moved. He was very thin, and the clothes he had on had become baggy. His arms were mostly bone. His eyes had sunk in, and the skin surrounding his eyes had become dark. His hair had thinned, and it seemed to Walt as if he had aged ten years in a few days. A smell of decay was also now noticeable in the basement.

Walt went upstairs and brought down a fan to get some airflow into the basement. He would have Ian bring some scented candles back the next time he went out.

Clack clack clack.

There was still no change in the speed of the typing. This meant to Walt that they were not near the end yet.

The next day, Ian came back to the house in the afternoon and brought some candles. He took them downstairs and lit them. It helped with the smell of the decay but did not remove it completely.

It had been six days since the man had started typing when finally the speed of the typing started to slow down.

Ian and Walt were sitting on the couch watching a basketball game when they noticed it. Going downstairs, they realized the smell had gotten much worse.

It reminded Walt of a dead dog he had walked by while going home from school as a kid.

On the first day he noticed the animal, it had been hit by a car and had either managed to crawl to the side of the road or had been thrown there by the blow from the car. Its back was bent in an *L* shape, and its two rear legs had been broken. The skin on the back legs had been torn off, leaving the broken bones exposed.

Walt stared at the dog for a few minutes every day on his way home from school. On the second day, ants covered the dog. By the third day, the ants were gone, and the smell of the decay hit. Walt had to move upwind when he was looking at the dog to keep from smelling it.

The smell of the man who was typing brought back the memory of the dog. At least the dog had been dead. This man was still alive and typing.

"I'll start getting things ready," Ian said. He brought in a tarp. "I think we should just toss the body whole. If we cut him up, it will be obvious if anyone ever finds him. We want it to look as natural as possible."

On day seven, the typing had slowed to only a few words a minute, and on the morning of day eight, the man fell to the floor, dead.

Ian didn't waste any time. He laid the tarp out on the floor next to the body. Walt grabbed the dead man's feet, and Ian grabbed his shoulders, and they moved him onto the tarp. Walt removed the diaper, and they put a pair of underwear and some pants on the body. Walt even put a belt on the man and tight-ened it.

Ian then rolled the man up in the tarp, and they carried him out to Ian's car and placed him in the trunk. Ian had lined his trunk with plastic. If anyone made him open the trunk, even without a body in it, there would have been questions.

Ian slammed down the lid of the trunk, turned to Walt, and said, "I've scouted out a couple of places I can drop the body where no one will find it for a few months. The only risky part will be dropping off the body. I'll come back by afterward."

"OK," Walt said.

Ian got into his car, started it, and drove off. Walt turned and went inside without waiting for the car to be gone.

7

How many times over the years had Ian and Walt done that same thing? Walt wondered. It would be easy enough to figure out: one for each book. But no good would come from that kind of thinking. Each of his books represented death, and he had made the decision long ago to live with it.

The first time they had done it, it was amazing how lucky they had been. Now they had it down to a system.

It turned out that one missing homeless person a year caused very few ripples. By their own nature, homeless people were not easy to track, and Ian was very careful in whom he selected.

A few of them over the years had fought, but a gun to the head had persuaded them to stop fighting and start typing. Even homeless people didn't want to die, it seemed, and the feeling of the cold barrel of a gun touching the head persuaded even the most ardent fighter.

Walt had grown to think that if he were ever put in that position, it might be better to take the bullet to the head than to have the slow death dealt out by the typewriter.

Ian had not changed much over the years. Walt and Ian had developed a very good working relationship but purposely did not see each other at any other time.

Aside from when they were working, Walt knew nothing about Ian other than what he had found out in the beginning, and after more than twenty years, he was sure a lot had changed. But he did not care. Walt had given Ian a lot of money for the work, which was only done once a year, for the most part.

Sitting by the pool, Walt's thoughts went to Marie. Since that night they had met in New York, he had never met anyone like her. She was everything he wanted. Now that he was in his early forties, he was thinking about marriage. He had started to think that it would not be so bad to have a kid.

Of course, there were some problems. First, he would need to tell Marie about the typewriter. He was not sure how she would take it. Telling someone you make your living by causing people to die would not be an easy thing to do. Marie had never reacted the way he figured she would about anything he had ever told her. He was constantly surprised by her.

When he had found out years ago that she was in Southern California and was a personal trainer, he had gone out of his way to be her client. She had remembered him right away and had agreed that their night together had been wonderful. But she was resistant at first. She was focused on getting her business going and did not want the distraction of a man.

He had been persistent, and they spent half of each session talking with each other. Eventually, she had asked him out. He had not been expecting it, but she was having him plank one afternoon when she said, "So, I was wondering if you would like to get dinner sometime?"

Walt was focused on keeping his midsection straight and was in a lot of pain holding it up. He nodded quickly and then collapsed to the floor.

Marie smiled and told him to stop resting and get back up.

At dinner he realized he already knew all about her. He had talked to her so much during the training sessions that they had grown very close.

Walt had already told her about his brother—how he had been in the medically induced coma for ten years when he died. He had gotten a bedsore that turned into an infection and killed him. It was probably for the best, he explained to her. There was nothing really left of him. He had gone crazy and was no longer the brother Walt had grown up with.

Marie had told him about her abusive father and how happy she had been when he died of a heart attack when she was eleven He had collapsed to the floor in front of her. Marie admitted to him that she watched him there on the floor for ten minutes before calling for help.

Walt had become very familiar with death and did not judge her for that.

At the end of the date, they got a room at the nearest hotel and made up for the long break between their first time in New York and this time. At the end of the night, they were both exhausted, but he knew then that he loved her.

It took her a lot longer to admit her love for him. She was not an overly emotional person, and even though they kept seeing each other, she would always choose business over him.

After six months she finally admitted her love for him. It was during dinner. She took a sip of wine and set the glass down and looked at him.

"You know I love you," she said, looking into what Walt felt was his soul. She understood him so well.

"Not until this moment. I hoped you did. I have loved you since we met," Walt said. He reached his hand across the table and held her hand. Her hand was warm and soft in his, and he didn't want to let go of it.

The memory of that night and the feel of her hand in his made Walt smile.

They'd of course had their ups and downs over the years. Both of them were strong-willed and had very clear ideas of how they wanted the other person to be in the relationship.

Luckily for Walt, each time they had a major fight, they had been able to work it out.

His cell phone buzzed in his hand. It was a text from Marie, asking how it was going.

He texted back "good" and sent her a selfie of him smiling. He always sent one of himself, hoping to get one back from her.

She sent one back a few minutes later. In her selfie, she teased him by showing her bare shoulders, hinting at the fact that she was naked. A few seconds later, a text came in.

"Just getting in the shower…wish you were here :)"

"Wish I was there too," he texted back.

Walt set the phone back down beside him. Yeah, he thought, he would need to tell her about the typewriter soon. He wasn't sure how she would take it, but if he wanted to keep going in this relationship, he didn't really have much of a choice.

Walt had gotten the burner phone earlier and held it in his hands. He typed in one word, "now," and hit Send.

A few minutes later, the text was returned. "Tomorrow night. Same as always."

Walt stared at the message for a while and then put the phone away. He would not be able to sleep tonight and would not sleep well until he watched Ian drive away with a dead man in his trunk.

It occurred to Walt that over the years they had never picked out a woman. Walt knew there were homeless women. Ian must have made a conscious effort to never use a woman. Walt was glad for that. He did not know if he could watch Ian put a gun to a woman's head. It was sexist, Walt knew, but it was something he couldn't change.

He poured himself a drink, went into the front yard, and sat on his porch. The trees were trimmed and dark green. Whatever the gardeners were costing him was worth it. His accountant paid most of the bills, including the yearly sum to Ian. Whenever Walt had been asked about it, he said that Ian helped him with security and was a consultant on a lot of his novels. Usually that satisfied whoever was asking the question.

A bird flew down and sat on the railing of the porch next to Walt. Motionless, Walt watched the bird. Its head made quick, jerking movements as it looked around. Ignoring Walt, it hopped along the railing, looking for something that Walt would never know. There was something soothing about watching the bird. Walt unconsciously sipped his drink, but his movement scared the bird, and it flew off.

The wind picked up, and Walt got a little chill, so he stood up and went inside.

First thing in the morning, Walt called Marie.

"Hey, you. I didn't expect you to call," she said.

"I know. But I'm about to start writing for the day, and I wanted to hear your voice before I started."

"Aw, how sweet. You OK?" she asked. Normally, he never called her when he was writing.

"Yeah. I'm just feeling a little down. Thought talking to you might cheer me up."

"Is it working?" Marie asked.

The sound of her voice was working. He was feeling better at the sound.

"Yes, it is."

"Good. What's the book about?" she asked, knowing with certainty that he would not answer, but she asked anyway. At times she was annoyed that he wouldn't talk, and she would ask questions like this. It was passive-aggressive, she knew, but she didn't care. If he loved her as much as he claimed, he could put up with the questions.

"You know I don't talk about that. But I think you'll like it," Walt said.

"I like everything you write, so that's not a tough guess," Marie said. "I need to get going. I have a client meeting in…" She paused for a second—Walt guessed to check the time—and then said, "Oh shit, ten minutes. Love you, bye," she said, and with that he heard the sound of the phone disconnecting.

For the rest of the day, Walt watched TV. There was nothing on that was interesting, but he watched to kill time until that night.

Daytime eventually gave way to night, and finally Walt got the text message letting him know Ian would be there in an hour.

When the headlights pulled up the driveway, Walt was already standing outside. He wanted this part to be done quickly. This was the part he dreaded the most. It only took fifteen minutes at the most, but he hated it.

Up until this person started typing, Walt could tell Ian to stop, and they could turn back. Once the person started typing, that was it, and Walt would feel better.

Ian got out of the car and nodded at Walt. They said very few words to each other.

Ian popped the trunk, and the smell hit Walt. This person was not clean, and Walt noticed his clothes and skin were caked in dirt.

Walt looked at Ian. "You couldn't find someone cleaner?"

"This was the best of a bad lot that fit our requirements," Ian said.

"Right," Walt said and grabbed the man's feet.

Ian picked up the man by the shoulders, and they carried him inside and downstairs. Walt had unlocked and opened the door to the basement before going outside.

Ian untied the man's hands, and they sat him in the chair. Walt held him while Ian woke him up.

When he woke up, he started to yell. "Who the fuck are you? Where am I? Fucking let me go!" the man said.

Ian pulled out his Glock and pointed it at the man.

"We want you to type a sentence on this typewriter, and then we will let you go," Ian said.

"Fuck you. I ain't fucking afraid of you. Fucking shoot me."

Ian aimed and fired a single shot at the man's ear. The bullet tore off the bottom part of his ear. Blood splattered over his shoulder, and pieces of his ear landed on the floor behind him.

"*Argh*! You shot my fucking ear!" the man screamed, grabbing his ear with his hand. Blood dripped from between his fingers.

"Start typing, or I shoot the other ear," Ian said, with no anger in his voice. He was calm as he explained to the man what he would do.

The man stared at Ian and then started typing. All the fight left his body, and he began to start writing the book. The blood from his hands smeared on the keys of the typewriter and then disappeared.

Ian and Walt watched him for a second to make sure he wasn't going to fight anymore. Walt then went upstairs to get a bandage.

Walt cleaned the man's ear and bandaged it. They needed him to type as long as possible, and blood loss would cause him to type less, so they cleaned up the ear to prevent any additional bleeding.

Walt put on gloves and picked up the small pieces of the man's ear and scrubbed the blood off the floor. He would need to patch the bullet hole later.

Ian stood watching the man typing and Walt cleaning up the mess. Ian had made it clear long ago that he would not do any cleaning unless absolutely necessary.

After Walt was done cleaning up the mess, he stood next to Ian. "Jesus. This guy was a fighter," Walt said.

Ian nodded.

They both went upstairs, leaving the man to type.

Ian sat on the couch and turned on the TV, and Walt went outside to the pool. Time to play the waiting game.

Thoughts of Marie and what she would think of him when she found out how he really wrote his books crossed Walt's mind. She would not understand, he thought.

Then an idea crossed his mind. He would need to buy a second place and tell her that was where he would write. It made sense. There was no way Marie would understand him killing people. They had just shot a man to make him do what they wanted. Marie was kind and could not do that.

But if Walt bought a second place—a cabin in the woods somewhere—he and Ian could do what they needed there, and Marie would never have to know.

He had established with her the rules already, and nothing would change. If he married her, she would understand that he needed a private place to write.

Feeling that he had just solved a major problem, he relaxed. The wind had picked up, and the cool breeze felt good.

Walt decided he would finish getting this next book published and then ask Marie to marry him. At that point he would find another place and move the typewriter. He did not want Marie to ever be alone with it. He knew he couldn't explain it, and he did not want her to ever press one of its keys.

Walt went inside and sat next to Ian and listened to the faint clacking sounds coming up from the basement. It was strange to him how soothing he now found that sound.

"Hey, Mitch, it's Walt."

"I know. I saw your name on the phone," Mitch said.

"Hey, I just wanted to let you know the next book is almost finished and will be ready for editing in the next few weeks."

"That's great. So we may be able to publish by the end of the year. Do you have a title for it yet?"

"Not yet. I'll call you next week with a title."

"OK. Thanks for the heads up. I'll talk to you later."

"OK. Talk to you later," Walt said and hung up.

Walt walked inside and listened. The clacking sound had started slowing last night, and he guessed the man didn't have much longer to live.

Ian and Walt always got tense near the end. Worry about someone coming by kept them both on their toes. If anyone came by, there was always the chance that they would smell the decay.

Walt had a vent and fans in the basement, but even that didn't always get rid of the scent. Someone with a good nose might smell it. Marie had never come by, and Walt knew if she ever did, she would smell it. Her nose was quite good.

"I think I'm going to ask Marie to marry me," Walt said to Ian.

"Congratulations. What are you going to tell her about this?" Ian said, motioning toward the basement.

"I'm not. I think I'll get a cabin in the woods somewhere where we can do this," Walt said.

"That's not a bad idea. We would be a little more secluded, and it would be less likely anyone would stop by for a visit. Not sure why we didn't think of doing that sooner," Ian said.

"True. It does make a lot of sense."

It was silent. The man had stopped typing, which meant only one thing.

"He's dead," Ian said with no emotion.

"Let's get him out of here."

Following the same pattern they had followed since the beginning, they wrapped the man in the tarp and loaded him into the trunk.

Ian always kept alert for one of the bodies they had dumped to be found. Only a few had been found over the years, and each time the death was ruled as natural causes.

Ian was nervous the first time one of the bodies was found. He followed the case closely up until the point that it was ruled a death by natural causes. Neither Walt nor Ian was sure what the cause of death was going to be, but once it was ruled a natural cause, they both rested much easier.

After that they kept the system the same. There was no one looking for them.

Ian was a little concerned about the ear on this guy. If they found the body before it decayed, they would notice the gunshot wound. After a few weeks, the ear would decay enough that it wouldn't matter, but he worried about the two-week window.

For that reason he was a little more cautious about where he dumped the body. He needed it not to be found for at least six months—or preferably, for it not to be found at all.

Ian had a list of dump places. When he wasn't with Walt, he scouted out places to dump bodies. California was a big state with a lot of different geographic features, which worked well for Ian. He had buried several bodies in the Southern California desert.

That was a safe way to dispose of the bodies, but digging a hole took time and was a very suspicious activity. If someone happened to see him digging the hole, the outcome would not be good.

Most of the time, he would drive north and dispose of them in the Sierras. This was his preferred choice, since there were homeless people living in the Sierras, and it was not uncommon for them to get lost and die.

Strong winters were also good and bad. Snow hid the bodies, but the cold stopped the decay. For bodies that had no marks on them, snow didn't matter, but for this man it mattered.

Ian made the choice to bury the body. This was going to be the dangerous part. He stopped at a small hardware store in a small town and purchased a shovel. He paid in cash.

When he checked out, the man had made small talk. Ian hated small talk and usually did not engage in it. But he needed to not be remembered for doing anything odd. Being an asshole caused people to remember you.

For that reason Ian was nice and polite and made small talk. He hated every second of it.

Ian did not buy lime. In the past he had purchased it when he needed to dispose of a body, but he had quickly learned that although it did help to hide the odor, it slowed down the decomposition of the body. It was not likely that someone would find the body buried in the middle of the desert, so smell was not really a concern. But he wanted the body to decompose as fast as possible.

Ian drove for an hour on the small road, farther into the California desert. When he felt he was far enough away from the main roads, he turned off and drove at fifteen miles per hour for about twenty minutes. The desert was rough, and the driving was not easy.

Ian stopped the car and got out. It was dark out, and he turned off the car lights. He stood silent in the dark night and listened, worrying that someone might have seen his lights. He waited another twenty minutes to make sure no one had seen his lights and then decided to check it out. When nobody came, he got a pair of gloves from the glovebox and put them on. Then he grabbed the shovel and started digging.

After about fifteen minutes of digging, he heard the sound of a car in the distance, and dropped to the ground, letting the shovel fall to the ground next to him.

He could see car headlights in the distance coming toward him. He reached around to his back and pulled out his gun. He pulled the slide back and checked to make sure there was a round chambered and ready.

Then he waited.

The car drove slowly. It had the same problem Ian did in that it was night, and even though the desert wasn't bad terrain, it was still not as nice as a road.

Watching the lights get bigger, Ian figured he would have to kill whoever was in the car. There was no way he could explain what he was doing. After he had killed whoever was in the car, he would put them in the backseat and then finish burying the body. He would then need to figure out what to do.

Fuck, he thought. Stay calm, he told himself. He took a deep breath.

When the car was almost close enough to see him, it veered off to the right and started driving away.

Ian watched the car go. After a little while, the car disappeared from his sight.

"Jesus," Ian said out loud.

Letting his heart rate return to normal, he got back up, picked up his shovel and continued digging.

It took him an hour to get the hole deep enough. He crawled out of the hole, went to the back of the trunk, and opened it. The smell of decay hit him immediately, like a shot to his nose. No matter how many times he smelled that smell, he never got used to it.

Ian picked up the body from the trunk and hefted it over his shoulder.

He stood at one end of the hole and slid the body in headfirst. The body went about halfway across the hole, and Ian had to go to the other side and get inside the hole. He then pulled the body the rest of the way in.

He climbed back out, stood, and looked around. There were no further lights, and the night was quiet.

Ian went back to the trunk and grabbed the plastic he had lined the trunk with, along with the tarp. He put those inside the hole as well. Then he picked up the shovel and began the long process of filling the hole back in.

On the drive back, he wondered about the other car he had seen. It was strange that anyone would be that far out in the desert without a reason. He had not gotten a good look at the car, so he had almost no way to figure out who it was. It was still strange, so he would be taking a different way back toward LA.

Paying close attention to his rearview mirror, he took a long way back to LA. He saw no one, and the trip home was uneventful.

He decided he would stay at a motel for the night, not wanting to go straight back to his place. He parked in the lot of a Holiday Inn and went inside.

First he went to the front desk and got a room. Checking in was uneventful. After checking in, he went back out to his car and grabbed a duffel bag with a change of clothes and a toothbrush that he kept in the backseat.

After he went into his room, he threw the duffel bag on his bed and moved a chair close to the window. He had asked for and gotten a room on the first floor, facing the parking lot.

He dragged the chair to a location where he could see his car, and then he sat and waited. Nobody came by to check out his car, and he didn't see anyone he recognized in the parking lot. At around two in the morning, he let himself fall asleep. He slept in the chair.

Sunlight hit his face at around seven, waking him up.

He stood, grabbed the duffel bag, went into the bathroom, showered, and got dressed. Then he placed his dirty clothes back in the duffel bag, zipped it up, and went outside. He wore jeans and a plain white T-shirt.

The parking lot was busy as people checked out and got on the road. Ian did the same.

On the drive home, Ian thought about the cabin Walt had talked about purchasing. He had some requirements he'd want to make sure Walt met. It had to be somewhere secluded. Ian still wanted there to be a basement. Sound was best controlled from a basement. Gunshots from inside homes tended to attract attention. A basement provided the best dampening of gunshots.

Ian also wanted a single long driveway—something that would allow him to see any car approaching. If someone walked up to the house, there was nothing he could do, but since most people would drive up, the longer and more open the driveway was, the better.

Opening the new burner phone, he texted his requirements to Walt.

Walt always slept best the first night after Ian took the body away. This was the time when he was farthest from the task. The closer he got to doing this, the more he would drink and the less he would sleep and eat.

Walt got up and went downstairs. This was the first time he would read the story the man had written. It usually took him a few days to get through the story. Walt was not a great reader, and aside from these books, he never read anything.

He looked through the pile of papers the man had left on the table, found the point where the man had written "The End," and separated out the pages.

Before he had died, the man had gotten about twenty-five pages into a new story. Walt didn't even bother to read those. He had learned that if he started reading, he would want to know how the story ended, and it would be harder for him to wait until the next time. As long as he read only the story he wanted to publish, he would be fine.

He placed the start of the next book in the cabinet and took the finished story upstairs. He set the story on the kitchen table and went downstairs to make sure everything was neat and clean.

The bullet hole could not be seen, and there was no blood visible anywhere. He wiped down the table, centered the typewriter on the table, and shut off the light.

Back upstairs, he put the lock on the basement door and then sat at the table and began the task of reading the book. It was a good book, but he had known it would be. The stories were always great. He got about a quarter of the way done and stood.

He went outside to the pool and thought about Marie. Now that he was done with the first part of the book, he would call her and let her know he had finished. At that point she would come over. She always asked to read the book, and he always said no. He had to read it a few times to get the meaning. Marie was very smart and would absorb the book's meaning, and if she read it, she would ask him key plot points that he would not always know.

This had happened a lot when they first started dating. He'd had to get good at dodging her questions. At one point he had considered maybe letting her read it after he had memorized the story, but he did not want her to figure out he wasn't the one writing the stories, so he'd said no.

Still, she would always get a copy after it was published and read it. That never failed. Everything he ever published, she read.

Once, during an argument, she had wondered how someone so dumb wrote such beautiful books. He had been taken by surprise. Did she really think he was dumb? he had wondered. After the argument ended, she had apologized, and it had not come up again.

Not that he cared. He knew he wasn't that smart and that he was lucky to have her. If it weren't for the fact that he wrote the novels, she would probably have left him long ago, but she loved what he wrote so much that she had fallen in love with him.

Walt loved her without question. He knew he would marry her, and he began to think about how he would propose to her.

A few years ago, he'd had one of the nightmares in which he had been falling off the cliff, and he had woken up covered in sweat. She had been there with him, and he had described the dream to her. He told her that in his dreams he often stood at the edge of a cliff with wind blowing him toward the edge. In the dream everything felt so real, and he could feel the wind, and most of the time he stood at the edge of a cliff by an ocean, and he could feel the water from the waves hitting. The dreams always ended with him falling off the cliff to his death.

When he was done, she had told him that he should face his fear. At the time, he was not sure what that would mean. Now he had an idea. It was a simple idea, but he thought she would love it. He could propose and face his fear at the same time.

Several things had to happen before he would be ready. He had to get the latest book published. Each book had a hard birth, he knew.

Working with Mitch, he would decide on the cover, and they would arrange the release date and the book tour. Tours were the hardest part. He needed to have the story memorized and have some creative things to say about it. That was always the hard part for him.

After the tour he would need to get Marie a ring. Picking a ring would be a challenge. He knew she had strong opinions on diamonds—especially blood diamonds. Finding a diamond she would like that had been obtained humanely would be very important. Most women dragged men into jewelry stores at some point and looked at rings with them, giving them some idea of what ring to buy. She had never done that.

Marie hated the mall and shopping and felt it was a waste of time. She got most of her clothes online. A lot of them came from a monthly clothing service that sent her a few new outfits every month. She would pick the ones she liked and send the rest back.

Most of the time, he loved that she hated the mall because he felt the same way. Now it meant they had never been to a jewelry store together. All he really knew about her taste in diamonds was that she hated blood diamonds—which was not useful at all.

Finally, he would need to find a perfect location to propose, an area that reminded him of his dream but looked beautiful—something she would remember.

Working with Mitch and a designer, it took him about two weeks to come up with a good cover for the book. It was the silhouette of a man and woman holding hands. Their outline on the cover was dark, and the moon could be seen above them. Walt was very happy with the cover. He thought it reflected the story nicely, and the splash of light in the moon was a nice contrast to the dark couple in the silhouette.

After that the book tour went as expected. One of the things Walt noticed was that since he had decided to propose to Marie, he had no desire to go out and find other women. Not thinking about other women made him feel he was making the right choice in asking her to marry him.

While on the road, he also started to write his proposal. As he began to come up with what he would say, he realized he had never really written anything. Going through each draft, he felt like a child attempting to write.

"Fuck, I'm bad at this!" he yelled to himself in his hotel room, throwing his pencil and notebook against the wall. He got his backpack and pulled out his laptop. He sat the laptop on the desk and turned it on. Watching it come on, he laughed at himself. The world's best-selling writer—and he sucked at writing.

Funny, he thought, I'm not even sure if that's ironic.

Once the laptop was on, he put in his password and opened up a web browser. It took him a few minutes to figure out how to connect to the hotel's wireless Internet connection. He had to find the paper with the Wi-Fi password and then connect.

He went to Google and searched for proposal-writing tips. A lot of ideas came up. Reading through them, he began to put something together. He had to get up and go get the pencils and notebook, and then he started writing.

Wanting something sweet yet meaningful, he took his time. He went over his life without her and then what she meant to him. Basing it on several different proposals he'd read and keeping it personal, finally he came up with something he thought was good.

He read over it a few times and corrected some mistakes. Once he was happy with it, he copied it into his laptop and made sure the file was saved. He did not want to lose all this work. Glancing at the clock, he realized several hours had passed. He smiled and thought about how hard writing was.

Before going to bed, he browsed YouTube and watched some videos. That led him to stay up a few more hours, and he was dead tired when he finally went to bed. As he lay in bed, he realized he had not had a drink all evening—and then he fell asleep.

Now that he had the proposal written, he needed to start looking for a ring. After he went to his morning interview, he went to the mall. The mall was crowded and big. There were small stands in the center, and as he walked by, the salespeople would try to get his attention to come buy various things. At first he said a lot of no-thank-yous, but by the end, he just ignored them, looking forward as he walked by.

Now he remembered why he avoided malls.

There were four jewelry stores, and at each one, he explained what he wanted.

"I'm looking for something that is humane. No blood diamonds—and I have to be able to prove it's humane," Walt said to the first clerk.

"Yes, of course. The best way to do that would be to go with a man-made diamond. They are made in a lab but are humane. No one is sent down into a mine to get them, and they don't come from countries where people are abused," the clerk said.

Walt nodded. "I'm not sure she will like a man-made diamond. Can I see a few of them?"

Walt then got his first speech on diamond buying. He learned about the various cuts and about diamond clarity. It was kind of fun. He liked looking at the diamond using the jeweler's eyepiece. The eyepiece magnified the diamond, and he could see the small imperfections in it. Walt thought the man-made diamonds looked just like the standard diamonds, and he could not tell the difference.

"You can also get fancy colors, if you think she would like that. One of the most popular is yellow. It looks beautiful," the clerk said.

"It's important to her that it's not a blood diamond. I think the yellow color assures her of that. I don't think they sell yellow-colored blood diamonds," Walt said.

"True. Most diamonds dug from mines are clear-colored," the clerk said.

Man-made diamonds started to make sense to Walt. This was something he could do for her that he thought she would like, with no one getting hurt for what was essentially a clear stone.

Pricing was still the same, it seemed. He wanted to get her a two-carat diamond, which was still very expensive. He decided he would go with the princess cut. He liked the heart-shaped diamond but knew Marie would find it gaudy. She had no reason to wear a heart on her finger.

In the end Walt went with a light-colored, yellow, two-carat, princess-cut diamond. He chose a basic white-gold band. Marie could change the ring later if she wanted.

Walt thanked the man for his help and left. On his way out, the same people in the center stands tried to stop him to buy their items. No wonder everyone was buying their gifts online, although now even online you got bombarded with ads.

Walt laughed to himself. Hey, if he really was a writer, noticing those kinds of things would have been important, he thought. Too bad he wasn't really a writer.

At home Walt found he was spending a lot of his time thinking about Marie and proposing to her. He only had a few drinks and managed to sleep in bed and not fall asleep on the couch. Most importantly, he had no bad dreams. He slept soundly through the night.

8

Marie had let her curiosity get the better of her. She had suspected for a while that something odd was going on with Walt. Not wanting her around while he was writing was fine. She had dated a lot of artists, and they often got weird when creating something. She imagined it was like giving birth. The idea was like a baby growing inside you, and getting that baby out into the world was a painful process. Most of the time it was worth it, so she understood.

With Walt, though, there had to be something else going on. On the surface, everything seemed normal. But once you started any kind of digging, things got a little murky.

First, he didn't like to talk about what he wrote. Getting one book out a year made him a fairly prolific writer, but he seemed to hate what he wrote.

She loved his novels and read them with great interest. But she had the opportunity to discuss them with the author, and he never once seemed interested in talking about them.

Being a little conceited, she thought she had some good insights into the novels and wanted to discuss them with him, but he never reciprocated. He had no desire to discuss his own books.

Second, he did not read. She had never once seen him pick up a book and start reading. For people who love books, the sweetest reward is to find a book you can't put down. You want to devour it as you would a fine meal, with the story sucking you into a world you never want to leave.

Although he wrote many books that had made that happen for her, he never read a single book. Once, early in their relationship, she had given him a book as a gift. He had not read it, and it sat on a bookshelf he had in his library.

While he was sleeping one night, she had gone into the library to look at his extensive collection of books. Most of them were gifts, and she noticed two things. All of the books were in pristine condition, with no creases in the binding indicating the book had been opened and read. They were also dusty. Moving the tip of her finger along the top of the book she had given him, she pulled away a line of dust.

Not one book he had been given had been read.

Third was that he kept the typewriter he used behind a locked door. Nothing was as odd as that. She had seen the typewriter once, but he had watched her closely and would not let her touch it. It was an old-looking typewriter, which made it even more odd. Who the fuck writes on an old piece of shit when there are so many options available? Pushing the keys of the old-style typewriter could not have been easy.

Of course, when she had asked him about it, he was evasive.

"I just like the feel of the old typewriter," Walt had said to her.

What the fuck did that mean—the feel of it? Bullshit.

She needed to know what he was doing. For sure he wasn't an author. He couldn't be. No man could be that talented yet not like to talk about it.

So this time she decided she would try to find out what he was doing during the times he told her he didn't want to see her. It would be difficult. His house was secluded. You could not see it from the road, and there were a lot of trees surrounding it.

An idea came to her one morning while she was working out. She was thinking about her first client and the workout she wanted to put him through when the thought came into focus.

She would treat it as though she were a hunter. Hunters had to sit for hours and wait for deer to show up. They would bring snacks and sit up in a tree in a stand and watch for deer. In this case, the deer would be Walt.

Once she had the idea, she started to work at it. Like everything else in her life, all it took was patience and effort. She thought about her dad for a second and pushed him out of her mind. At the thought of her dad, she clenched her fists until her knuckles turned white.

Taking a deep breath and opening her hands, she focused on her thought. I will figure out what you are doing, Walt, she told herself. Now she was determined.

Sipping a glass of wine that night, she was using her iPad to read up on following people. Surprisingly to her, there was a lot of information online. Most of the time, people were looking to catch a cheating spouse. There were a lot of available tools for following people and spying on them. You could install apps on their phone. These apps would transmit the location of the person without his or her knowing it was installed.

Installing the app on the phone was the tricky part. Walt, like most people, usually had his phone on him or close by. Marie never used his phone since she had her own, so asking for it would be out of the ordinary, and it might make him suspicious. She knew his PIN from the few times he had had her look up something on his phone.

After she had worked out the basic idea of what she was going to do, she put her iPad away and turned off the lights. It was close to eleven, and she had a client at eight in the morning. Her diet and sleep were something she monitored closely. She always made sure to get eight hours of sleep. She felt her best that way. Following the advice of sleep therapists, she did not have a TV in her room, and she had blackout curtains on her windows.

Once she put the iPad down for the night, she turned off the lights and lay in bed. Long ago she had begun using meditation to get to sleep. Breathing in, she focused on her breathing. For a second she thought about her father. She regrouped and focused back on her breathing. Deep breath in, long and slow, and the same long, slow exhale.

Her mind clear, she fell asleep on the sixth breath.

Her client was a man in his late forties. He had the small belly a lot of thin middle-aged men got. She was having him do a plank to help tighten up his midsection. He had started shaking after about thirty seconds, but she wanted him to do thirty more. She yelled at him that he could do it and to just hold on.

While she worked with him, her mind worked on the problem of how to get the app on Walt's phone. She had found that when she did something else, she could often come up with the answer to a problem.

She felt relieved when the solution came to her, and then she yelled at her client, "Thirty more seconds."

He moaned and held on, falling to the floor like a rock when Marie finally called time.

One night before Walt had started writing his latest book, Marie and Walt had been having dinner. They were enjoying some appetizers at their favorite restaurant when Marie looked at her phone. She was starting to type something on the phone when it shut down.

"Fuck," she said.

Walt looked at her and asked, "What happened?"

"My stupid battery just died in the middle of an e-mail. Can I borrow your phone? I need to get this e-mail out."

"Sure," Walt said, handing her his phone.

Marie had practiced this on her phone multiple times. In a mirror she had figured out the angle she could hold the phone at so that a person sitting across from her would not be able to see the screen.

Timing the installation of the app, she had it down to less than a minute. Two things worked for her. First, she knew Walt had rooted his phone. That meant he could install apps from anywhere without an issue. It was unsafe, she knew, but in this case it worked for her. Second, Walt had no reason to care what Marie was doing.

Most of the time, cheating was the main thing couples got suspicious about with each other. As with most murders, the two things that caused most fights between couples were sex and money. Since they had an open relationship, there was nothing on his phone to find that would make her mad.

Opening up the web browser, she went to the website that would install the app. Once she opened the site, she downloaded the app and answered yes to all the questions. Earlier she had created an account, and now she put in her e-mail address and password, which linked this to her account.

After the app installed, it hid itself. She knew it would now run in the background, feeding her all kinds of information. Location, apps used, and texts were all fed into the app. One of the reasons the app existed was so parents could track their kids and see what they were doing.

Walt was looking at her as she went through the motions of installing the app. Forcing herself to keep calm, she was glad she had practiced this. It was nerve-racking to have Walt stare at her as she installed the app.

Once the app was installed and hidden, she cleared the history of the web browser and handed the phone back to Walt.

"Thank you," she said.

He took the phone and then held her hand. His hand was warm and soft. She leaned across the table and kissed him. Sitting back down, she took her foot under the table and put it between his legs and smiled.

Walt began to get hard under the table as she rubbed her foot lightly on his crotch. The waiter approached the table. Marie took her foot down, and Walt's erection disappeared.

"Have you guys decided what you want to order?" the waiter asked, and Walt and Marie both picked up their menus.

Marie spent the night at Walt's, and in the morning, Walt told her that it was time for him to start writing. She hugged him and told him OK. She called for an Uber, and when it arrived she had it drop her off at a Starbucks a few miles away.

She pulled out her laptop from her backpack and opened up the web page that allowed her to see Walt's phone. There were no texts sent, he did not go anywhere, and there was only one phone call made, to Mitch.

She sipped her coffee and browsed the web. After an hour, she checked the website again. There was still nothing out of the ordinary.

It was only the first day. She would need to be patient. She finished her coffee, put her laptop away, and went home.

In the morning, she checked the web page again. Nothing. Absolutely nothing had happened. Walt was still at home, and nothing odd had happened—no unknown phone numbers, no texts, nothing.

Was she wrong, and Walt really was the writer he had everyone believing he was? That couldn't be. Walt was not a writer. She believed that deep inside.

Waiting one more day, she did not sleep well. She woke up several times during the night, thinking about what she was missing. In the morning she woke up and checked the web page for Walt's phone. Still at home, still no phone calls or texts.

Deciding she would need to go to his house to see if anything was going on, she called for an Uber. She made herself a cup of coffee and put it in a travel mug. She dressed in dark workout clothes and black running shoes, and she tied her hair back.

To anyone seeing her, it would look as if she were just out for a run. Men would usually look twice just because of how she looked, but no one would be suspicious seeing her walk around Walt's neighborhood.

Calling the clients she was supposed to meet with that day, she told them she was not feeling well and would not be able to work out with them today.

She had the Uber driver drop her off what she guessed was about a mile from Walt's house. Her adrenaline was high, and she felt good. She liked sneaking around, and it surprised her that she was having fun.

When she got to Walt's place, she looked around, and then, when there were no cars or people, she climbed over the wall. She was up and over in a second and landed on the other side with a soft thud.

She knelt down and listened for a few minutes. When she was convinced there was no one around, she crouch-walked over to where she could see the front of the house.

Sitting in the driveway close to the front door was a car she did not recognize. It was a plain car and reminded her of something an old person or teenager might drive.

Moving as quietly as possible, she went around to the back of the house. Walt was sitting by the pool where he often sat. He did not have a drink. If Walt was sitting by the pool, the majority of the time he would have a cognac with him. Watching him sit there, she wondered what was going on.

After thirty minutes, Walt stood and went inside.

Now she needed to decide whether she should go back up to the front of the house or wait here by the back of the house and the pool. Knowing Walt was home, she knew he would eventually come back out to the pool, but she wanted to know whose car that was out front.

Moving slowly, trying not to make any noise, she went back to the front of the house to watch the car. She found a spot where she was concealed by a large bush, and she sat down and waited. She was mad at herself for not bringing something to eat. She had never done this before and was not prepared for a long wait. She told herself she could go one day without eating. So she waited.

A bird flew down and landed a few feet from her and hopped around on the ground. Marie watched the bird. It had not seen her, and she sat motionless. The bird came closer.

The front door to the house opened. Marie swung her head up to the door, and the bird flew off.

Standing in the doorway was a man she had never seen before. She had seen many men like him. He was wearing jeans and a T-shirt that were formfitting and showed off his strong physique. He was either current or ex-military.

She watched the man as his eyes narrowed, and he scanned the area slowly. She knew he could not see her, but when his eyes passed over where she was sitting in the bushes, she got nervous.

When his eyes moved on, she exhaled. She had without realizing it held her breath. After the man finished looking at the front yard, he went back inside and closed the door.

A military man. This was not what she had been expecting. In reality she wasn't sure what she had been expecting. She still didn't know if there was anyone else. She wished she had hidden a camera somewhere inside the house.

Now that she knew there was someone there, her next thought was to follow this person when he left so that she could find out who he was.

Marie had to work, and she could not keep taking days off. She would need to find a way to follow him even if he left when she wasn't watching. Also, she couldn't track a person in an Uber. She would need a car.

Moving slowly, she reversed her tracks and went back over the wall. She paused before going over, to listen and make sure there was no one coming. She pulled her head up over the wall first and looked around. When she was confident no one was around, she went over and landed once again with a light thud.

She then turned and started jogging. She called for an Uber and ran to the Starbucks a few miles away.

It took her about twenty minutes to run the few miles, and the Uber showed up a few minutes later.

She had worked up a light sweat and apologized to the Uber driver, who said not to worry about it. He then rolled down the window and offered her a water, which she accepted.

At home she thought about following someone in a car. She had seen enough movies that she was worried. The movies that seemed the most accurate to her had multiple cars following one person. That way, the person would not repeatedly see the same car in the rearview mirror as he or she drove.

For Marie that was not an option. She had to come up with a way to follow the car without being right behind it and without having multiple cars. She knew that some phones had tracking options available. They would report their location as long as they were turned on and had power.

Of course, the app she had installed on Walt's phone reported location. Why not just get another phone and put that somewhere in the car, using the same app to track it?

This endeavor was costing her. So far it had not been a big cost, but now she was about to buy another phone.

She called for an Uber and went down to AT&T. She got an Android phone. The man said it was the most basic but reliable phone they had. Holding the phone, she thought it seemed thick compared to the iPhone she normally used. It also had a cheap plastic feel to it,

229

but there was a good chance she would lose this phone, so she wanted something cheap. The second line on her account did not cost her as much as she had feared, so she purchased and activated the phone.

She then got in another Uber and went to a rental car location. After what seemed like a long wait, she had a car. It was a small, two-door, white car. The person at the counter made her fill out a ton of paper work. Since she didn't know what all she would be doing, she got the highest level of insurance they offered. Better to be safe, she thought.

She took the keys and went out to the parking lot where the rental cars waiting for drivers were kept. It took her a few minutes to find her car—in row F, slot 15. Sitting in the car, she got familiar with it. She turned the headlights off and on, looked over the air conditioning and heating settings, tested the windshield wipers, and disabled the door lights.

Satisfied that the car would meet her purposes, she left. She had to go through a gate on the way out, where she gave the person her paper work for the car. After a quick check, she let Marie out.

Marie drove back to Walt's neighborhood. She parked what she figured would be about a ten-minute walk away and went back up to Walt's. On the walk, anytime a car passed her, she got nervous. She was worried Walt would leave and see her.

Thinking about what she would say occupied her, and then she was at the wall again. She took a quick look around and went back up and over the wall. She had not done this much climbing over walls since she was a kid. She still enjoyed it.

She hunched down and made her way back to the front of Walt's house. The porch light was on, as was the light in the living room.

She felt her heart thumping in her chest. She had not brought any tape and cursed herself for it. She lay down and started crawling toward the car. When she got to the rear of the car, she felt under the rear bumper to see if there was any place she could put the phone. There was a small ledge under the bumper, but it wasn't big enough for the phone. Crawling around the side of the car that was farthest from the house, she saw there was no place to put the phone. It was dark, and she could not see underneath the car. She felt the best she could, and there was no obvious place.

She knelt next to the car and looked at the house. The curtains were closed, and she could see that the TV was on through the crack between them.

She lay back down and pressed the button on her phone that turned on the flashlight. She found a place under the car where she could wedge the phone. She took out the plastic phone and shoved it into the crack. She felt the phone scrape as she wedged it into the crack. When she was confident it would not come out, she stopped pushing.

She heard the front door open and flipped off the light on her phone. She held her breath and did not move. She did not hear the front door close, and she waited. It had to be the military-looking man performing the same search he had when she was there earlier.

After a minute the door closed, and she took a breath—slowly, to not make any noise. She did not move for a few minutes. She wanted to make sure whoever it was did not come outside.

When she heard nothing, she knelt by the car and peered through the window. There was no one there. She crawled away from the car, and once she was back by the bushes, she low-walked as fast as she could back to the wall. Peeking back over the wall, she saw a man walking a dog, and she waited. When the man was out of sight, she went over the wall.

This time she walked back to her car. Using the walk to calm her nerves, she made it to the rental car and got inside. She felt exhilarated. On the drive back home, she played her music loud and danced in the seat the best she could. A person in a car next to her smiled as he saw her. Waving at him, she smiled back. She had not felt this good in a long time.

Once she was home, she poured herself a glass of wine and got out some cheese. She enjoyed the cheese and wine without any crackers. No carbs tonight—it wasn't a cheat day.

She opened her laptop, logged in to the web page, and looked at the tracking information. Two devices were registered at Walt's place: one inside the house and one outside. The location tracking was very accurate, she thought.

She then installed the app on her phone that would allow her to track the phones. The app showed the same information as the website.

Marie sipped her wine. She was ready to follow the military man wherever he went.

She woke up early the next day and worked out, and when she was finished, she sat at her desk. First, she checked the tracking software. Both phones were still at Walt's house. They had not moved.

Next, she checked her schedule for the day. She had two clients in the morning and one in the afternoon. She showered and got ready. While she dressed, she thought about Walt and the strange man. The idea that Walt was lying to her had settled with her a while ago. People lied, and she knew that.

Once when she was young and her father had whipped her with a belt, she had called the police. Her father had lied and talked his way out of being arrested. Marie had thought at the time the police would be able to help her. But she was a child, and her father had left no marks except for a red bottom, which the police had not looked at.

When the police had left, her father turned to her and glared down at her. She was seven at the time, and he was a big man.

She was shaking as he glared down at her, tears coming down the sides of her face. Her father had done nothing to her after that but had taken it out on her mother. He had used the belt on Marie's mom, chasing her into a corner and whipping her with it. Making sure not to use the buckle end, he folded the belt and whipped her with the folded part.

Her mother wept as she was whipped, but her dad made no noise. When he was finished, he turned back to Marie and stood over her again.

"Are you ever going to do that again, Marie?" her father asked in a soft, calm voice.

"No, sir," Marie answered.

He nodded at her and handed her the belt. "Put this away and go to bed," he said.

She nodded and grabbed the belt. Taking it upstairs, she hung up the belt in his closet and went to bed. Falling asleep, she listened to the sound of her mom crying.

Marie hated the memories of her father that came back to her without warning. For years the sound of her mom crying after her dad had whipped her would come to her in nightmares. Or if one of her friends cried, the sound triggered something in Marie.

Marie thought of her dad on the floor, twitching as he died with a look of pain on his face. A smile came across her face. Knowing her father died in pain was the only good memory of him she had.

"I got you in the end, you fuck," she said to no one.

With that she went to her gym and met with her first client.

On most days she would Uber to work, but now she was driving a rental car. This caused a few questions when she arrived and one of her employees saw her getting out of the rental car.

"Good morning, Marie. New car?" Ashley asked. Ashley was one of Marie's personal trainers. She was polite and hardworking, and Marie liked her.

"Just a rental. I have some stuff to do this week and didn't want to wait for Ubers."

Ashley nodded. Inside the gym Marie grabbed a cup of coffee and called the morning team meeting. There were no immediate issues that Marie needed to address, so the meeting went quickly, and everyone got to work.

Marie sat at the computer at her desk and checked the tracking software. Nothing had changed. Both phones were still at Walt's house.

After her first client, she checked again, then after lunch, and again after the last two clients. Nothing changed at all. Both phones sat in the same location.

On the second day, Marie was getting worried about the battery in the phone in the car. Walt would charge his phone, but the phone in the car would soon run out of its battery.

She drove to Best Buy at lunch and asked the man about long-running battery packs. He sold her something that would last over seventy-two hours. She got two of them.

Back at her office in the gym, she charged the first one while she worked. After work she put the other one on to charge and drove over to Walt's neighborhood.

She hated that she had to risk going back. She had hoped that Walt or the man would have gone somewhere yesterday. Whatever it was they were doing, they were doing it at Walt's house.

Marie did not believe in luck, and things like this always affirmed that lack of belief. If she had been lucky, Walt or the military man would have gone somewhere the first day, and she would have followed them and found out everything. But of course that would not happen for her.

Walking back to Walt's house, she looked around and went over the wall. She got to the closest bush again and waited. Knowing the military man peered outside periodically, she would not move until she saw him scan the area. So she waited.

It was about thirty minutes before the front door opened. This time, instead of just looking outside the house, he walked down and around the outside of the house. He checked each direction to make sure no one was there. It took him about ten minutes before he went back inside.

Marie then waited a few more minutes and crawled back to the car. This time she had brought duct tape, and she plugged the phone in to the charger and taped both the phone and the charger inside the crack where she had shoved the phone.

Cutting her hand when she pulled the phone from where she had wedged it, she bit her lip to keep from making any noise. After the phone and charger were in place, she crawled back over to the bushes. At the bush, she knelt and watched the front of the house again. Nothing. All was quiet.

She went back to the wall, waited until she didn't hear anything, peeked over, looked around, and then went over it.

As with anything else, she learned quickly and adapted. Telling herself she would have made a good spy, she walked back to her rental car. Inside it, she checked her phone, and both phones were still at Walt's house.

Good, she thought.

On her way home, she stopped and got a salad and took it home to eat.

Sitting on her couch, she pulled out her phone and checked the tracking software again. There was only one phone at Walt's house.

The military man's phone was no longer there. She clicked on that phone, and it showed the car on the freeway.

Marie left her salad and ran out to her car. She set the phone on the dash with the tracking app left open. She pulled out of her driveway and drove as fast as she could to the freeway. The man was heading northeast, so she got on the freeway going the same direction. She had no way of knowing how fast he was going, so she went fast.

Continually checking her rearview mirror for police, she stayed in the fast lane, passing cars as she came up to them.

Looking at the map in the app, she was closing the distance between her car and the man's. He was now five miles ahead of her. When she closed the distance to four miles, she slowed down. She had been doing eighty-five miles an hour. He must have been going the speed limit.

That was interesting. He did not want to get pulled over. Whatever he was doing was most likely not legal. Why else did anyone go exactly the speed limit? Marie thought the police would probably do pretty well pulling over people who were going exactly the speed limit.

Dropping down to seventy-five so she would have a much lower chance of getting pulled over, she would gain ten miles an hour on him. Not sure how far they were going, she had made sure to keep the gas tank full. She had filled it up before going home each night. Better to be safe, she thought.

Now it was good. They had been driving for two hours, with no sign of stopping. When she was less than a mile from him, she slowed down to the speed limit.

Keeping the car at a distance of about a mile turned out to be easy. Whoever was driving kept the car at the posted speed limit, and she just needed to do the same. Driving at the speed limit was boring, so she turned on the radio and rolled down the windows.

The initial excitement of following someone had worn off, and now she had to keep herself engaged in following him.

After a few hours on the freeway, the app showed the car ahead of her getting off at an exit. Marie had no idea where they were. She had never gone this far north.

Now that he'd gotten off the freeway, he was heading east and had slowed down about ten miles more an hour. She did not want to get closer than a mile behind him, so she slowed down as well.

She got in the slow lane and drove at fifty-five miles an hour. In less than a minute, she was at the exit and pulling onto the same road his car had. At the bottom of the freeway exit was a stop sign. The car had gone right, and she saw the headlights of the car ahead on the road disappear into the dark.

The app showed that the car was about a mile away.

She had two concerns now. This was open space out here, meaning he could see her coming from a long distance. Second, she was worried about the cell phone signal. She now had to be ready to follow by sight in the event the phone stopped being able to transmit its location.

Turning right, she sped up. Marie could not afford to lose this man. Walt wrote one novel a year. Only once or twice had he written more, and she did not want to have to wait another year to figure out what the fuck was going on.

The app still registered the car, and she closed the distance. She got up to where she could see the headlights in the distance, and then she let the car get just out of sight.

It was difficult to keep close enough. The road was not straight like a freeway, so if she was not careful, she would get close enough that she could see his taillights. She had to assume that if she could see him, he could see her. She dropped back a little more. Being seen would be just as bad as losing him.

Watching the app and the road—all her focus was on this.

All at once, the car turned off the road. It made a hard left turn and drove on.

Marie pulled to the side of the road and stopped. If she had kept going, he would have seen her. Now she waited. She was not sure how far away he could see her, but now the driver's side of the car would be facing her headlights.

She looked at the map. It allowed her to place a marker down by touching the screen and holding. The map did not show a road. His car was still giving its position, but she guessed that wouldn't last long.

She drove forward slowly until she got to the marker on the app. There was a dirt road where he had turned off. She got out of the car and looked at the dirt road. It was solid dirt, and she would be able to drive on it. In the car, she went down the same dirt road the man had taken. She drove slowly and carefully. It was a bumpy ride.

After a few minutes, the car ahead of her stopped giving her its location. Now she was blind.

Slowing down more, she continued on. It was dark, and the headlights did not give her enough light to make her comfortable. Looking ahead as much as she could, she got to the last known location of the car from the app. She still did not see it.

Her car was a big bright beacon in the desert night.

Marie felt her heart in her chest as she drove through the desert.

Then it was there. She could see the outline of the car parked in the desert. She was not aware of how long she had been driving, but she could now just make out the outline of the car she had been following. Its lights had been shut off, and it had pulled off the dirt road.

Looking to her right, she saw flat earth. By now, she was sure that whoever was in the car had seen her. She drove forward a little more and then made a right turn. Leaving the road was the only option. She was not sure what the man would do if she came up on him in the middle of the night, but it would not have been good.

Fifteen minutes later, she guessed she was about two miles away. It had been slow driving in the dark desert, but now she hoped the man could no longer see her car.

She stopped the car and got out. Cool desert air blew her hair and brought up dust, causing her to squint. She only had sunglasses with her, and if she put them on, it would diminish her sight further. She ran as fast as she could back the way she had come, following the tracks her car had made.

On her phone she had a flashlight app that allowed her to turn the screen red. Using a red light to see the ground in front of her would make it hard for someone to see her.

When she had gone a little over a mile, she started walking and looking for the outline of the car again. As soon as she saw it, she dropped down. She could see the silhouette of a man in the distance next to the car. It looked to her as if he was digging a hole. No, not a hole—or not just any hole.

Why would someone come out to the middle of the desert to dig a hole? There was only one reason someone went out to the desert in the middle of the night and dug.

A grave. The man was digging a grave.

Holy shit, had this man killed Walt? That was the first thought that crossed her mind. No, that wasn't what this was. That didn't make any sense.

She crawled closer and was lying next to a desert plant, watching.

The man finished the hole. Then he went to the trunk of his car and lifted something out. It looked like a body, but it was difficult to see. The man lowered the body into the hole and then went around and jumped into the hole and pulled the body the rest of the way in.

The man climbed out of the hole, went back to the car, got some other items, and threw them into the hole as well. He then grabbed the shovel and filled the hole back in. It did not take him long to fill the hole.

He put the shovel in the trunk, and she heard the trunk door slam and then the car door open. After a few seconds, the car started up, and the headlights came on.

Marie rolled behind the bush as the car turned around and the lights passed over where she was lying. Once the car passed by, she watched the taillights until they disappeared into the distance. She then stood and walked over to where the man had been digging.

The hole had been filled in, but she could see where it had been. She knew that in a few days, it would be impossible to find. Now she had a choice. Should she mark the hole and come back and dig it up later to see who was in it? Or should she follow the man and ask him directly?

She did not relish the idea of digging up a dead body. It could still be something else in the hole, but she was fairly certain it was a body.

It was an easy choice in the end. She wanted to speak to a live person to find out what was going on, and she did not want to speak to Walt. Walt was a practiced liar who had been concealing whatever was going on from her for years. But the man who had dug the hole—he was an unknown to her, meaning that it could go either way.

With men, her looks and personality got her far. So she would take a chance.

There was no sound, so she stood for a little while, enjoying the calm of the desert. The wind blew her hair, and she felt good standing there.

After a few minutes, she left the hole, walked back to her car, and left the desert.

In a little while, she was back on the freeway, and she drove home.

According to the tracking app, the man had gone to a hotel. Marie would go home and get some rest and then wake up early and track the man if he looked as if he was heading back toward the city.

Falling asleep proved difficult for Marie. She was excited and nervous about confronting the man about Walt and about the hole in the desert, so at four in the morning, she got up and looked at the app to see where the man was.

He was still at the hotel.

This surprised her a little. She wasn't sure what she had expected. She guessed she thought he would have gone to wherever his house was or maybe even back to Walt's.

Had she spooked him that much when she drove up on him in the night?

Thinking about it, she guessed if she had been doing what he had done in the middle of nowhere in the middle of the night, she would have been a little spooked as well.

She closed the app and set down her phone. There was nothing she could do now. Not wanting to confront him until she knew a little more about him, she went back to bed. Focusing on her breathing and calming herself, she managed to fall back asleep.

In what seemed to her like a very short amount of time, her alarm went off, and it was time to get up. Purposely, she did not check the app for the man's location. She wanted to give him some time to get wherever he would go next. Noon, she told herself. Do not check the app until noon.

If he didn't go home by tonight, she would start to get worried about the battery and would have to go to wherever he was to change it.

But for now, she focused on her work and on her clients.

At noon she went to lunch. She went to one of the local restaurants. It was bright and well lit, and the waiters all wore the same red outfits. Marie normally avoided chain restaurants, but today she only wanted somewhere to sit where she could check the app and plan her next moves.

She ordered a salad from a cheerful young lady with long blond hair held back in a ponytail. After taking her order, the waitress walked away with her ponytail swinging behind her.

Marie pulled out her phone and opened the app. It showed the man's car parked at a house on the beach in Santa Monica.

Her salad arrived, and Marie hid the screen of her phone. She was not sure why. Anyone looking would have just seen her staring at a map, but she still hid the screen.

She got the address of the house from the app, put it into Google Maps, and went to street view. Outside, the house was a wall with an entrance controlled by a gate. It was hard to tell anything else from Google Maps, but she looked at as much as Google had.

Next, she opened up another app that she had needed to purchase access to. It was designed to track people. All she had was an address, and she was not sure how much information she would be able to get. Turned out there wasn't a way to search for someone by address. The app was more for getting information on people based on their name.

OK, she thought, this is not an issue. Her idea was that if needed, she would steal some of his mail to get his name.

Looking at his house in Google Maps, she figured out where the mailbox was. There was a small slot on one side of the wall near the gate. The thought that maybe this wasn't his house came and went. There was a good chance this was his place. Still, she wanted to be certain.

She finished her salad and paid the check, once again admiring the blond waitress and her cute ponytail. Then she left the restaurant.

Work went by quickly, as she had several clients whom she really liked working with that day. They liked a challenge, and she enjoyed meeting the challenge.

After she finished work, she drove out to Santa Monica. She parked at the pier and walked around for a while. There were people walking around the pier, eating and laughing and enjoying themselves. It was a fun atmosphere, and Marie thought it would be a good place to come on a date.

Standing at the edge of the pier, she watched the sunset. Listening to the sound of the waves hitting the pillars on the pier along with the sunset was beautiful. Once the sun had set, she pulled out her phone and looked at the app. The car was still parked at the house by the beach.

She walked along the beach. At some point there was a sign that said that the beaches ahead were private and you could not trespass. She turned and walked out toward the street that ran along the beach. Cars drove by her as she walked. She could feel the wind from them as they passed.

When she arrived at the man's house, she stopped and looked. It was a beautiful home. The wall outside and the gate were clean and looked well maintained. She went over to the wall and pulled herself up and scanned the yard. Inside the yard were several palm trees and a well-kept lawn.

This was an expensive house. That was the only thought she had. It wasn't one of the larger homes and was probably on the small side, but the location made it most likely worth several million dollars.

Curiosity about what this man did flooded Marie. Was he in the Mafia or some other crime organization? Or maybe he sold drugs. Was Walt one of his clients? If so, why had he been at Walt's house so long? Were they doing drugs together? Looking at this house had just created more questions and did not answer any.

She walked over to the mail slot. She knelt down and lifted the flap and peeked inside. There was some mail visible at the bottom. Her hand would not fit into the slot past the wrist. If she wanted to grab the mail, she would have to at least get it to her elbow. That was not going to happen.

Climbing over the wall was not an option. She knew nothing about this man except that he was paranoid. At Walt's he had come outside every time she had been there, meaning that he was vigilant and most likely would have some kind of alarm system at his home. So she would need some way to get the mail without climbing the wall and without using her hand.

She left and walked back toward the pier. What she would need was one of those claws that old people use to pick up things when they can't bend over. Ordering one on Amazon would take too long. She was in a hurry to find out who the man was and what the fuck was going on with Walt. It was still early enough that Target would be open.

She left the pier and drove to Target. She got the gripping arm, and, since she could never go to Target without doing a little shopping, she got some other items she needed. She found a cute shirt and got a couple of books.

She drove back to the pier, parked, and made the same walk back down to the man's house. She opened the flap, and the mail was still there. It crossed her mind that this was a federal offense, so she tensed up. She pulled up one of the envelopes and looked at the name.

Ian White. To be sure, she grabbed a second envelope. It was also addressed to Ian White. After putting both envelopes back into the slot, she left.

Now she had a name and could run the search. Before doing that, she wanted to get back to her car. She was worried and would not feel relaxed until she was home.

Inside the car she checked for Ian White in Santa Monica. There was a lot of information. Ex-military was the first thing that caught her eye. She had been right about that. He had served for about a decade and had gotten out with an honorable discharge.

Now he owned a security company. Checking the company's website, she saw that they provided bodyguard services for celebrities. Having seen his house, she figured that must pay well.

Now she at least had a reason why Ian would have been at Walt's house, but it still didn't explain what or who was buried out in the desert. This was where it would start to get tricky. Her next move would either be to approach Ian directly or to try to get a little more information on him.

Following this man would be dangerous. He was an ex–US Navy SEAL, according to his website. He had served in Afghanistan and Iraq and had trained Iraqi police forces. His website biography was much more detailed than what she had been able to find in the background check. What she had found in the background check was that he had never been convicted of any crimes and had lived at the same place for the last ten years.

How long had Ian known Walt, and why had he been at Walt's house? The questions still came.

After finishing reading the website, she drove home. Not turning on any music, she drove in silence. Alone with her thoughts, she was nervous about confronting Ian. He was a trained killer who had buried what was most likely a person out in the middle of the desert.

Marie now realized she was lucky he hadn't had night-vision goggles or some other way of seeing her. If she was smart, she would go to the police right now and tell them what she had found. She'd give up both Walt and Ian and let them know what she had seen in the desert. But she did not want to give anyone up until she knew what exactly it was she was going to be giving up.

At home she sat in the dark, thinking, her legs folded beneath her. She took several deep breaths to clear her mind.

She knew what she would do. It was never really in question. Confronting Ian was the only way to find out about Walt—Walt, who had been lying to her for years. She knew something was going on with him. There was no way he was writing the beautiful stories she had been reading. It all came down to that.

The man she knew could not have written some of the beautifully moving stories she had come to love. Because of that and the anger it brought, she would confront Ian. Dangerous as Ian was, he had the answers she needed.

Now she only had to figure out the best way to confront him. Again, the answer was simple. Playing games was not in her nature. She would confront him directly.

She was not afraid of him. The problem was that he could slam the door in her face and then call Walt and let Walt know about her. She did not want that. If anyone was going to tell Walt, she knew it would be her.

Marie decided she would wait a few days to confront Ian. Let him get comfortable again. Since Ian had stopped at the hotel when he lived close by, she assumed she had spooked him by coming up on him in the desert.

She fell asleep with her thoughts. Sometime during the night, a knock at the door woke her up. At first the knock incorporated itself into her dream. She was dreaming about Walt's house—standing in his kitchen, looking at the door with the lock. In the dream she picked up a hammer off the kitchen table and was about to smash the lock when there was a knock at the door.

As she turned to the front door, the second knock woke her up. By the third knock, she was standing. Her heart raced, and she went to the front door and peered through the peephole.

Standing on the other side of the door was Ian.

Holy shit. At least now she wouldn't need to go confront him, she thought.

"I know you're there," Ian said through the door. "The peephole went dark when you looked through it."

Marie's thoughts raced before she answered, "One second."

Ian said nothing in response.

"If I wanted to hurt you, I would not have knocked," Ian said.

Marie had a gun in her nightstand, and she went upstairs to get it. She grabbed it. Its cold weight felt comforting in her hand. Holding the gun in her right hand, she opened the door with her left hand. Ian had been one step ahead of her, and he pointed a gun at her face as soon as she opened the door.

Ian looked at her.

Marie was wearing a tight-fitting T-shirt, a pair of underwear, and nothing else. She saw him stare, and in that moment she relaxed.

"Drop the gun," Ian said.

She did as she was told, and the gun fell to the floor with a thud.

Motioning with the gun, he directed her away from the door and pointed for her to sit down on the couch.

Once she sat down, he reached down and picked up the revolver she had dropped.

Ian held the snub-nose thirty-eight revolver for a second, and then he opened the cylinder of the revolver and dumped the bullets out onto the floor. With a flick of his wrist, he closed the now-empty cylinder and set the gun on the small table by the door where she kept her keys.

He gently closed the door behind him. The gun in his hand never moved off her.

"I'm not going to hurt you," Ian said.

"I know," Marie answered.

"It was you out in the desert." Ian stated this as fact, not as a question. He then reached into his pocket and pulled out the phone and the battery she had taped under his car.

"These belong to you," he said, showing them to her and then setting them down on the same table where he'd put her gun.

"You didn't call the police. Why?" Ian said.

"I want to know what's going on," Marie said.

"You don't know? Walt didn't tell you about me?"

"No. Walt's never mentioned you. What did you bury in the desert?"

"You don't know?" Ian said.

Marie was quiet. Why did Ian seem surprised that she didn't know?

"Why would I know?"

"I always assume, whenever I am working with a couple, that if one knows they both know. You and Walt have been seeing each other for a long time. I figured he would have told you about me and about the typewriter by now."

"What about the typewriter?" Marie said.

Ian sat on the couch at the opposite end from where Marie was sitting, his gun still pointed at her.

His gun was black, and the hole on the front looked large to her. She noticed that his finger was not on the trigger, but he held it straight next to the trigger. He had been telling the truth when he said he was not going to hurt her.

"What about the typewriter?" Marie repeated.

"Do you know how Walt writes his books?"

"No," Marie said.

Ian lowered the gun.

"I followed you because I'm trying to find out who helps Walt write the books," Marie said. "I know he doesn't write them himself."

Ian looked at her and waited.

"I have known Walt a long time, and I love him," she went on. "I think he wants to marry me. But I know that man could not write those books. Have you read his books? They are amazing and insightful. Whoever writes those books sees the world as it is. Walt is not capable of that level of sensitivity. He can barely discuss the books."

Ian nodded. "He doesn't write the books. You are right about that."

He had just confirmed what she had known.

"Then who writes the books? You?" Marie asked.

With that, Ian let out a quick laugh. "No not me. I'm no writer. I just help Walt."

"Help Walt with what?"

When Walt had first started dating Marie, Ian had done a background check on her. There was nothing suspicious about her. Her dad had died when she was eleven of a heart attack in front of her, and there was some doubt as to how long her and her mom had waited to call 911. But it came out later that the dad was physically abusive, so no one looked too deeply into them not calling 911.

She was beautiful and smart. She ran her own business and had double-majored in business and kinesiology. Putting her degree to work, she ran a successful personal-training business and gym. All this he had been able to find out about her.

What he had not been able to find out was what he was now realizing. She did not fear him. Even when he had the gun pointed at her, she had not been afraid. Most people who had a gun pointed at them showed fear. She had not been afraid, and he could see her looking at him, waiting for an answer.

"I'm not sure you will believe me if I tell you who writes them," Ian said.

Marie looked at the gun, and then her gaze moved off the gun and onto Ian.

"What did you mean about the typewriter?" Marie said.

Ian, who had never been one to mince words, said, "The typewriter writes the books."

"You mean he uses the typewriter to write the books," Marie said. "I figured that out. Why else would he have such an old typewriter?"

"No. The typewriter writes the books. Walt has people sit at the typewriter, and then the typewriter uses them to write the books, and in the process it kills the people who write the book," Ian said, watching Marie's face to gauge her reaction.

Marie heard what Ian said and thought about it. "So that's who you buried in the desert? The last person to write a book for Walt?"

"Yes," Ian said.

"You're full of shit," Marie said.

"That's what I first thought when Walt told me. His brother found the typewriter in an old storage locker and was its first victim. After typing on it, he I guess became addicted to the typing. Once you start typing on it, you don't stop until you die," Ian said.

"Paul died in a hospital. He had some kind of mental breakdown," Marie said.

Marie realized for the first time that Walt had never gone into detail about what had happened to his brother. All Walt had ever said was that he had gone crazy and would hurt himself and others.

"Yes, he died because he would not do anything other than try to get back to the typewriter," Ian said.

"So then, if you let someone type on it, you are killing them," Marie said. She was not judging, just stating a fact. She still wasn't sure what Ian was lying about this for. There was no real reason to lie about this.

"Yes. You are killing them if you let them type on it. Walt has me kidnap homeless people, and we make them type on it. They aren't missed when they disappear. Homeless people disappear all the time," Ian said.

It was the way Ian talked about this that made her question herself. Long-term, a story like this made no sense. Lying about something that was impossible and could be disproved so easily didn't make sense.

"The typewriter caused him to go crazy," Marie said.

Ian wasn't sure whether it was a statement or a question, but he answered anyway, "Yes."

"I—" Marie started and then stopped. What Ian was saying made sense, but it was difficult for her to believe. It was impossible.

"So you kidnap someone once a year? What do you get out of it?" Marie asked.

"Walt pays me very well. One death a year—and I get to live in a very nice place, and it also helped me get my bodyguard business going," Ian said.

Ian sounded very cold to Marie.

"Why are you telling me this?" Marie said.

"You will find out eventually," Ian said. "Walt has an idea about moving the typewriter to a cabin so that you won't find out. But if he marries you, eventually you will find out. And look at the trouble you just went through to find out about me. It makes no sense to lie to you anymore. I will let Walt know you now know, and he can decide what to do. I'm sure he will show you next time."

"Why wouldn't I go to the police?" Marie asked.

"You won't. You saw me bury a body in the desert and didn't," Ian said.

Ian was right, of course. Marie had no desire to go to the police. She didn't know what she wanted to do. If Ian was telling the truth, as impossible as it sounded, she had to know more about this typewriter.

"Don't tell Walt I know," Marie said.

"Why wouldn't I tell him?"

"Let me tell him in my own time," Marie said. "I want to find out about this typewriter first. If you are telling the truth, Walt can't be the only person to ever use this thing. Give me some time before you tell him."

Ian thought about Marie. He didn't mind waiting to tell Walt. In reality he would not hear from Walt until it was almost time to write the next book, and he had no desire to rush out and tell him Marie knew. He liked Marie. She had not been afraid of the gun, which was something he respected.

"OK. I won't tell him until I see him next."

"When will that be?"

"I only see him when it's time to write his next book, which is about once a year. You have a lot of time. But if you haven't told him by then, I will tell him," Ian said.

Marie nodded. "OK."

With that, Ian stood, put his pistol in his waistband, and walked out.

Marie stood and looked out her front window and watched him leave.

"A magic fucking typewriter?" she said out loud.

Marie couldn't sleep. Her mind tried to think of reasons why Ian would lie to her. Making up a story about a magic typewriter that wrote books was insane. She needed to figure out what the fuck was going on. She would start with Walt's brother and work forward. There had to be something in the past that would help her figure out what was going on.

In the morning before she went to work, she called a private investigator. She had done a search online and looked at several websites. One of them went into detail on how he could find out information about anyone—even secrets that person didn't want found. Marie called the number on the web page.

"Out of the Weeds Investigations," a perky-sounding voice answered.

"Yes. Hi, I'm looking to speak to a private investigator," Marie said.

"OK. One moment please," the perky voice said.

There was a click as she was transferred.

"This is Mick," a deep male voice said.

"Hi, yes, I'm wondering if you can help me," Marie said.

"Depends on what you need help with," Mick said.

"I need to find out everything I can about Paul Erickson," Marie said.

"Do you know where he lives presently?" Mick asked.

"No. He passed away a long time ago. I'd like to know everything you can find out about him. And I'm not sure what I'm looking for. I just want information," Marie said.

"Sure. That should not be a problem. I need everything you know about him, so I have a good starting point and don't go looking into the wrong Paul Erickson," Mick said.

Marie told Mick all she knew. It wasn't much, but Mick said it was enough. He told her his rate for this, and she agreed to the price. He then asked a bunch of questions and got a credit card number and contact information from her.

"It will take me a week or so to complete the research. I'll give you a call when it's ready. I'll e-mail you a report with everything I find," Mick said.

"OK. The faster you get this done, the better. I am willing to pay extra for you to expedite," Marie said.

"Let me see what I can do. I'll let you know," Mick said and hung up.

So much of life involved waiting. Now she would have to wait again.

Marie thought about the typewriter. She had seen it, and to her it looked like an old antique typewriter. It was in remarkably good shape. That was all she remembered thinking about it.

Walt had refused to let her get near it. If there was any truth to what Ian had told her, that made sense. All she would have had to do was press a key, and then she would be trapped by it.

Telling herself that was impossible and that Ian was lying to her, she got ready for work. In a few days she would find out about Paul, and then she could start tracking the typewriter. So she would wait.

On the fourth day, she had still not heard back from Mick, and she was starting to get anxious. Marie would give him one more day, and then she would call him to check on the status.

Mick got back to her on the fifth day.

"Hi, Marie. It's Mick," Mick said.

"Hi, Mick."

Mick did not preamble but went right into it. "Sorry it took so long, but it took me a little bit to get the medical records. Since you paid extra, I wanted to get as much detail as I could. I'll be sending the information over in a little bit. I got the medical records, the death record, and a bunch of other information. Since I didn't know what you were looking for, I am going to send over everything. It's a lot of information. Most of it is probably not interesting."

"No problem. I don't know what I'm looking for, so the more info the better," Marie said.

"Great. Give me a call if you have any questions or need anything else," Mick said. He confirmed her e-mail address and hung up.

An e-mail arrived a few minutes later with a web link, which she clicked on. It opened a web page, and inside were a bunch of documents, which she downloaded to her computer. She closed the browser and went through the documents.

Paul had died of an infection from being trapped in a bed. Reading through the medical record, she saw that it first went through the story of how the police had arrested him and had to sedate him to keep him from lashing out at them. Several specialists had written diagnoses on him.

The police report explained how Paul had become fixated on a typewriter, and he had to be sedated for them to get him away from it. Paul had assaulted the police when they had tried to get him to stop typing.

As Ian had said, anytime Paul had woken up, he seemed to try to escape. He never attacked anyone directly but only tried to escape and would hurt himself or others in his efforts. He had dislocated an arm while trying to escape, and he had not stopped. Even with the pain of a dislocated arm, he continued to fight to escape.

Marie knew that Walt and his brother at some point had bought storage lockers at auction and sold the contents. There was not much information on any of the storage lockers they had bought.

Fuck, she thought. Aside from proving that Walt's brother had indeed lost his mind in the way that Ian had described, there was no other information on their finding a typewriter.

Now she had to figure out another way to find out about this supposed magic typewriter. She thought back to the few times she had seen it. Walt was very protective of it, and she never saw it for long. She pictured it in her head the best she could. It looked like an antique but was new looking. That was something, she supposed. She thought about its color, the look of the keys, and the label: *Wordsmith.*

That was something. An old Wordsmith typewriter that wrote books. Again the doubt about the typewriter writing the books crept in.

She jumped onto Google and did a search for Wordsmith typewriters. It turned out there was a typewriter company named Wordsmith that made a typewriter that looked like the one in Walt's house. They were in business from 1928 through 1940. Wordsmith System One was the name of the one in Walt's basement, from the looks of it. Google had pictures of restored versions of the typewriter, and you could still buy working models on eBay.

So far, nothing she found made her think that the typewriter would write the stories. Ian could still have lied to her.

Now she started looking for authors who were famous during the same years the Wordsmiths were made. It was doubtful, she thought, that there would be any pictures of the typewriter with the authors. It was a fair assumption on Marie's part to think that they would do the same thing Walt was doing and hide that they were using the typewriter.

What she did find was an author named Thomas Smyth, who died under suspicious circumstances. Thomas wrote multiple books, and he was one of the first writers to appear on the *New York Times* best-seller list when it started in 1931.

After his death, his cousin became a writer. This was noted in one of the articles on Thomas that Marie found. Thomas's cousin was named Robert, and Robert wrote two books a year for ten years, and then he died when he was hit by a car crossing a street. Every book he wrote had appeared on the *New York Times* best-seller list.

After Robert was killed, his son Louis became a writer. It took about a year, but his first book was a best seller. Once again it appeared on the *New York Times* best-seller list. Writing under a pseudonym, his son wrote for an additional ten years. Abruptly, he stopped writing, and a few years later, a man by the name of Dale Woods started writing.

It turned out that Louis was in an accident in which he was paralyzed from the neck down. Louis lived a few more years after becoming paralyzed, but he died in a hospital bed in New York. Dale had been by his side when he died.

Dale's first book was a number-one best seller. After that he wrote a book every two years, and each time the book was on the *New York Times* best seller list. It was interesting that Dale only wrote one book every two years. It was like clockwork, and it went on for twenty years. Dale looked to have a total of ten books in print. After ten years he abruptly stopped writing. No other authors fit the pattern of the typewriter.

Dale lived another fifteen years off the money from the books he had written. He lived on the East Coast and was something of a recluse. Marie found several articles on him in which multiple people had tried to persuade him to write again. In one article Dale had said that it took too much out of him to write.

The area where Dale had lived was the same area on the East Coast where Walt and his brother had lived.

Marie picked up the phone and called Mick.

After the receptionist transferred her, Mick answered. "Hello. Mick speaking."

"Hi, Mick. It's Marie again. I have someone else I want you to look into."

"Hi, Marie. Sure, what's the name?"

"Dale Woods. He lived on the East Coast and died sometime in the midseventies. He was a writer. One of his book titles was *Strange Places*. I need everything you can find about him."

"Got it. I'll need a few days," Mick said.

"I need to know every property he owned and where he lived," Marie said.

"OK. Anything in particular?" Mick said.

"Is there any chance you can find out if he rented any storage lockers in the same area where he lived?" Marie said.

"I'll see what I can find," Mick said.

They hung up.

Marie went back and did some more reading on each author she suspected of having the typewriter. None of them had done any writing prior to showing up on the best seller list, and all of them except for Dale had something happen to them that stopped them from writing.

Marie still wasn't convinced. Why had Dale stopped writing if he had the typewriter? And why had he said that writing had taken too much out of him? Dale had died in bed surrounded by family and had seemed to have a good life. Maybe he hadn't used the typewriter. Maybe she was wrong, and Dale had written the books on his own.

In a few days, Mick got back to her.

"Hello?" Marie said, answering her cell phone. She saw it was Mick, and she was excited.

"Hi, Marie. It's Mick. I have the information, and I'll be sending an e-mail in a few minutes," Mick said.

"Great. Thanks!" Marie said, her excitement coming through in her voice.

"You're welcome," Mick said and hung up.

Marie sat at her computer, opened the e-mail, and clicked on the link to open the files. Mick had done his job well. There were pictures and articles she had not seen. As she read the articles, Dale came across as warm and friendly. Every article said the same thing about him. He was nice and warm and open with the people conducting the interviews.

Pictures were included with the articles. Most of them were standard and not that interesting to Marie. In the background of one of the pictures, sitting on a shelf surrounded by books, was the Wordsmith.

Marie gasped slightly and felt her heart beat hard in her chest. Proof of the typewriter. Looking at it, she studied the typewriter. For the first time, she noticed what made this typewriter different from any of the other Wordsmiths she had seen photos of in her research. This typewriter had no ribbon.

On older typewriters, two spools sat on the top, one feeding ribbon and the other rolling up the used ribbon.

Everything else on the typewriter looked the same except for the missing ribbon.

Walt's typewriter was also missing the ribbon. This was the same typewriter. This picture was at least forty years old, and the typewriter looked identical.

An article on Dale's death explained that his family had fought over the money Dale had after he died. It took a long time for the courts to work it out. At some point the house was taken by one of the family members, and all of Dale's items were put into storage.

According to the article, there was some additional fighting, with claims that not everything he had owned had been put into storage. So the storage was locked in the legal argument, and someone paid the storage fee for years. Eventually the family resolved their issues, and everything was forgotten. Some of the family members passed away over the years, and Marie guessed that at some point, whoever was paying for the storage passed away. Then the storage was auctioned off, and Walt's brother found it.

Now that Marie knew that Dale had owned the typewriter, she read through everything about him again.

Writing took so much out of him, Dale had said. That statement meant something. Marie was not sure what yet, but her mind focused on it and began to work on its meaning. In any of the articles written about him while he was writing, his hands did not show in any of the photos. But in articles after he had stopped writing, he would have his hands in the photos.

Now she had an idea, but she needed to talk to Ian.

Marie pressed the buzzer at Ian's gate and waited. She knew he was home. She could see there were lights on in the house, and his car was in the driveway.

After a few minutes, she pressed the buzzer again, and Ian answered. "Yes?" his voice came through the speaker.

"Hi, Ian, it's Marie. I have a couple of questions for you, if you have some time," Marie said.

Nothing happened for a few seconds, and then there was a buzzing sound and the driveway gate began to slide open. When it had opened far enough, Marie walked through and followed the path along the driveway.

Behind her she heard another buzzing sound, and the gate stopped and then began to close. Ian stood in the doorway of his house, waiting for her.

Marie smiled and said hello when she saw him.

Ian smiled back. The smile was warm and inviting. For someone she knew to be a killer, he seemed very friendly, she thought.

Ian invited her inside. The house was neat and clean. A white leather couch sat in the middle of the living room. There was a simple glass coffee table sitting in front of the couch, and a TV hung on the wall. Pictures of people in military uniforms, along with people she guessed were his family, hung on the wall. Among the group of pictures was a photo of Ian shaking hands with George W. Bush.

"You know the former president?" Marie asked.

"I've met him a few times. Nothing personal, mostly just as part of a unit as we received awards. Kind of boring, really," Ian said.

Marie studied the rest of the photos. Aside from the picture of the former president, there wasn't anyone she knew. No pictures of Walt.

"No one knows of your relationship with Walt?" Marie asked.

"What would I tell them? That I help Walt kill someone every year? Doesn't seem like a good thing to mention in conversation," Ian said with a hint of sarcasm in his voice.

Marie had an idea of what she wanted to do, but she would need Ian's help.

"I think I've figured out something about the typewriter. I'm not one hundred percent sure it will work, but I want to try. Before I can try, though, there is something I need to do, and I think you can help me," Marie said.

"What is it you want me to do?" Ian said.

It took Marie a while to persuade Ian to help. But she was beautiful, and she was persuasive, and for Ian, saying no was never really an option. So after a while, he agreed. It then took them a few more weeks to work out the plan.

One night while they were working on the details, Marie purposely sat closer to Ian. She was wearing a tight T-shirt and short, tight, workout shorts. At times she would touch his arm and smile. It worked, and eventually Ian kissed her.

Sex was fast and rough. Marie enjoyed it. Ian was not gentle, and she returned the favor.

Marie scratched up Ian's back, and afterward they both were lying on his bed, covered in sweat—and with Ian covered in scratches. His breathing sounded as if he had just sprinted up a hill.

Sex with Ian was exactly what Marie had expected it to be, and it was what she needed.

For the next few nights, they repeated what they had done until Marie said they needed to stop for a while. Once everything was done, they would figure things out, she told him.

Ian was unhappy, but he understood the need.

After everything was planned out, Marie hugged Ian and said they couldn't see each other anymore until everything was done. Walt had been working on finishing editing his new book, so Marie had a lot of time with Ian. But now Walt had finished up with the book and it was about to go to print, so Walt would want to spend his time with Marie.

Ian said he understood, and Marie hugged him and left.

Walt was relaxed. The book was about to go to print, and he was ready to propose to Marie. He had been dropping subtle hints to her. He knew how he wanted to do it. His dreams of falling off the cliff had inspired him.

He would face his fears for her, proving his love for her by overcoming his fear. It had taken him a while to find a place. Up north on the coast was exactly what he was looking for.

He drove up there one Monday and parked in a dirt parking lot. There was a sign that warned of hazardous cliffs ahead, and if you entered, it was at your own risk. Walt walked up the path. There were trees along the side of the path, and in the distance he heard the sound of waves hitting rocks.

Walking along the path, he felt relaxed. No one was around, which was expected. This trail was not commonly known. Walt had a friend who had told him about it. Knowing his friend lived in the area, Walt had asked if he knew of any cliffs with a view where he could propose to Marie.

Walt's friend described this area and gave him directions. It was not easy to find. The road to the parking lot was long and winding. But it had been worth it. It was exactly what Walt was looking for.

When he got within fifty yards of the edge of the cliff, Walt froze. Memories of years of dreams came crashing down on him, and he couldn't move any farther.

Waves crashed on the rocks below, and the sound was exactly like what he would hear in his dreams. He sat on a log that lined the path and listened to the sound of the waves crashing on the rocks below. Without Marie, he would not get any closer. All he could think about was falling off the side.

There was no wind coming from behind him. It was the opposite. The wind came from the ocean and would not push him toward the ocean; it pushed him away.

Everything else was the same. There was even grass near the edge.

Walt did not want to stay any longer. He got up, listened to a few more waves crashing on the rocks, and then left. On the walk back to the car, he thought about Marie and knew she would love this. She was fun and daring, and this was the kind of place she would love. Doing this for her would show how much he loved her.

Walt drove home in no rush. Lost in his thoughts, he went over how the cliff looked compared to his dream. It was eerily similar—from the sound of the waves to the grass that covered the ground. Even the wind was similar, with the only difference being the direction it was blowing. Not as much of the water from the crashing waves hit him, but he could still feel a slight mist from where he had been sitting on the log.

He had the ring, and he had the location. Now all he needed to do was get Marie to agree to go on a trip with him. She did not like to travel and was always worried about her business when she wasn't there to watch over it. She had put so much of her life into getting it up and running that she thought of it as a baby and did not like to be away from it.

Getting her to go away for a weekend would be difficult, but he believed he could talk her into it. Marie was smart, so she would know something was up. Walt had never asked to take a trip with her.

They had gone on a few trips together, but they had been Marie's idea. On the trips, Marie would check in with her business a few times a day, calling to make sure everything was going OK. She would also check her e-mail and answer any critical e-mails that had come in. She had a fill-in trainer for her clients, so they would not miss any workouts while she was traveling.

Marie prided herself on her clients' progress, so she made sure there was nothing to slow them down. She would go over the details of each client with her replacement trainer before she left, letting the trainer know what her goal was with each client for the sessions she would miss and long-term, to make sure the trainer understood.

Walt knew he would need to give her notice, even if they were only going away for a few days. He would ask her tonight. They had a date arranged for tonight. First, a nice dinner at their favorite steak place, and then they had tickets to go see *Beauty and the Beast*. It was a musical, and Marie had been wanting to see it for a while. Walt had gotten them the tickets, and he knew she would be in a good mood afterward, so that was when he would ask her about going away for the weekend.

Dinner and the musical went perfectly. Each of them ordered a steak, medium rare. Marie liked hers a little more on the rare side, and Walt liked his a little more done. Both were good, and Marie didn't finish hers. She packed it in a to-go box with the potatoes and vegetables that remained.

Marie was always careful with her diet, and she stopped herself when she had finished half the meal.

Outside she found a homeless man lying down with a sign that said, "Need money for food and weed." Marie gave him five dollars and the remains of her meal.

"Thanks!" the man lying on the sidewalk said.

Walt looked at the man longer than he should have, thinking about all the homeless people he had killed over the years.

"You OK?" Marie asked.

"Yeah, I'm fine. Just full from the dinner," Walt said.

They walked in silence the few blocks to the theater. By the time they arrived, Walt had pushed the guilt down into wherever those kinds of feeling go when you aren't thinking about them.

Enjoying the musical was not difficult. It was well done and never dull. The audience cheered and laughed, and when Gaston fell to his death at the end, they cheered. Overall, it was an excellent musical.

After it let out, Walt and Marie walked along by a lake that was near the theater. Even at night there were people out jogging and walking.

"I was thinking we might go away for a few days. I know a place up north in the redwoods. It's really nice," Walt said.

Marie tensed. "When do you want to go?" she asked.

"I was thinking we could go in a few weeks," Walt said. "Leave on a Thursday and come back on Sunday.

Just spend a couple of days away before my book goes to print and I have to go on the book tour."

"That sounds lovely. Let me know when, so I can get a sub trainer to fill in for me," Marie said.

Walt was pleased she had said yes so quickly. "That was easy. I was expecting to have to persuade you," he said, smiling.

"I could use the time away. A short break would do me some good," Marie said.

Walt turned and hugged her. She hugged him back and put her head against his shoulder. He could smell her strawberry shampoo.

After a few minutes, they started kissing. She put her hand down his pants.

Walt looked around, and there was nobody close by, so he did not stop her.

In the morning, Marie was gone by the time Walt woke up. Everything last night had been wonderful. It could not have gone better, Walt thought. He was sure she knew something was up. She was smart and figured things out quickly. It was OK if she had an idea. If she knew what he was planning and still wanted to go, there was a good chance she would say yes.

He wondered if their open relationship would end once they were married. It had worked for them, and he would want it to continue once they were married. Walt knew a lot of marriages ended because of affairs, and he did not want to be another statistic. Marie was a realist, so he figured she would be OK with it. He knew she liked to be able to see other people as well.

It wasn't something to think about now. He needed to focus on the proposal and make sure the trip was fun and romantic.

For her to enjoy any trip, there would have to be some outdoor activities. He had learned early in their relationship that she liked outdoor activities. Walt did not care either way. He could stay at the hotel and relax by the pool with a drink, or he could go on a hot-air balloon ride. It didn't matter to him. But Marie would get bored sitting by a pool all day and would want to go out.

He had enjoyed the hot-air balloon ride but worried about the balloon getting a hole in it and them plunging to their deaths. That did not seem to worry Marie at all.

They had been on their first trip together, and Walt was sitting by the pool with Marie. Each of them had a drink, but Marie had not touched hers.

"I'm bored out of my mind," she had told him.

"OK. What do you want to do?" Walt had asked.

At that she handed him a pamphlet she had picked up in the lobby. It was for a hot-air balloon ride. "I want to try this," Marie told him.

"Um, OK," Walt said.

"Great. The bus leaves in twenty minutes. I booked the ride this morning. Let's go change, and let's get the fuck out of here," Marie said.

Two hours later, Walt found himself up in a hot-air balloon. From that point on, anytime they went on a trip, Walt made sure to have some excursions planned. He did not want to end up in a hot air balloon like that again. The ride had been fun, but he had been scared out of his mind before they got up in the air.

For this short trip, he would hike with her to the area where he would propose to her. It would be perfect. She would not think there was anything weird about a hike, and he knew she would like hiking to the edge of a cliff.

Marie left Walt's place that morning and drove to Ian's house. Ian had told her the code to the gate, and she walked up to the front door and knocked. Ian answered the door in boxer shorts and nothing else.

Marie loved how lean and muscular he was compared to Walt, who rarely worked out except for swimming a few laps in his pool. Ian worked out every day.

"I can't stay long, but Walt wants to go away on a trip. I'm going to install the app on my phone so you can track us," Marie said.

Ian told her to hold on for a second and went back into his office. He came out a few minutes later and handed her a phone.

"This is a burner phone," Ian said. "It can't be traced, and you can use it to text me when you leave. Do not let Walt see this phone. He will know what it is. I use them with him all the time. After this weekend is over, you need to get rid of this phone. Once it's no longer in your possession, it will be almost impossible to prove it was you who was using it."

Marie took the phone and put it in her pocket. She hugged Ian, turned, and left.

On the ride to the gym, she went over everything in her head. She knew what she was going to do, and she was nervous. This would be the second time in her life that she had done something like this. The first time had worked out. It was important to make sure to plan everything out as much as you could. Never lose focus of what you want the outcome to be. Go over all the details as much as possible.

The other important part about anything was to be able to change when the circumstances changed. Oftentimes—hell, most times—things did not go perfectly to plan. Being able to adapt was what she considered her greatest strength.

Until they left, Marie would go over everything. Knowing Walt, a lot of the plan would not be done until last the last minute, so she would need to adapt as she went along.

Yes, she was nervous, but if this worked out, everything she had always wanted would be open to her.

Taking a deep breath, she calmed herself down. There was a lot riding on this.

Walt called that night and let her know the trip was set for two weeks from now. He had booked a suite at a hotel in the middle of the redwoods.

Marie looked up the hotel online. It was a nice hotel. They would be close to a lot of activities and about three miles from the ocean. Walt had picked a wonderful place for a weekend together. She had to give him credit for that.

Now Marie sent a text using the burner phone. She gave Ian the name of the hotel and the check-in and check-out dates. Ian replied with a single answer: "OK."

Marie would not text Ian again until it was time for her to leave.

The next two weeks went by quickly. On the day they were leaving, Marie wished she could have had a few more days. She loved Walt, but that would not stop her from doing what she was going to do. She thought back to her father, whom she had also loved. But he had been abusive, and Marie was someone who did not take abuse.

9

Packing her bags, Marie remembered the last time her father had whipped her with his belt. She had left a small plastic hairbrush in the hallway. It had fallen from her bag. Of course she would not have left it there deliberately. Knowing how her father would react, she was always careful with all of her things. Never leaving anything out was one of the first rules he had taught her with the belt.

She didn't know about the brush, but her father stepped on it in the middle of the night when he came home. He was drunk, and she was lying awake in bed and heard him come home.

Marie knew her dad was always an angry drunk. Some of her friends' parents got silly when they drank, laughing and joking with their friends. Some of their parents didn't even drink. Marie wanted her dad not to drink. He was mean sober, and the drinking just made it worse. Marie's dad would use the belt on her when he was sober. It just didn't go on as long or happen as much as it did when he drank.

Better sober than drunk, she thought.

That night he was very drunk.

Listening in the dark, Marie heard the door open and close and then heard him put his keys in the bowl by the front door.

Everything got quiet for a few seconds, and then she heard his footsteps come down the hallway. When he stepped on the hairbrush, he stopped and yelled.

"Ow, Fuck! Marie, you left your fucking hairbrush in the hallway."

Marie took a breath and lay in bed as still as she could, waiting for whatever would happen next. Her door opened, and her dad threw the hairbrush at her on the bed. The hairbrush hit the thick blanket and came to rest on the bed. It did not hurt.

Her dad stood in the doorway for a second, looking at her. "I've told you before to clean up your shit, you stupid little shit."

Her dad then lifted his shirt and unclasped his belt and slid it off. Folding the belt in half, he held it in his right hand as a loop.

Wrapping herself in her blanket, Marie began to cry. "Daddy, I'm sorry! Please don't hit me. I won't do it again."

Her dad did not say a word as he walked over and pulled the blanket off her. He grabbed her and lifted her out of the bed, and then he turned her and began to hit her in the back with the belt. He swung the belt over and over, hitting her back. She tried not to scream, and she struggled to get out of his arms, which held her in place. He was a strong man, and she was a little girl. Most of the time, he stopped after fifteen or so swings. She would cry, but she had learned to take the pain.

Tonight he was drunk and kept going. Fifteen swings, twenty swings, twenty-five. At twenty-five, she screamed, "Daddy! Please! I won't do it again."

Marie's mom came into the room and saw what her dad was doing and went over and grabbed him.

"Stop it! Mark, stop hitting her!" Marie's mom yelled.

At that her dad turned and hit her mom in the arm with the belt a few times and then stopped.

"I told her not to leave her shit on the floor. She's too stupid to listen. Maybe now she won't forget," her dad said and left the room.

Marie's mom grabbed Marie and hugged her. Marie was sobbing, and she put her head against her mom's shoulder.

"Shhh, it's OK," her mom said, hugging her.

After she slowed her crying, her mom lifted up her shirt to look at her back. Marie's back was red, and there were small cuts covering it. Her mom had seen the blood soaking through the shirt.

"Come on; let's get you cleaned up," her mom told her.

Marie did not say anything to her mom, but she followed her into the bathroom.

Marie bit her lower lip while her mom dabbed antiseptic on her cuts. She washed each cut and then dabbed the antiseptic, and finally she put a large Band-Aid on each cut.

Neither of them said a word, and Marie forced herself to stop crying.

As her mom worked on her cuts, Marie thought of something she had been told a few months ago. One of her friends had told her that apple seeds contained a small amount of cyanide. She had freaked out and asked her mom if it was true.

"Yeah, I think so. But you'd have to eat a lot of seeds all at once for it to hurt you, I think," Marie's mom told her.

Marie loved apples, but when her friend told her about the poison in the seeds, she didn't eat the apple she had brought to school that day.

Poison in seeds. That fascinated her, and she began to read about it.

Marie begged her mom to take her to the library. Her mom relented, and Marie read as much as she could about the poison in apple seeds. It turned out a lot of different fruits had a chemical in their seeds that broke down into cyanide when digested.

Her mom had been right about eating the apples. Two things prevented people from getting poisoned by apple seeds. First, the shell of the seed needed to be broken for the poison to be dangerous. It was advantageous for the plant seeds to pass through the digestive tract of whatever animal ate them, so they could spread and grow other plants. Killing the animal was not the goal of the plant. So if you didn't chew the seed, you didn't get poisoned.

Second, killing someone required a large dose of apple seeds. One-third of a cup of seeds would be lethal half of the time, according to the book she was reading. Marie thought that a half cup would be lethal most of the time. It turned out that raw bitter almonds, cherries, and nectarines all had poison in the seeds. The almonds were poisonous on their own.

The interesting part to Marie was that cyanide poisoning resembled a heart attack. That thought stuck with her.

Marie began collecting the seeds of the apples she ate. She would keep the seeds in her pocket, and when she got home, she would put them in a plastic bag she kept in the freezer. Putting the bag in the back of the freezer under old bags of frozen french fries and peas, she was certain they would not be found. Her mom and dad never cleaned out the freezer that she had seen.

Collecting the apple seeds was a slow process. She pulled out the measuring cups her mom kept in the kitchen drawer and placed the frozen bag of seeds inside. After two weeks, she had barely covered the bottom of the one-third-cup size. Marie would need to step up her collection.

Her goal for collecting became five apples a day. Instead of eating lunch with the lunch money her mom gave her, she would save the money and buy apples from the supermarket. Instead of eating the apples, she would cut them in half and pull out the seeds. She would then go out and throw the apples around the neighborhood.

Her parents were not interested in what she was doing. Her dad left her alone unless she did something he didn't agree with. Then he would beat her with the belt and leave her alone again.

From an early age, she had learned to steer clear of her dad. When she was young, she would get hit with the belt about once a week, and then as she got older and more cautious, it would be as low as once a month.

It was the fear of getting beat with the belt that kept her going. As an adult she figured out that she'd had the same fears as someone living in a war zone—the constant fear of something bad happening that was beyond your control.

Now, focusing on collecting the apples kept her occupied. On most days she met her goal of five apples. Some days she would get more, and on rare days she would get fewer. On the days she got fewer, she would not sleep. That would mean another day of living in fear of her father and his belt.

Her cuts and bruises from the last beating were almost healed. After the last beating, she had been careful not to do anything her father might explode at.

On nights he had been out late drinking, she would get up and check the hallway and make sure all her items were put away.

When she would hear the door open, she would lie in bed as quietly as she could and wait. She would not breathe until she heard the door to her parents' room open and close. He rarely came back out of their room once he had gone to bed. The alcohol put him into a deep sleep.

Only once did someone mention the number of apples she had been buying. It was a clerk at the store she was getting the apples from.

"You must really like apples," the clerk said, grinning.

"Uh, yes," Marie said.

She smiled back at the clerk, paid, and took the bag with the apples.

After that, Marie did not go to that checkout clerk again. She also changed her habits and began going to different stores as much as possible. Because she used different stores and tried not to use the same clerks, no one else commented on her buying apples.

In preparation for what she was going to do, she also started cooking dinner for her parents twice a week. At first, what she made was not very good. She made spaghetti for them and overcooked the noodles.

Her father commented on the noodles. "You overcooked the fucking noodles. They taste like mush."

"I'm sorry. I will do better," Marie said. Her father demanded she answer like that.

"Don't let it happen again," he said.

Knowing he meant it as a threat, she took it as a threat. From him she always got one warning—and then the belt.

She practiced cooking the noodles before giving them to her father again. She asked her mother to show her how her father liked them.

"You need to cook them al dente. That means they are cooked but firm," her mom told her. She showed her how to cook the pasta and let her taste al dente pasta.

Marie went to the library again and got a book on Italian cooking. It turned out that pasta and vegetables both tasted better when cooked al dente. Marie followed the recipes from the book on the nights she would cook dinner for her parents, double-checking the pasta before serving it to her father.

She would then sit at the table and wait for him to try the food. Once he had taken his first bite and did not say anything, she would eat hers.

After two months, she had enough seeds and had gotten good enough at cooking that she felt ready. The night before, she lay awake in bed thinking about what she was about to do when her father came home.

Lying in the dark, she realized that she had forgotten to get up and check the house for her things. Fear gripped her as she listened to her dad close the door, and she saw the living room light turn on from under her door. After a few minutes, she knew her dad was taking off his shoes.

Holding her breath out of fear, she saw the living room light turn off and heard him walk down the hall. He stopped at her door and opened it.

Marie closed her eyes. She could feel him standing there looking at her. After a minute he closed the door, and she heard him walk down the hall to his room and go inside and close the door.

Only then did she start breathing again.

At school that day, she thought over and over about what she would do. She had thought about telling her mom she didn't feel well so she could stay home from school, but she didn't want to do anything out of the ordinary. Everything had to look normal. Police looked for things that didn't make sense.

When she got home from school that afternoon, she took the bag of seeds out of their hiding place in the back of the freezer and took them to her room. She laid them out flat on the top of her dresser to let them warm up. While the seeds were warming up, she got the spice grinder out from the cabinet and took it into her room.

After the seeds had warmed up, she placed them in the grinder and ground them up. Marie had hoped they would turn into a powder, but they became more of a paste.

She cleaned the seeds out of the grinder and put them back in the bag. She put the bag in the top drawer of her dresser, went to the kitchen, cleaned the grinder, and put it away.

Her mom came home at her normal time, and then, an hour later, her dad came home. Once her dad came home, she started cooking dinner.

She placed a large pot of water on the stove, added salt, and turned the water on to boil.

In a frying pan, she placed ground beef and started to brown it—everything she normally did when cooking them dinner.

While the meat was browning, she went to her room, got the bag of seeds out of the dresser, and put it into her pocket.

Her mom was in her parents' room watching TV, and her dad was sitting on the couch watching basketball.

The water in the large pot had started to boil, and she added the spaghetti noodles whole, not breaking them in half. She pulled out a loaf of bread and placed it in the oven to warm. Her dad liked to have warm bread with his dinner.

The only thing she did differently was to get out a second, small frying pan and place some of the browned meat into that pan.

Next, she added the sauce and some Italian spices and let both pans simmer.

By that point the noodles were ready, and she strained them out and put them back in the pot with a spoon of butter.

She took the seeds out of her pocket and mixed them with the sauce and meat in the smaller frying pan, stirring the seeds into the meat sauce until they were gone and adding a little extra garlic to the frying pan with the seeds to help mask the flavor.

She put noodles for her dad on a plate and then poured the sauce from the pan with the seeds on top. Finally, she put some Parmesan cheese on top and placed the plate at her dad's spot at the table.

From the other pan, she served her mom's portion and then her own portion, placing the plates at each of their spots at the table. She cleaned the extra pan she had used and put it away, leaving the other two pans on the stove.

She pulled the bread from the oven and used an oven mitt to hold the bread while she sliced the loaf. She then set the bread on the table with butter on the side, and she was ready.

Marie went into the living room and told her dad dinner was read. Always tell Dad first, her mom had told her when she was little, and she had followed that instruction since she had been told.

She then walked down the hallway and told her mom.

Once, when she was little, she had yelled across the house for her dad, and he had sprung up and come at her. "Do not fucking yell for me! You come into the room I'm in if you want to tell me something," he had yelled at her as he pulled the belt off and hit her with it a few times.

It was one of the few times she had gotten no warning before being hit. She had never yelled for him or her mom again.

Marie went back to the table and sat down and waited. Her mom came and sat down, and a few minutes later, her dad came and sat down. Her dad had a beer in his hand. He sipped his beer and then twisted the spaghetti on a fork and ate some.

Marie was not sure what to expect. Trying not to watch him, she wondered how long it would take.

Her dad got a piece of the bread and put some butter on it and then used it to pick up some sauce from the side of the plate. Her father ate the entire plate of spaghetti, finally using the bread to clean up the rest of the sauce.

Marie had been worried her dad would taste the seeds and stop eating and tell her the spaghetti tasted like shit. But he had eaten everything.

Marie had eaten only three bites of her spaghetti. She knew she needed to keep eating. Nothing could stand out as different for this meal. She knew the police would ask a ton of questions and try to find out if there was anything suspicious.

Her father then stood up and stopped. He made a loud inhalation and grabbed his chest. He then turned and sat back in the chair. He looked first at Marie and then at his wife, and then he fell to the floor. As he fell, the chair he was sitting on tipped over.

For a few seconds, Marie stared at her father lying on the floor. She did not want to help him, but she knew she had to act the way a normal person would in this situation.

She got up and ran to her dad. "Dad? Dad, are you OK?"

Marie saw that her mom had not moved. She sat staring at her husband with no expression on her face.

"Marie, come here," Marie's mom said to her. There was no worry in her voice. Just a calm call for Marie to come over.

Marie looked at her dad and then did as her mom said.

When she got over to her mom, her mom stood and hugged Marie.

"Go to your room," her mom told her.

Marie was surprised at her mom, who was not making any effort to help her dad—not that it bothered Marie, but it still surprised her.

On the way to her room, Marie heard her mom pick up the phone. After a brief pause, she heard her mom say, "I think my husband is having a heart attack. Please send someone."

Later, during the investigation, the lack of emotion her mother had in the 911 call would be noted. It would make the police focus on her mom for a little longer than they would have normally, but they did not find anything.

Marie realized she had not thought about how her mom would react. She had assumed her mom would panic and freak out, but she had been wrong about that. Her mom almost seemed happy that her husband was dying.

Marie could not blame her. She had felt the belt on her back as much as Marie had. Yet she had never done anything about it. Marie and her mom would never discuss the abuse, and her mom never mentioned her dead husband after the funeral.

Everything went exactly how Marie had thought it would go, except for her mom's reaction.

A cursory investigation was done, and nothing out of the ordinary was found. In the autopsy, the cause of death was ruled to be cardiac arrest. It turned out her father had very high cholesterol, and it was likely he would have eventually had a heart attack on his own. All Marie had done was move up the event.

Cyanide poisoning was never mentioned.

Her mom sold their house after her dad's death, they moved to a new town a few hours north, and the rest of Marie's childhood was uneventful.

Marie thought about her father frequently and how he had looked at her when he was dying. It made her sad at times, but then she would think about the small scars on her back from the belt and the sad feeling would turn to anger.

Marie was happy with her decision and never regretted killing him.

10

As she packed for the trip with Walt, Marie thought about Walt asking her to marry him. Even if she had not found out about the typewriter and how Walt wrote his books, she was not sure she would have wanted to marry him. Now that she knew about the typewriter, her feelings were clear that she did not want to.

Marie called for an Uber and went to Walt's house. When she saw him, she smiled at him, and they hugged.

He kissed her, and then he picked up her bag and they went inside.

"I still have a couple of items left to pack, and then we will get going," Walt told her, and then he went to his room.

Marie sat on the couch and waited. She cleared her mind and focused on her breathing while she waited, repeating her mantra over and over in her head.

Everything's normal.

She had used that as her mantra as long as she had been meditating. She had always felt she was different, but she knew that came from the abuse. To get over that, she acted normal. The more she acted normal, the more normal she felt. She had said that mantra to herself thousands of times.

When Walt was ready, she grabbed her bag, and they went out to his car. Walt had a silver Mercedes-Benz, but he rarely drove it. Most of the time when Walt went out, he liked to drink, so it was always easier for him to use Uber. Before Uber, he had used taxis.

Marie sat on the passenger side after she put her bag in the trunk.

Getting out of Southern California was always a slow process. Over the years it had seemed to get worse, to the point that even on weekends traffic would clog up, and everyone would drive at a snail's pace.

Once they were over the California grapevine on I-5, traffic picked up, and Walt drove the car like a rocket, passing slow-moving cars as fast as he caught up to them. With his radar detector on the dash, he slowed only when it beeped to let him know there was a cop somewhere close.

Marie fell asleep, and when she woke up, Walt was pulling over for gas and lunch. Knowing Marie did not like fast food, he had stopped at a restaurant, and Walt ordered a burger and fries for himself and a salad with the dressing on the side for Marie. Sitting at the table,

Marie ate the salad as fast as she could, and Walt asked for a to-go box for his burger and fries.

Marie took over driving to let Walt get some sleep. Driving across the street from the restaurant, she filled the car with gas, and then they kept going north.

In Marie's purse, buried at the bottom, was the burner phone Ian had given her. She had made sure it was charged, and she knew Ian would not be far behind them.

After a while they had switched from I-5 to Interstate 101, which took them along the coast. Driving along the coast of California was beautiful, and when they drove close to the ocean, Marie could not help but slow down to look. It was not a smart thing to do, since the road was winding, but she could not help herself.

According to the GPS, they had only two more hours to go before they got to the location where she knew Walt was planning to propose to her. If it was anything like the area they were driving through now, Walt had chosen well.

Walt had fallen asleep shortly after they ate lunch, and Marie felt he'd had enough sleep, so she pulled into a gas station. Before she got out of the car, she woke up Walt and told him that it was now his turn to drive, letting him know that he had only an hour or so left.

After she filled the tank, she got in the passenger seat. She was not tired, but she wanted to take some pictures of the redwoods and beaches as they drove past.

"Look how beautiful this is. Pull over," Marie said.

Walt drove a little farther, looking for a safe place to stop the car. When he found a place, he pulled the car to the side of the road and Marie got out.

"This is amazing," Marie said.

She took pictures using her cell phone. After each shot she checked the photo to make sure it looked how she wanted.

"Get out of the car. I want to get a picture of us together," Marie said.

Walt opened the door and stepped out of the car. He walked over to where Marie was standing and stood next to her. She handed him the phone, since his arms were longer.

"Take a selfie of us," Marie said.

Walt looked at the screen of the phone. Holding his arm out straight, he made sure both of them were on the screen, along with some of the trees, and took a few photos.

"Thanks," Marie said, and she took the phone back.

She looked at the photos Walt had taken and liked them.

"OK, we can go," Marie said.

The rest of the trip was uneventful, and Marie fell asleep.

Walt woke her up by touching her arm when they arrived at the hotel.

He pulled up to the front of the hotel, and a bell-hop opened Marie's door and then ran around to the other side to open Walt's door.

Marie got out. She could smell the redwoods.

The bellhop got their luggage out of the car, and Walt paid for valet parking. The valet took a tip from Walt, handed him a slip with their car's information, and then got in the car and drove off.

Inside the lobby, Marie admired the beautiful redwood pillars, and she sat on one of the chairs in front of a small table. The chairs were big and soft—dark brown in color, to match the redwood pillars. To the right was a fireplace, but it was not lit.

After a few minutes, Walt came and told her the room was ready. They rode the elevator to the top floor. Walt had gotten the penthouse suite. Looking out the window after they got into the room, Marie could see they were surrounded by redwood trees.

Their luggage had already been brought up and was sitting in the small hallway that led into the main area of their room.

Inside the bedroom was a queen-size bed, and Marie lay down on it. Walt came in and lay down next to her. Turning their heads to the side, they looked at each other. Marie then climbed on top of Walt and began kissing him. They pulled off each other's clothes, and ten minutes later they were both sweating and breathing hard.

When they had finished, Walt told her that he had a long hike planned for tomorrow, so they would need to get some sleep.

Marie grabbed the room service menu and ordered herself a salad and Walt a steak.

After dinner, Marie lay in bed. She had trouble sleeping, so she meditated, going over her mantra in her head.

Everything's normal.

After a while she fell asleep.

In the morning, Marie woke up first and showered and got dressed. After she was dressed and ready to go, she woke Walt.

Walt got out of bed and showered and got ready.

While he was in the shower, Marie pulled the burner phone out of her purse and texted Ian. "You here yet?" She pressed Send.

After a few minutes, Ian replied, "Yes. I'm a few miles away."

"OK. Stand by. I'll let you know when I'm ready," Marie texted.

"OK," Ian responded.

"OK. Ttyl."

Marie plugged the phone into her charger until she heard Walt turn off the water to the shower. At that point she put the phone back in her purse.

Walt came out of the bathroom a few minutes later, wrapped in a towel.

He got dressed in hiking shorts and a lightweight hiking shirt. Putting on his shoes, Walt felt good. Everything on this trip was going exactly as he had planned.

"Are those new shoes?" Marie asked when she saw him putting on his shoes.

"Uh, yeah. I needed some hiking shoes," Walt said.

"You didn't break them in?" Marie asked.

"I didn't think to," Walt said.

"Hopefully you won't get blisters," Marie said.

Marie was right, Walt thought, cursing himself for not wearing them a few times. This could turn out to be a painful hike.

Once Walt was ready, they went downstairs. He handed the valet ticket to the valet, and their car was brought to them in a few minutes. Walt hugged Marie as they waited.

Marie put her head against Walt's chest. He always smelled good after a shower in the morning.

Walt drove, taking them to a different trailhead than the one he had used to scout the place he would propose to her. He wanted a long hike to the area, so he parked at a trailhead that would give them about a two-hour hike before getting to the location.

On the first hour of the hike, everything was fine, but then Walt got a blister on his right foot.

"Shit, I got a blister," he said to Marie.

"Do you want to stop and check it?" she asked.

Marie was wearing a small backpack she had filled with some water bottles and a couple of energy bars. She had also placed her phone and the burner phone inside.

Walt had his own backpack with water and energy bars inside. He had also packed some sandwiches, which they would have for lunch.

Walt sat on a rock on the side of the trail and took off his right shoe and his sock. There was a small blister on his heel that had not yet popped.

Marie searched her bag and pulled out a small first aid kit she kept in it. She opened the kit, pulled out some Neosporin and a Band-Aid, and handed them to Walt.

Walt picked at the blister with his fingernail until it popped. He then pressed out the fluid from inside and put the Neosporin and Band-Aid on it.

While Walt worked on his foot, Marie reached into the bag and turned off her cell phone and the burner phone.

Walt stood up and walked a little. "Much better," he said.

Marie smiled, and they proceeded on the trail. The redwoods were beautiful, and Marie saw a banana slug crawling on a fallen log.

Walt was getting nervous about the proposal as they got closer to his planned location.

Marie calmed herself with slow, deep breaths and went through her plan in her head. Both of them were quiet, moving at a slow pace on the trail.

When they were a quarter of a mile away from where Walt wanted to propose, they were close enough to the cliff shore that they could hear the waves crashing on the rocks, and the smell of the salt air broke through the smell of the redwoods.

When they came to the clearing, Walt walked into the center and stopped. Marie walked over to the edge and looked down. There were rocks, and every few seconds a wave came in and crashed against the rocks, covering them briefly. The water would then recede, and they would be visible again.

Marie turned and walked over to Walt.

He grabbed her hands and knelt before her, kissing her hands as he knelt.

"Marie, I've loved you for a long time, and I can't picture my life without you. Every time I see you, my heart skips a beat, and I know my life is complete," Walt said, looking up at her.

Marie smiled and squeezed his hands as he spoke.

"I don't want to live my life without you in it, and I want to wake up every day with you lying next to me," Walt said. "Would you marry me?"

Marie had tears in her eyes. "Yes," she said.

Walt took the ring he had been carrying from his pocket and placed it on her finger.

Marie wiped her eyes and looked at the ring. "It's beautiful," she said.

Walt stood and hugged her and then kissed her. It was a long kiss, and Marie hugged him tight.

After a while Marie let go of the hug and walked back over to the edge. She stood at the edge and looked down at the water crashing below.

Walt watched her walk over to the cliff. He wanted to follow her, but he was afraid. He'd had so many dreams in which he had fallen from a cliff that looked just like this one.

Marie turned to him and held her hand out and gestured for him to come over.

Now it was Walt's turn to take a deep breath and steady himself. He then walked over to Marie and hugged her.

They both turned and looked out at the ocean.

It was beautiful, Walt thought, feeling the sturdy cliff edge beneath his feet.

Marie went around behind him, and Walt felt her arms around his waist.

She hugged him tight and placed kisses on his neck, moving from low on his neck to his shoulder and then up to his ear. When her mouth was by his ear, she said, "I know about the fucking typewriter, you fucking liar." With one swift motion, she put both her hands on his back and pushed with all her strength.

Walt tumbled over the side of the cliff. He turned and screamed and tried to reach for her.

Marie flung herself back, fell to the ground, and watched as Walt disappeared from the edge of the cliff. For a brief second, she heard a scream—and then only the sound of the waves below.

Tears came hard, and she cried. The wind from the direction of the sea dried the tears, and she stood and walked to the edge of the cliff. Looking down, she saw no sign of Walt. She took the ring off her hand and threw it out into the ocean.

Walt had taken off his backpack, and it sat in the center of the clearing where he had proposed. Marie walked over and picked it up. She took a quick look inside. His phone, the sandwiches, water, and some energy bars were inside.

She zipped the bag closed and tossed it over the side.

Now came the hard part, she thought. She turned and ran, continuing on the trail. She ran for forty minutes, which was a little over four miles, along the coast. She stopped at the next clearing. This one did not have the nice grass of the first one, but that didn't matter. She just needed something close to the ocean that was not close to the first clearing.

She then turned on the burner phone, leaving hers off. The phone had a signal, and she texted one sentence to Ian.

"It's done."

They had planned this out, and she sat on a rock and waited.

She didn't know how far out he was, but Ian had told her he would be there as fast as he could once she texted.

Marie had been worried there would not be a signal, but her luck held, and there was a decent signal from her location.

It took almost an hour for Ian to show up. He came running up the trail. She heard him before she saw him.

She stood and ran to him when he came into the clearing. "It's done. He's dead, and his body is in the water," Marie said. She hugged Ian.

Ian hugged her back, relieved that this was done.

"Is the typewriter in your car?" she asked.

"Yeah. In the trunk," Ian said.

Ian walked to the edge of the cliff and looked down.

"Those fucking rocks look nasty. How are you feeling?" Ian asked.

Marie thought about the question and then answered, "I feel like shit. I loved Walt." She teared up again. She had loved him, but she had also hated him in the end. The man she had loved was a great writer, and Walt was just a fucking fraud.

"I don't see his body. You threw all his stuff in with him?" Ian asked.

"Yes. Everything went in, including the ring he got me. It was a beautiful ring," Marie said. "Did you see anyone on your way here?"

"Nope. I think we are good," Ian said. "Now you just need to get back to the room and wait."

Marie nodded.

Ian came up and hugged her again. "You did great," he said.

Marie hugged him and felt the gun against his lower back. She pulled it out, using her left hand to unbutton the holster and then her right hand to pull the gun.

She pointed it at Ian's chest and fired once.

The sound of the gunshot was muffled by being so close to his chest, along with the sound of the waves crashing on the rocks below.

Ian looked at her for a second and then fell to the ground. His breathing slowed and then stopped after a few minutes. Marie stood over him, watching. It was the same thing she had done with her father when he died from the cyanide poisoning.

Marie walked over to the cliff and used her shirt to wipe her fingerprints off the gun and then threw the gun as far as she could. It landed out in the water with a small splash that Marie could barely see.

She searched Ian's body and grabbed his keys. She took the car key off the ring and put it in her backpack. She then tossed the keys over the edge. Then she emptied Ian's pockets and tossed everything into the ocean. Once the body was found, she did not want it to be easy for the police to identify him. Since he had been in the military, they probably would have his DNA, but she wanted to do what she could.

Now came the hard part. She had always done a lot of pushing and pulling of heavy objects when she worked out, and now she hoped it would pay off. She grabbed Ian's feet and pulled his body toward the edge. When she was close enough, she turned his body parallel to the edge and rolled it until it went over the edge. She watched it land on a large rock below and heard it hit with a loud thud. A wave then crashed over the rock, and his body disappeared into the ocean.

Marie then looked around to make sure she had not left any traces of what she had done. She took the burner phone out of her bag and tossed it over the edge to join Ian. She then turned and ran back in the direction of the hotel as fast as she could. As she ran, she thought about Ian and Walt.

Ian she could not give a shit about. He had been a cold man who killed people for money. Killing him, she thought, was just balancing the universe. Walt she had loved.

When she got to where she had killed Walt, she pulled her phone out of her backpack and called 911.

"My boyfriend fell. Oh my god, Walt fell!" she screamed into the phone.

"Ma'am, please calm down. What happened?" the 911 operator asked in a calm voice.

"We were taking a selfie by the edge of a cliff, and he slipped and fell. Oh my god; I think he's..." Marie trailed off.

"Where are you, ma'am?" the operator asked.

Marie explained where she was, and the operator told her to get back to the hotel. The operator would have the police and paramedics meet her there.

Everything that happened the rest of that night was a blur.

Marie took the police and paramedics out to where she had pushed Walt off the edge. Looking down at the rocks and the waves, they discussed the best way to retrieve Walt. All of them knew there was no possible way he had survived the fall, but no one said anything about him being dead. They all worked as if there were some hope of finding him alive.

A rescue boat showed up a while later, outside the waves, and divers looked where they could. A helicopter flew low over the water, looking for a body.

On the first day they searched, they had only a few hours before it got dark, and nothing was found.

When it got dark, Marie went back to the hotel with a warning from the police not to go anywhere.

Reporters started to show up. Walt was a best-selling author, and this was worthy of some news.

Marie cried as they interviewed her, tears streaming down her face as she talked to them. She watched herself on TV that night. She thought she looked convincing, but you never knew. She had read enough and seen enough cop shows to know that if anything out of the ordinary turned up, they would expand their search.

Marie worried about being found out, so she fell asleep trying to figure out if she had missed anything.

In the morning the reporters were in the hotel lobby, wanting to interview her. She declined to be interviewed.

Walt's body was found early the next day. It had gotten stuck between two rocks, and during low tide the search teams were able pull it free.

Upon seeing Walt's body, Marie burst into tears. She reacted harder than she had wanted to, but she felt a wave of sadness wash over her.

They would not let her near the body.

Once Walt's body was found where she had said it would be, they confirmed the contact information she had given them and let her go.

They had taken her phone, and she had given them the PIN to unlock it. Someone told her it was evidence. Marie was not sure how, but she complied. She would get a new phone when she got home, having heard stories of evidence not being returned for years at times.

By the end of the day, the reporters were gone, and the police and everyone else left as well. Mitch had shown up that morning, but she had not had a chance to speak with him until now.

"How are you doing?" Mitch asked.

"I think I'm still in shock. I don't—can't—believe he's gone," Marie said.

Mitch couldn't believe Walt had died taking a selfie. It seemed like a bad dream to him, and he wanted to scream at Marie *Why couldn't you have been more careful?* But he didn't. He knew Marie loved Walt, and Mitch could not blame her.

"Don't worry about Walt's body. I'll take care of the arrangements to have it brought back home," Mitch said.

"Thank you," Marie said.

Marie was grateful, and she hugged Mitch and went up to her room. She did not feel like talking with anyone. Alone in her room, she had one last thing she needed to do before she could leave the area.

She went to her backpack and pulled out the key to Ian's car. All she knew was that it was in a parking lot somewhere close to where she had killed him. It had already been parked there one night. Not being sure what the rules were for parked cars in the area, she worried that it might get towed.

Marie packed her items and went down to Walt's car. She had her own key that Walt had given her. At one point they had been on a trip and Walt had been too drunk to drive, and she'd had to use his keys.

"Better to have your own key," Walt had told her, handing her the key he'd had made for her.

She got into Walt's car, adjusted the seat, and left the hotel. She drove along the coast, checking all the parking lots where Ian might have left his car. It took her almost two hours to find it. It was parked in a lot a mile north of where they had met and where she had shot him.

Marie clicked off the alarm and popped open the trunk. Sitting in the trunk, looking shiny and new, was the Wordsmith typewriter.

Staring at the typewriter, Marie realized she was nervous about picking it up. She reached in and placed her hands on the sides and then pulled them back. Of course, the typewriter was warm to the touch. She had known it would be, but it still surprised her.

Putting her hands back on it, she let the typewriter warm her hands for a second, and then she picked it up and put it in the trunk of Walt's car.

Now she thought about what to do with Ian's car. The car would eventually be towed. It would end up sitting in a lot, waiting for its owner to pick it up.

If she moved the car, her hair or some of her DNA could be left in the car, and that would be suspicious. Better not to have any of her DNA or anything that could be traced back to her in the car.

When they found Ian's body, they would look for his car. She was not sure how that would work, but if they found it, they would check the car.

Marie wiped off the parts of the trunk she had touched. Then she got in Walt's car and left.

After she had driven for an hour, she rolled down the window and tossed the key into the redwoods.

Over the next few weeks, everything worked itself out. The cause of death for Walt was ruled as an accident. The body was released, and the funeral was held on a Saturday.

Walt's fans placed flowers all over outside his driveway.

Marie went by Walt's house once and looked at the homage his fans had left him. It was beautiful, she thought, seeing the pile of flowers and cards.

Talk shows discussed in depth death from selfies. It was a common occurrence, and they went over how to take selfies safely. One main point was to never take them where there was a danger of falling.

Marie spoke at the funeral, expressing her love and the loss she felt now that Walt was gone. She also talked about how his writing had affected her and how she would miss reading his novels.

It was a moving funeral, and Marie found herself crying through most of it.

Mitch, who had been very close to Walt, also cried and spoke. He talked about Walt's work with children's hospitals and the great charity work Walt had done— a lot of it without wanting any recognition for his donations.

At that point, Marie felt real guilt for the first time about killing him.

When the funeral was over, Marie hugged Mitch. "That was beautiful," she said.

"Thank you. I was worried, but once I started talking about Walt, it felt good to say what he meant to me," Mitch said.

"He affected a lot of people. It's wonderful to see so many people come out to say good-bye," Marie said.

They were both quiet for a time, and then Mitch said he had to go. He hugged Marie once more and left.

Marie went back to work the following week. She had done as much as she could now that Walt was gone. It turned out that since she wasn't his wife, she had no legal rights to do anything.

Walt's trust gave most of his money to the children's hospital. He had no family.

11

arie felt good being back at work. Her clients understood her time off and welcomed her back. All the conversations started with condolences on losing Walt. She was tired of the condolences, but there was nothing she could do about that.

Marie had the typewriter in her bedroom, sitting on her dresser. She had placed it there after removing it from the trunk of Walt's car. Every night when she came home, she would touch the sides, feeling the warmth and letting herself get used to the feeling of the typewriter.

After a few months went by and Marie began to feel normal again, she thought about what she was going to do next. Since she had the typewriter, she knew what she wanted to do. She wanted to type on it.

All her research led her to believe one thing. It was possible to type on the typewriter and stop. She believed that one of the authors, the one who wrote the greatest books, had written them himself with the help of the typewriter.

Marie did not want to kill anyone else. In her life she had killed three people, and in her mind all of them deserved it. She would not go down the path Walt had of killing innocent people.

She knew that typing on the Wordsmith would be risky. There was a good chance she would type herself to death. Was that something she was willing to do?

After a few months, she decided it was. She wanted what Walt and the other authors who had used it had.

Marie decided she would take two weeks off and try using the typewriter.

First, she needed to find a place where she could use it and not be disturbed. It turned out that was not difficult. There were cabins she could rent for several weeks. She found one on a lake, and she paid the rental fee.

Two weeks should be enough time. If she died, they would find her body slumped over the typewriter. If not, she would be left alone long enough to finish a book.

She told her clients she needed a break for a few weeks, blaming Walt's death. They all understood. Marie worked out the schedule so that each training day for her clients was covered by a substitute trainer.

On the day she left for the cabin, Marie packed light. She was not sure what would happen, but she prepared the best she could. She stopped eating the day before the trip. Ian had mentioned that once you started typing, you would not move for anything, and Ian had said that people would not stop even when they needed to go to the bathroom.

Marie figured that meant she would not stop even if she needed to go to the bathroom. She did drink a lot of water, knowing that you could go much longer without food than you could without water.

When she got to the cabin, she put the typewriter on a small plastic table she had brought with her. She also brought a mesh chair that liquid would pass through. She did not relish the idea of sitting in her own pee or poop. The floor of the cabin was wood. Marie laid towels down around the chair to soak up the mess she was sure she was going to make.

Marie stood outside, at the front of the cabin, and took a look around. There were trees surrounding the cabin, and a small driveway was the only way up to the cabin. In the back there was a large lake that she could see from the bedroom.

She put the table and chair in the living room. The view of the lake would not matter.

She placed a few reams of paper on the table behind the typewriter.

Now she felt she was ready, and she sat down in the chair.

Touching the sides of the typewriter, she felt the warmth of the smooth surface.

Taking a deep breath, she pressed the letter *M* on the typewriter, with the intention of writing her name.

As she pressed the key, she felt a sharp pain in the tip of her finger, but before she could pull it away, an overwhelming feeling came over her as though she had taken a shot of a powerful drug. Her mind became cloudy, and her thoughts were foggy. The only thing clear in her mind was the next word she needed to type.

To her, the words seemed to come from nowhere, and she just typed them, not being able to stop—one word after another. With the first key pressed, each finger would feel the same sharp pain—and then nothing. All the pain went away, and she felt drunk.

She could not stop typing.

Time lost meaning, and all she focused on was the next word she needed to type.

In the distance she could make out the faint sound of the typewriter clacking as she typed. She fought to stop, but after a while she gave in and let the typewriter take over. For an amount of time she was not sure of, she let the words come and typed them as they came.

Her own thoughts were there, but they came as slowly as a snail crawling over a lawn. Fighting the feeling was a pointless endeavor, she knew. People had died using this. But maybe she could guide the story.

She focused her thoughts only on what she was writing, and the story the typewriter wanted to tell took shape in her head. If she thought of anything else, the story would disappear from her thoughts. All her focus had to remain on the story. No other thoughts could be allowed in her mind.

Marie would focus, and then her mind would wander, the story would be gone, and the words would be forced out of her. Clearing her mind, she focused on the story, and what had started as a brief moment began to get longer and longer.

She began to understand what was already written—even the parts she had not done herself—and then she began to understand what the story would be.

What she wanted was to be able to make the story her own.

She found that she could not focus on what she wanted to write; she had to focus on an idea of the story she wanted to tell. When she did that, the typewriter would adjust the story with her thoughts.

Getting the story she had in her mind to work with the typewriter was painful. It reminded her of trying to figure out a difficult math problem.

When she was in school working on something difficult, she would take breaks and let her mind work on the problem, and then she would go back to work on the problem. With the typewriter there was no such option. If she let her mind drift even a little, the typewriter would take back over, and the words would be pulled out of her.

Focusing only on the story, she knew she was coming toward the end. At some point while she was writing, she saw the end of the novel become clear in her mind, and she added what she thought would be a good ending to what the typewriter wanted, and the story was pushed out of her.

Knowing now that she would only have a brief moment to stop, she concentrated on the story and let it begin to reach the ending. When she felt herself typing the words *The End*, she pulled her hands up off the typewriter and threw herself to the floor. When she did that, she screamed.

On the floor she was on her hands and knees, taking deep breaths and crying. She began to dry heave, but she had nothing to throw up. Her stomach hurt each time it tried to push out something that wasn't there.

After a few moments, the dry heaving stopped, and her hands started to hurt. The tips of her fingers were raw and red. They felt as if each one had been hit with a hammer. Only her left thumb, which hadn't really done any typing, was unhurt.

A strong smell of urine and shit filled the room. She did not remember going to the bathroom, but the towels under the chair were soaked with urine.

As soon as she felt strong enough, she stood, and her legs wobbled beneath her.

Walking slowly, using whatever object was nearby to steady herself, she went into the kitchen. She filled a glass with water, drank it down as fast as she could, and then filled another glass. Marie felt instantly better and went to the bathroom to take a look at herself.

Most noticeable was how much thinner she was. Her face looked like a skeleton, and there were dark, black circles under her eyes. Her hair looked dirty and greasy.

She needed to eat something. She went back into the kitchen and found an unopened bag of chips. She opened the bag and ate the chips as fast as she could. Her stomach started to hurt again, so she slowed down her eating. She did not want to throw up.

She finished the second glass of water, filled the glass again, took the water and chips back into the living room, and sat down on the couch.

When she looked at the typewriter, she felt the urge to continue typing but was able to push the feeling away.

She did not remember changing the paper as she typed or opening a new ream. The only thing she could still remember was the story. What she had written about was clear in her mind.

Marie picked up her phone and looked at the time and date. It had been five days. She had typed for five days straight.

She took off her clothes and put on a thin robe she had in her bag. She was dirty and desperately needed a shower, but she had something to do first. She wanted to read what she had written.

The pages had been neatly stacked beside the Wordsmith, facedown, with the last page still stuck in the typewriter. She pulled the page out, placed it facedown on the stack of paper, picked up the stack, and went to the bedroom, worried that if she stayed in the living room, she would want to start typing again.

Sitting on the bed, she looked out at the still water of the lake. Her fingers still hurt, and she needed to be careful using her hands. Any time she bumped the tips, a sharp pain radiated through her hands.

Someone who was now dead had written the first part of what she had finished. It was good, and she found it reminded her of Walt as she read it. It matched his style—which she now knew to be the style of the typewriter.

Everything written for the first part reminded her of Walt until the point where she had figured out how to add her own voice to the story. From that point on, the story felt as if it was written by a new voice. Part of it was her voice, and part of it was something new and unrecognizable to her.

She loved it.

All the pain she felt seemed worth it now. She had created something that was unique and was her own voice.

Her thoughts turned to Walt, who had killed, or at least helped to kill, people to get the stories that had made him very wealthy. In truth the stories told were not his, but now she knew you could make them your own.

Now she found herself wanting to share her story. She wondered if all authors who wrote something wanted to share what they had written. Were there authors who wrote and never shared what they had written? It didn't matter. She wanted to share.

After finishing the bag of chips and the third glass of water, she began to feel a lot better. It was amazing how quickly the body could recover.

Now she had to do what she had been dreading. She went back into the kitchen and got out a plastic kitchen bag. The owner of the cabin did not have any rubber gloves, so she picked up the pee-soaked towels barehanded. When she moved the first towel, the smell of stale urine hit her, and she almost threw up. Her fingers stung when the urine touched the tips where there were small cuts from typing.

The chair she had been sitting on had piss and shit smeared on it. She cleaned the chair as much as she could and then decided she would have to throw it away.

She placed all the towels in the kitchen bag and tied the top. Then she took the chair outside to remove the smell from the house.

She opened the front door and the windows to let the smell out, mad at herself for not doing that right away.

The floor was discolored where the pee had soaked through the towels, and she realized she would have to pay for the damage.

She then took a shower, taking time to soap and clean the tips of her fingers. She did not want to get an infection on top of everything else.

When she was done showering, she put on a clean set of clothes and threw the old clothes away in another plastic trash bag. Her old clothes were soaked with sweat and urine, and she did not want to wear them again.

She went back into the living room and touched the side of the typewriter, feeling the warmth. She then picked it up, took it out to the car, and put it in the trunk.

Going back inside, she picked up and then cleaned up the rest of the house, making sure she could not smell any urine in the living room.

Finally, before leaving, she picked up the story and wrapped it with a large rubber band she had brought. She made one final walk through the house, locked up the door, and left.

On the way back home, she thought about Mitch. She would need to be patient before presenting her story to him. For now, she thought, she would bring it to him as something Walt had been writing and that she had finished. Legally, she was not sure who owned the first part of the story, but if she went through Mitch, it was unlikely she would get into trouble. Time was on her side now.

She had the typewriter, she knew how to control it, and she had survived typing on it.

Now she would go back to her personal training business, and when enough time had passed, she would show the story to Mitch.

Driving home from the cabin with the story sitting on the seat next to her, she felt joy. This story she had just done was good, but she had another story she wanted to tell—about a little girl's abuse—and this typewriter would help her to do that. She just had to be patient.

EPILOGUE

Marie stood on the edge of a cliff. She knew this was a dream, but everything about the dream felt real. She could feel the water drops from the waves that were hitting the rocks below. Beneath her feet she felt the cool, wet grass. A light breeze blew from behind her.

She turned from the cliff, walked back about fifteen paces, and then turned around to face the cliff once more. The wind behind her grew strong. Walt had described a similar dream often. He would wake up covered in sweat, and sometimes he would be shaking. Walt had described the wind pushing him over the edge to his death, at which point he would wake up. Marie had never understood the dream until she found out his secret.

Marie stood and put her arms up, letting the wind flow around her. She stood in the wind and enjoyed the feeling of it as it blew her hair.

The strength of the wind picked up.

When she felt the wind start to move her, she put her arms down and sprinted to the edge of the cliff and jumped off, laughing as the wind took her.

CPSIA information can be obtained
at www.ICGtesting.com
Printed in the USA
LVOW07s1617270417
532419LV00001B/15/P